TO SEIZE A QUEEN

Also by Fiona Buckley

The Ursula Blanchard mysteries

* available from Severn House

TO SEIZE A QUEEN

Fiona Buckley

SEVERN
HOUSE

First world edition published in Great Britain and the USA in 2024
by Severn House, an imprint of Canongate Books Ltd,
14 High Street, Edinburgh EH1 1TE.

severnhouse.com

British Library Cataloguing-in-Publication Data
A CIP catalogue record for this title is available from the British Library.

ISBN-13: 978-1-4483-1356-3 (cased)
ISBN-13: 978-1-4483-1357-0 (e-book)

All Severn House titles are printed on acid-free paper.

Typeset by Palimpsest Book Production Ltd.,
Falkirk, Stirlingshire, Scotland.
Printed and bound in Great Britain by
TJ Books, Padstow, Cornwall.

Praise for the Ursula Blanchard mysteries

"A lively story with excellent historical detail and atmosphere"
Booklist on *Golden Cargoes*

"Plenty of action"
Kirkus Reviews on *The Net of Steel*

"Lovers of Tudor fiction will enjoy the carefully researched details of daily life woven into the suspense . . . Highly entertaining"
Publishers Weekly on *The Net of Steel*

"Buckley's vivid portrayal of the resourceful, clever, and devious Ursula carries the plot. Readers will hope to continue seeing more of her"
Publishers Weekly on *Golden Cargoes*

"The queen of Elizabethan historicals"
Publishers Weekly on *The Scent of Danger*

About the author

Fiona Buckley is the author of twenty-two previous Ursula Blanchard mysteries including *Forest of Secrets*, *Shadow of Spain*, *Golden Cargoes* and, most recently, *The Net of Steel*. Under her real name, Valerie Anand, she is the author of numerous historical novels including the much-loved Bridges Over Time series. Brought up in London, she now lives in Surrey.

For Renee
In memory of the good days at ERT

Prologue

1594 AD, Constantinople

The Constantinople quayside was busy and also noisy. Ships were loading and unloading while passengers, often laden with bundles, hurried to board or disembark. A family who had just come ashore and were apparently waiting to be met, had brought snacks with them to eat while they waited and seagulls swooped and cried, hoping for scraps, their white wings flashing in the sun. Half a dozen languages criss-crossed in the air. Overseers shouted at the sweating porters; on the decks, orders were shouted at toiling sailors.

On the *Mary Pengelly*, an English merchant vessel, sails were being unfurled and the rowers, on the little tugs that would ease her away from the quayside, were in their places. A few last crates of lemons were being taken aboard, watched intently by Captain Tredgold, who was standing on the quay.

Captain Tredgold was a stocky Cornishman with slate blue eyes and a short temper. His ship was bound for Bristol as usual, and he was anxious to be sure that his cargo would arrive there intact. As usual he meant to call in at Penzance on the way to visit his kinsfolk and stock the galley with fresh fish. When someone behind him called his name, he turned round in an irritable fashion. A tall, thin, Turkish gentleman, with a bushy grey beard and sparklingly clean white robes was hurrying towards him.

In passable English, the gentleman said, 'Captain Tredgold, Master Mustafa is anxious to be sure that the lemon crates are stacked securely this time. He understands that when the last consignment reached Bristol, about half of it had come adrift, with the lemons spilt, most of them damaged or rotten. These consignments are paid for in advance. He has received the payment for this one, but minus the value of the spoilt goods last time. This is not satisfactory. I have orders to go aboard and see for myself that the stacking has been properly done.'

'It has, and so it was last time. We met bad weather. It happens at sea. If you want to inspect, you'll have to hurry,' said Tredgold in surly tones. 'We'll be off in half an hour.'

From a newly arrived vessel further along, a line of new slaves, men and women, roped together, were being disembarked. A sense of misery wafted from them; a young man in the middle of the string had a face full of the bitterest anger. Poor sod, Tredgold thought.

'If you would lead the way . . .' said the Turkish gentleman, with gentle but determined persistence.

Captain Tredgold took his irritating visitor aboard but not to the hold. Instead, he led the way to his own cabin. On entering, his visitor observed that although the cabin was tidy enough, the valuable rug with its rich blue and crimson pattern had been moved from its place in front of the beautifully carved walnut armchair and replaced by a sheet, as if to protect the floor in some way. Behind the chair stood a red-haired seaman with a gap-toothed and wicked grin.

He was stropping a razor.

ONE
Call To Duty

The morning was misty but it was going to lift. The sun was out, albeit in a hazy fashion, and would soon burn those vapours away. It was the second of May. Yesterday, there had been May Day celebrations in the village down in the valley, with a maypole and dancing, to rejoice in the final departure of winter and the burgeoning all round us of new life, as the crops sprouted and young animals were born. May Day was always a happy occasion.

I was standing, as I so often did, at my bedchamber window in Faldene House, overlooking Faldene valley. The house faced south and beyond the valley, between Faldene and the sea, were the rolling downs of Sussex. Sometimes, though, the wind carried the tang of the sea even this far inland.

Faldene was the property that had been left to me after the deaths of my Uncle Herbert and my Aunt Tabitha. It was also the house in which they had brought me up, not always kindly but, because my goodhearted grandfather was then still alive and insisted, very adequately.

My mother, sister to Uncle Herbert, had promised to be an ornament to the family when she became a lady-in-waiting to Queen Anne Boleyn, but, when she was dismissed and sent home, pregnant with a child whose father she wouldn't name, she was an ornament no longer but a disgrace. The child she bore was myself and from the day I was born I was a cuckoo in the nest. The truth about my paternity didn't emerge until years later. If my uncle and aunt had known from the first that my father was King Henry the Eighth, their attitude might have been different.

As it was, because of my tolerant grandfather, my mother and I were fed, clothed and housed and I was allowed to share my cousins' tutor. There were limits to my grandfather's power – or knowledge – and I was often harshly treated, but I did have an

education. My poor mother was always treated coldly and after
my grandfather's death, she was made to work in the house as
though she were a servant. When I was sixteen, she died. I really
believe her death was due to sheer unhappiness.

Four years later, when my cousin Mary became betrothed to
a young man called Gerald Blanchard, he fell in love with me
instead and I with him, and one summer night I crept out of my
bedchamber window, slid down a low roof, scrambled down some
ivy into his arms and we ran away to be married. Later on, I
sometimes wondered whether a desire to avenge my mother, and
maybe to pay for the unjust birching I had received as a child,
had something to do with that.

But whatever my secret motives, I really did love Gerald and
he loved me, and we were happy, until the smallpox came and
took him from me. I still had our daughter Meg, however. Now,
I was approaching my sixtieth birthday and Meg has long since
married and is living in Buckinghamshire with her family, but
over the years, much had also happened to me. I too became a
lady-in-waiting to a queen – this time to a queen regnant, Queen
Elizabeth – and a desire to augment my stipend in order to support
Meg had led me into undertaking unusual duties for Elizabeth.
I had become one of her secret agents, sometimes going into
danger on her behalf. I had married again, twice, and had borne
a son, Harry, who was now grown up and married in his turn
and was living at Hawkswood, the house I inherited from my
third husband, Hugh Stannard.

And, as though life had turned in a circle, I had returned to
Withysham, now as its mistress. I had of course brought my
personal servants with me. The Brockleys, husband and wife,
had been my good companions for a good thirty years. Roger
Brockley had started out in life as a groom and then a soldier
and was now my right hand. We had been in danger together
and struggled out of it together; we had once come near to being
lovers and though it didn't happen and now never would, there
was a bond that never broke between us.

His wife Frances was my tirewoman and my companion. Her
original surname was Dale and I still called her that, out of habit.
I couldn't imagine life without either of them. Also with us –
brought from Hawkswood after Harry's marriage to our

neighbours' daughter, Margaret Blake – were Eddie Hale, who was an excellent groom and had also shared some of my moments of danger, and the maidservant Bess – formerly Hethercott and now Mrs Hale and expecting their first child.

I hoped the marriage would be a success, for at Hawkswood Eddie had been something of a philanderer and already had two children in the village there. Here, the village of Faldene was well away from the house, which stood high above it on a hillside. I hoped there would be less temptation for Eddie and I kept an eye on him myself.

Though for the next six weeks I wouldn't be keeping an eye on anything or anyone at Faldene. Today, as I had to do twice a year, I must set off for the royal court to attend on my half-sister, the queen. She didn't always summon me to her at the same times of year, but the calls always came. Now, as I watched the mist rise and swirl and dissolve in the soft blue sky I realized, wryly, that three years ago, when I first left Hawkswood to live here, I hadn't wanted to come. Now, I didn't want to leave.

I would call at Hawkswood on the way to the court, of course, to see Harry and Margaret and their two-year-old daughter Helen, but I wouldn't want to go back there to live. It was a different house from the one I had left. For one thing, there were now far more servants, who in my opinion didn't have enough to do, although Harry maintained that a place as dignified as Hawkswood should have a good-sized staff and 'not the stingy one you always insisted on, Mother'.

I had reminded him several times that the reason for my apparent parsimony was because Hugh had once lost a great deal of money in a trading venture when a laden ship sank, and that life had surprising twists and one should always be prepared for them, but he shook his head and said he didn't go in for seagoing ventures. Well, Hawkswood was Harry's now and he would do as he pleased. In his last letter he had said that Margaret was enceinte again and they hoped for a son. I had a gift for her. But I would linger just for one night, and no more. Hawkswood was no longer home.

The mist was almost gone. I had stood at this very window, looking into mist, on the morning of Uncle Herbert's burial. It seemed a long time ago. I turned away and called for Dale. We still had some packing to do.

At Hawkswood I found all in good order. The steward Ben Atbrigge, a former ward of mine, was still young but had been well trained, while Margaret and her personal companion, Katherine Fitzjohn, both knew how to run a good household. There was nothing slapdash about this one. I had feared, of course, being old enough now to make the mistake of underrating the young; I should have known better.

I stayed longer than the one night I had planned, because on the very day of my arrival, Margaret went into labour. She hadn't indulged in any prolonged lying-in but had been visibly blooming and going about her normal tasks. We were at supper and my daughter-in-law was presiding at the table and inviting me to take some more roasted duckling in a sharp sauce that the cook, John Hawthorn, had invented that very day, when her eyes widened and she sat down suddenly, saying, 'Oooh!'

After that, things moved fast. The oldest member of the household, Gladys Morgan, a Welshwoman who had attached herself to me after Brockley and I, years ago, saved her from a charge of witchcraft, for once did *not* prophesy disaster. In any crisis, one could usually rely on her to croak foreknowledge of calamity like a pessimistic raven. This time she merely brewed a pain-relieving herbal drink, which Margaret swallowed willingly, saying that it tasted rather nice.

Meanwhile, Harry sent a messenger to Cobbold House, a few miles away, where Margaret's parents lived, to summon his mother-in-law to her daughter's bedside. But, by the time Mistress Blake arrived and all but fell off her hard-ridden horse at our door, her grandson and mine had come into the world, with the gentle and practised assistance of Katherine Fitzjohn. He could hardly have come more easily.

'I *told* you I was good at this,' Margaret said chirpily, sitting up in bed and addressing her mother and an exhausted and anxious Harry. 'Please thank Gladys for that warm drink she brewed for me; it helped. I think I can hear Helen crying. I expect she's frightened of all the disturbance, poor little lass. Tell her that all is well and she has a new brother. Bring her here and

I'll introduce him to her. And tell Hawthorn to make a careful note of the recipe for that new sauce of his. I think it may have miraculous powers!'

At that moment we heard a clatter of hooves in the courtyard below and the voice of Arthur Watts, Hawkswood's now aged head groom, loudly welcoming someone. I went downstairs to see who it was and met Ben coming up, with two well-known people behind him.

The Speltons, who lived a few miles away on a farm called West Leys, had been part of my life for years. Christopher Spelton, who had formerly been a Queen's Messenger and sometimes one of her agents, had once asked me to marry him and I probably would have done except that while I was dithering, he met another of my former wards, Kate Lake, fell in love with her instead, and lived in a state of hopeless adoration until, in most unhappy circumstances, she was widowed. He let a little time go by and then began to court her. They married and were happy until Kate died, in childbed. Since then, he had married Mildred Atbrigge, the widowed stepmother of my young steward, Ben Atbrigge. The Speltons had known all about the impending happy event at Hawkswood.

'We rode over to wish her well,' said Mildred, 'knowing that she must be near her time, but according to Ben we're too late! How is Margaret?'

'Come and see,' I said and led the way back upstairs. As we emerged into the light at the top of the stairs, I turned and hugged them both. Christopher's head was nearly bald by now but his nice brown eyes were as friendly as they always were, and I knew that he had been happier with Kate and Mildred than he would ever have been with me. Mildred who as a girl had been so awkward and difficult, was now a calm and sensible woman, who had known trouble and danger, had survived them and learned wisdom from them. She was a wife any man might value.

I peered into Margaret's room, asked if she would see them and was instantly urged to bring them in. Soon, we were virtually having a party in the birth chamber, although Margaret couldn't share the wine and drank her son's health in a harmless camomile tisane, another of Gladys' concoctions.

The Speltons stayed for some hours and we all enjoyed their

company. I had left Faldene several days before I actually needed to, just in case of delays. From long experience, I knew that unexpected things could happen. Because of that early start, I was now able to spend two extra days at Hawkswood, long enough to see my new grandson baptized.

He was a vigorous baby even though he had come a couple of weeks before he was expected, and there was no need for great haste. Harry and Margaret, however, thought I would like to be present. The Speltons came over again for the occasion. Dr Joynings, the Hawkswood vicar, came to the house and performed the ceremony in Margaret's bedchamber.

His parents named him Matthew, after Harry's father. It sent a pang through me, for Matthew de la Roche, my second husband, had given me physical joy and a beautiful son but had also been a sworn enemy to Queen Elizabeth and therefore to England. It had wrenched us apart but I would always remember our good days. Since then, I had married Hugh, who was a blessing to me, but I would never forget Matthew.

However, by the time little Matthew had been baptized, all the spare time I had built into my plans had been used up. I had been called to duty and I could delay no longer. I hoped that no unexpected events would hinder my journey to the queen at Hampton Court. However, they didn't.

The unexpected events manifested themselves after I got there.

TWO

Petroc's Tale

We arrived at Hampton Court in a thin drizzle. The only member of the party who was really dry was Dale. Because she could no longer ride for long distances, she had travelled in our little carriage, along with the baggage that among other things contained our elaborate court clothes. Her little blue roan ambling mare, Blue Gentle, had been tethered behind the carriage, which was drawn by Red and Rufus, a pair of smart matched bays that I had lately bought for the carriage. Over the years, the queen's court had grown more and more formal and these days, her kinswoman couldn't arrive at court with her baggage in a mere cart, with only one horse in the shafts.

Laurence Miller was driving. Miller was once a stud groom at Hawkswood, in charge of the trotters' stud I had established there. He was also a kind of guardian to me, for he made regular reports to Sir William Cecil, otherwise Lord Burghley, on events surrounding me. As the queen's half-sister, Cecil insisted that I must have such a guardian and Miller now lived at Withysham, another of my houses, three miles along the valley side from Faldene and continued his watchful duties from there.

Dale might be dry, but Brockley and I had made the journey on the backs of our horses Jaunty and Firefly and, although we were huddled in thick hooded cloaks, we still felt damp. We were glad to arrive and be directed to our guest quarters. I had the right to stable three horses at court, which meant that Firefly, Jaunty and Blue Gentle could be accommodated but no more. Brockley and one of the palace grooms took them away to stable them while Miller unloaded the baggage with the help of the page who served our rooms. After that, he would drive the carriage to Hampton village where he and the bays could rest overnight at an inn before he took the carriage back to Faldene. He knew on what date he should come to fetch me home. At court, in the company of the queen, I didn't need his guardianship.

Dale and I said goodbye to Miller and went to our quarters. These comprised a parlour and two bedchambers; fires were burning in the hearths of all three rooms. The page had evidently lit them when he saw us arriving. In front of one of the bedchamber fires, we arranged two chairs and hung our cloaks over them to dry. As soon as the baggage was in our rooms, we sent the page for wine and set a poker heating, to mull it with.

Half an hour later, Dale and I were taking our ease, seated by the parlour fire and sipping our warm wine, when the page reappeared with an air of haste. *A thousand apologies for the interruption but would Mistress Stannard come to the stable yard?* My man Brockley was involved in a disagreement over the stabling of our horses.

'I will come,' I said. 'Dale, you stay here and keep warm. I expect it's some trivial thing.'

It seemed so at the time. Its later repercussions were actually resounding but I couldn't have guessed that at the time. At any rate, I flung my hooded cloak on again and went with the page to find Brockley indignantly wrangling with a large, brown-bearded man whose penetrating voice was easily audible several yards away. A stocky young groom stood by, holding – or rather, grasping – the bridle of a grey gelding, a good-looking animal except for its laid-back ears and white-ringed eyes.

'. . . how many more times? That dark chestnut of yours must be moved. Your mistress may be entitled to stable three horses here but she can't use the stall where your dark chestnut is. That is the stall that my Grey Cornish here should have. I always put one of my horses there when I am at court and Grey Cornish is a nervous animal and needs a well-lit stall . . .'

At this point, Grey Cornish lunged at his groom and tried to bite him. The groom dodged and gripped the bridle harder.

'Can I help you?' I enquired frostily, from inside my damp hood, as I stepped between Brown Beard and Brockley.

The bearded gentleman turned a cold grey stare on me. 'And you may be . . .'

'I am Mistress Ursula Stannard,' I said. 'Master Brockley here is my manservant and groom. I most certainly am entitled to stable three horses here and these are the stalls I always use. It seems that there may have been some confusion.'

'I have heard of Mrs Stannard, yes. But that stall . . .'

'I always have this group of stalls. They are well-lit, true enough, especially the one where my own horse is now, and they are completely free of draughts. Where is the head groom for this section?'

The queen's stables were enormous and were divided into sections, each with its own head groom. I called to a stable boy who was passing by with a bucket and despatched him to find the one for this run of stabling. After some time, the head groom came hurrying to where the three of us were waiting and quietly simmering. He was full of apologies. He also had an air of authority.

'I am heartily sorry, sirs and madam. I have been with a horse that has had a fall and has injured its knees; otherwise, I would have been here to attend to you. Master Rowe, it is true that these three stalls are always allocated to Mistress Stannard. She is half-sister to the queen, you know.' The authority was in the final sentence. The head groom didn't intend to stand any nonsense. 'Your horse, Master Rowe, is to have the stall at the other end – it's just as well-lit as these. He'll be perfectly comfortable there and his feed is ready. In this dismal weather, we're giving new arrivals bran mash and there is no extra charge for it.'

Master Rowe's groom sidestepped again as his charge made another attempt to bite him.

'Why ever did you buy such a vicious animal?' Brockley enquired.

'He's only nervous. He's had hard treatment, apparently,' Brown Beard said. 'And I didn't buy him. He isn't mine. I've been put in charge of him for the time being until he can be tamed. He really belongs to a cousin of mine who got him cheap because he's so wild. And just because he isn't mine, I still want him treated with the greatest care. My groom Robbie there . . .' he nodded at the stocky young man who was still holding resolutely on to his unfriendly protégé, '. . . is a rare hand with difficult horses and we hope to calm this one down presently. That's why my cousin has left him with me.'

'He tried to kick me this morning,' remarked Robbie, apparently unperturbed by the grey's behaviour. 'But the kick didn't land. He has been very badly handled by a previous owner. We will quieten his fears eventually. May I take him to his stall now?'

'I suppose so.' Master Rowe did not like being defeated but with the head groom's eye on him, he had reluctantly recognized that he must accept it. He gave me a stiff bow. 'Please accept my apologies, Mrs Stannard.' Rowe was evidently one of those who had adopted the short forms of Mr and Mrs, which were now so very fashionable. 'Well, Mr Brockley, it seems that you may go on settling your three. What a pretty thing that blue roan ambler of yours is.'

Stolidly, Robbie said, 'If you will come this way, sir . . .' and led the grey gelding away. Mr Rowe gave us a parting bow and then followed.

'That's all right, then,' said Brockley. 'I'll give ours a rub down and a feed now.' He beckoned to the stable boy, who was hovering. 'If you'd like to earn a penny or two, come and give me a hand with these. They've come a long way in this dismal wet weather. They're muddy and they're tired.'

I left them to it and went rather wearily back to my rooms. Dale at once took my cloak and set it to dry again. While I finished my wine, she began heating water to wash with before we changed into court dress, remarking that she was glad that she at least need only wear a moderate-sized ruff and farthingale, 'While you ma'am, will have to endure the fashionable extremes.'

'Quite so,' I said, as she helped me into the vast farthingale and ruff that the queen's sister was expected to wear. We were hardly done, before our page was once more asking for me. Yet again, I was summoned as a matter of urgency, this time by Sir Robert Cecil, according to the page.

'Sir Robert?' I queried.

'His father Lord Burghley is unwell and remains at his house in the Strand,' said the page. He was a well grown and confident lad, very much a future courtier. 'For the time being, Sir Robert fills his place. Will you come, please? I understand that the matter really is urgent.'

I felt harried but there was nothing to be done about it. Once more, I threw my cloak on and followed the page out and across a courtyard, in a gateway, across another courtyard, in at another entrance, along a passageway, up some stairs and round a corner and eventually into a study, not very large but with beautiful linenfold panelling. I recognized it, for I had been to other meetings here. It was said, long ago, to have been Cardinal Wolsey's study. The page announced me, and from behind a desk, Sir Robert Cecil rose to greet me.

I knew him, though not well. I always felt sorry for him for he was a hunchback. His was not a severe case, more a matter of an awkwardly bulging shoulder, but it was definitely a deformity. I never showed my feelings, though, for he was known to reject any sign of pity with blistering resentment. I knew that his deformity had been a serious disappointment to his parents, although there was nothing wrong with his mind. He was looking at me now out of pale blue, very intelligent eyes. They were the same colour as his father's but without Sir William's warmth.

The page took my cloak away, promising to get it completely dry, and Sir Robert bade me be seated. At the same moment, the door opened again and in came another page followed by three men and then, after a slight pause, by a fourth, who at once went to a writing desk behind the one where Sir Robert was seated and made evident preparations to take notes. Sir Robert's secretary, presumably.

'Sir Robert,' said the page, 'I bring Sir Francis Godolphin, the Reverend John Poole and Master Petroc Roskilly.'

'Welcome, gentlemen. Be seated. Let me present . . .'

Sir Robert introduced us all to each other. I had never seen either Sir Francis Godolphin or his companions before, but I had heard of Sir Francis and knew him to be a Cornishman and a seaman. He didn't look like a seaman now, however, for he was most elegantly dressed, in the latest style. His brown velvet doublet had no puffs or slashes and instead of a ruff, he wore a lace-edged linen collar. I could see that he was middle-aged, but his movements were smooth and there was no grey in his hair, which was black and crimped and worn to his shoulders, hanging down the sides of his face like long, curly ears.

That hairstyle was a fashion I had heard of but not seen hitherto. It struck me as highly unsuitable for a sailor and yet a seaman he assuredly was. As he moved towards the chair that Sir

Robert had indicated, he had the rolling gait that sailors so often acquire from walking unsteady decks and he had the weathered complexion of exposure to sea winds.

The Reverend John Poole was another middle-aged man, this time a vicar, clad in black with the white bands of his calling. Petroc Roskilly was puzzling. He had a ruff but it sat uneasily, as though it didn't belong to him, and I had the impression that his plain fustian doublet didn't fit him properly, either. He had a pleasant face, however, though it was too lined for a man of his age which surely wasn't above thirty. He didn't have the air of being a man of position, but he didn't seem overawed by being in a queen's palace or in the presence of Sir Robert. His brown eyes were interested and, I thought, a little tired, but he wasn't nervous.

During the introduction, I gathered that his calling was that of an itinerant minstrel and that he normally worked back and forth along the considerable length of Cornwall. There were households that knew him and one or other of them could be relied on to shelter him during the winter. He had been offered permanent positions but he liked best to go on travelling through his county.

'Though I didn't reckon on the kind of travelling I've just done,' he said mysteriously.

When we all knew who we were, Sir Robert went straight on to business. 'Let us begin, and I will start with you, Sir Francis. How did you first make the acquaintance of Master Roskilly here?'

'I fished him out of the Atlantic, sir, about two miles south of the tip of Cornwall.'

'Thank you. Now, Master Roskilly, tell us how you came to be in such a dangerous position.'

'I was kidnapped, sir, by one o' they corsair pirate ships that's such a trial to us Cornish folk.' He had an agreeable voice, and a soft Cornish accent. 'Snatched I were, when I were on the road, in between Land's End and Penzance, makin' my way to a house in Penzance where they like to see me. I could rely on a week's stay with 'un and good pay, and they'd invite folks in to hear me and I'd get good pickings from them as well. Only time was getting along and I were thinkin' I wouldn't get to Penzance afore dark, and I'd best go to a village I was near to, where I'd likely get a bed for the night if I'd sing for it and give them all a musical evening. And then two fellows with masks over their damned faces just step out of the bushes and grab me! Took my pack off me, they did, with my lute and my spare clothes in it. I've lost all that. Sir Francis here has lent me what I'm wearing now. When those masked brutes grabbed me, they bundled me up into something that smelt like sacking, then dumped me in a cart. Well, I suppose it were a cart. I heard its wheels and the hooves of a horse. It bumped and lurched, goin' downhill, I reckoned – I were all over bruises – and then I smelt the sea and I guessed I were bein' taken aboard some vessel or other.'

He stopped for breath, exuding resentment at such treatment. Sir Robert said, 'Go on.'

'I were in that boat a long time. I heard oars and wind in sails, and then after a long time – seemed like forever to me – I were lifted up, started to swing in the air I did and I were scared like never before, and then I was thumped down on something hard. I realized later I'd been taken out to sea on a small boat and then shifted to a big one. They took the wrappings off me and there I was on a deck with huge sails high over my head. A brown man as wasn't English though he could speak it, sort of, told me I was aboard a ship with a name I couldn't make out, and she were bound for Constantinople. I never heard of such a thing!'

He sounded so aggrieved that it was almost funny. But Sir Robert didn't smile. He just said, 'Continue.'

'I said I didn't want to go to Constantinople but he just laughed and so did some others as had come up to help him. I was that stiff from the way I'd been brought there that I couldn't hardly walk but they got me moving and took me down into – not the hold, zackly, it were more like a big cabin. There were other folk there. They told me that my pack was safe; they showed it to me and said I'd have it back when we got there. I suppose they meant Constantinople. They said dinner was in an hour! You'd have thought they was running an inn! Ship were on the move by then. I could feel it.'

'Tell us who the others were that were in the cabin with you,' said Sir Francis.

'Sittin' in a row on a sort of long chest, they were. There were

a good-looking lass, all black hair and smouldering dark eyes,'
said Roskilly lyrically. His experiences clearly hadn't dampened
a healthy appreciation of female charms. 'And was she a wildcat!
There were three men as brought me in. She jumped up and tried
to go for them but one of them just got hold of her, laughing,
and snatched a kiss. She spat in his face. He wiped it off with
the back of his hand and said tut tut, naughty temper, smack you
if you're not good, and then shoved her back down on the chest.

'And there was a family: mother, father, three young children
– between ten years old and five, I'd say. Poor little things had
been crying; I could see it. Farming folk, they were; I learned
that while we were waiting for the dinner we'd been promised.
And there were a pair of twins, about twelve, 'dentical girls with
beautiful fair hair and the bluest eyes you ever did see, only
they'd been crying, too; their eyes were all reddened.'

He paused, apparently to let the busily scribbling secretary to
catch up. When the secretary gave him a nod, he continued.
'There were a tall, thin fellow, too. Must have been well past
fifty, I'd say. I gathered he were some sort of scholar, must have
studied languages. Leastways, he said he spoke Turkish and he'd
heard the crew talking and Turkey was where we were bound.
At least I'll be able to talk the language, that's what he said.
There were chains hanging from brackets on the wall – I think
we could have been chained if our captors wanted it but they
reckoned that none of us was much of a threat so we was left
loose.

'Then I made my mind up, sir.' Roskilly's voice changed at
this point. He stiffened his back and seemed to acquire a sudden
air of power and dignity.

'Sir, we'd all been taken as slaves, that was for sure and slave
I wouldn't be. I would *not.* I'm a free man. I walk the length of
Cornwall and back every year and say no when I'm offered
permanent places, 'cos I like the open road, the freedom, the
veering this way and that as my fancy takes me, thinking I'll try
this little village or that house as I can see in the distance, ask
if they'd like an evening of music in exchange for a bed and
breakfast and a coin or two. I'm a *free* man. I'd die afore I'd let
anyone make me a slave.'

His head went back and he looked Sir Robert straight in the

eyes. It struck me that he was a little like Brockley, in that Brockley was also a free man who considered himself inferior to none. Such men loosed the shafts that won the day at Agincourt.

'Please continue,' said Sir Robert.

'I didn't make me mind up right then,' Petroc said. 'I ate their dinner; not bad, it was. Fried fish, fresh out of the sea, and new baked bread and a cheese and cream tart. The dark girl said they'd all been kept chained up in a cave first of all and only brought aboard two days before. It seems the ship had stayed hove to as if waiting for someone or something – maybe me or the likes of me, anyhow! – but now we was sailing. Leaving Cornwall behind! Going to Turkey as slaves! So, when the men come to take away our dinner dishes, I upped and punched the nearest one on the jaw and threw myself past the others and scrambled up a sort of ladder affair that led up to the deck. I tore across the deck and afore anyone could get hold of me, I had dived over the side. I'd drown afore I was a slave! I meant to drown. Only,' said Master Roskilly ruefully, 'there were a problem. I can swim.'

That actually drew a snort of laughter from Sir Robert, and grins from the rest of us. Still in that aggrieved voice, Roskilly said, 'Bloody cold that sea were and it were dark but drown I could not. I just swam, or floated, couldn't damn well help myself. Clothes didn't drag me down; they'd taken my cloak and my shoes just fell off me. It was night. There were a full moon and I were glad to see her; lady of the night I call the moon. But, oh God, that cold! I'd have died of that instead of drowning except that the sea were near as bright as day and Sir Francis' ship come sailin' my way just minutes later and in that moonlight, his lookout saw me splashing about in the water and next I knew they'd lowered a boat and yanked me aboard and I were among honest Cornishmen again.'

'I'd seen that corsair vessel,' said Sir Francis. 'But I wasn't after her; ships from Turkey or Algiers are always coming and going in our waters; traders as likely as slavers, bringing in goods like silks and spices and gemstones. You can't tell the difference until you catch them actually grabbing people. We don't chase them unless we're sure they're slavers – at least, there's some, the Killigrew family, for instance, that will go for them if they think there's treasure aboard but not me. I'm no buccaneer. Anyhow, she was faster than my *Lucy Marie*. I was with my fleet, at sea, training sailor men for war. With these new rumours that Philip of Spain is planning another attempt on us, crews need to be trained. They've got to be able to sail by night, to sail near the wind, to get every ounce of speed out of a vessel, to know how to manoeuvre her. I had to finish my exercise, Sir Robert, or I would have brought Master Roskilly here ashore a month ago. I ask pardon for the delay.'

'Quite so,' said Sir Robert. 'I understand the need to train our seamen. Put against that, one wet minstrel weighs light in the scales.' It was impossible to tell from his tone whether he was being sardonic, joking or just stating facts. His face told us nothing. Godolphin smiled but did not comment. Sir Robert said, 'Now let us hear from the Reverend Poole. When all the witnesses have spoken, we will then decide what to do next.'

Will we, indeed? Sir Robert had assuredly heard the witnesses already, separately, and was already making plans. I knew, and my heart sank as I thought about it, that I would not have been summoned here unless Sir Robert had a use for me. Just as his father so often had, and Walsingham in his day. They had no doubt sought the queen's consent to their plans, but I don't think she would have resisted. Not now. Over the years, Elizabeth had become more ruthless. I might be her sister; in her way, she loved me. But she would let them use me all the same.

The peaceful days at Faldene that I so treasured were receding into the distance.

THREE
An Invisible Enquirer

All eyes now turned to the Reverend John Poole. 'I haven't heard Master Roskilly's tale before,' he said. He too had a Cornish accent but it wasn't marked, only a matter of intonation. This was a man of education.

'But his story ties up with mine,' he told us. 'I am the vicar of a small parish called Polwood, not far from Penzance. When I say small, I mean it. We have cottages and smallholdings but no forge. When I take my mare to be re-shod I have to go to Penzance. I was taking her there one morning about, six or seven weeks ago. The track goes past the gate to a smallholding called White Rocks, after a scatter of broken white rock near the farmhouse, if you can call it that. It's no more than a cottage. It's owned by a landlord in Penzance.

'The people there are my parishioners. Their name is Gray; there's a youngish couple and three children. When they took the place over, neither the cottage nor the smallholding were anything much. The previous tenants had grown old, couldn't look after it properly and finally the landlord realized the state it was in and ordered them out. I think they went to kinsfolk somewhere. The place was in a bad state already and I know that it was hard to find new tenants. A winter passed and by then White Rocks was almost derelict. Stock sold off, holes in the cottage roof, cowshed almost falling down, fields with more weeds in them than anything else. Then the Grays took over and in two years, they've done wonders with it.'

Like Petroc, he paused to make sure that the secretary was keeping pace with him. Then he said, 'As I was passing the gate that morning, I heard such a din, a dog howling, cows blaring – not just lowing, *blaring* – and even ducks quacking as if there was a fox around. So, I got off the mare, threw her reins over the gatepost and went to see what the matter was. There wasn't a human soul in sight but the dog was on a chain and it came leaping towards me, baying madly. I went to it and then it veered away from me and struggled against its chain as if it wanted to reach the ducks. Or the pond. I thought: the poor thing's thirsty. It had a water bowl but it was empty and dry. I scooped some water out of the pond and gave it to the dog and it drank every drop in half a second. Just then someone went past the gate – a labourer walking to work on some other farm. I called him in and we reckoned that somehow, for some extraordinary reason, the Grays had left the place, abandoning their animals. I said to the man I'd called to that I needed help and I'd make it right with his employer and then we went into the cowshed and dear God, there were two cows there, desperate to be milked.

'That labourer was a good fellow. Austol his name was. Between us we found some buckets and we milked the cows and there was a donkey, too, tied in his stall. We gave him water and a feed. We found what Austol said was food for the ducks and we fed them as well. Then we went into the house and looked round. I'd thought perhaps there'd been an outbreak of illness, plague or something. I dreaded what we might come across but we didn't find anything. Or anyone. There was no one there. Hadn't been for a couple of days, we thought.'

He looked round at us all. 'We turned the cows and the donkey out to graze and I took charge of the dog. I got to Penzance, trailing the dog after me, left it and the mare at the smithy and got a boatman to take me across the bay to Porthleven and there I borrowed a horse to get me to Helston, to report the Grays' disappearance to Sir Francis, since he is Sheriff of Cornwall. He was at sea but I left word. I sent word as well to the owner of White Rocks. He has now taken charge of the farm and the animals. I believe there are new people at White Rocks already.'

He paused once more to let the secretary catch up. Sir Robert said, 'Continue, Poole.'

'Two weeks back,' said the vicar, 'Sir Francis summoned me and said I must accompany him here; there were things to be reported at a higher level. I reached here three days ago, waiting for this meeting. Now I learn that this man here, Petroc Roskilly, when he was on that pirate ship, found a farming family of parents and three children. Well, that sounds like the Grays.'

He stopped again, looking at Sir Francis, who now took up the tale. 'The thing is Cornwall's a big county and it has a long coastline, too. Life's always uncertain, things happen; now and then, for this reason and that, people do disappear. There are accidents on cliffs, accidents at sea; people run off – go to sea or go to London. I know an innkeeper in Penzance whose daughter used to go fishing sometimes in her own little boat. Some weeks ago, she disappeared. But her boat came ashore, upside down, brought in on a high tide; everyone supposed she'd had an accident at sea. The innkeeper's still distraught. His daughter was beautiful, he said, took after her mother. Her mother was a gypsy, apparently, and when he married her he had to placate three angry brothers and what it came to was that he bought her. But she was a handsome girl with black hair and dark eyes and so was the daughter. Just like the girl Petroc here saw on the ship. When my ship picked Petroc up, he told me about his fellow prisoners and his report about the beautiful and furious girl made me think at once: was that the innkeeper's daughter?

'It stuck in my mind and when I came ashore again, bringing Petroc with me, I found the written report that Mr Poole had left for me, bringing me news of how the Grays had vanished. As he has just said, their description matches the family that Petroc saw on board the pirate ship. It matches too precisely to be a coincidence. So, I sent a few men round asking about any other disappearances and they came back within three or four days, with results. There have been quite a number of disappearances, too many to be normal mishaps or running away from home. At about the same time as Petroc here was seized, a scholar who lived in a house on the Lizard promontory, overlooking the sea, also vanished. I knew him slightly – I know everyone who lives on the Lizard. But I didn't know him well because he was inclined to be reclusive and never went into society. His name was Edmund Wells. He was aged about fifty and had made a lifelong study of languages, including Turkish. He was also interested in astronomy and had written a treatise about the movements of the stars. He had private means – rents from property somewhere – but he also visited certain houses in Penzance to tutor the children in various languages.

'That's how his disappearance was first discovered; he set out to Penzance to do some tutoring but never got there. His servants have tried to find him, in vain. He had an outdoor man who did the garden and fetched firewood, a groom for his two horses, a personal manservant and a couple of women servants to cook and clean.

'They all thought at first that he would come back soon, that something might have called him away. But when he'd been gone three weeks and there was no one to pay their wages, they dispersed. His manservant sent word to me about the disappearance. I was still at sea then but my steward filed the report and sent a groom to fetch the two horses. They're still in my stables.

'Petroc's description of the scholar he met on the Turkish vessel is another match! All those vanished recently, but one of my men brought back news of an earlier disappearance, last August. A gifted embroideress, able to do gold and silver embroidery, she vanished. It was the same pattern as with Wells. She used to visit various houses to instruct the daughters in her skills and she didn't arrive to give lessons when she was expected.

'Her clients were angry. I think they supposed that she had just tired of them and of Cornwall and had gone to live elsewhere without mentioning it, but my men took the trouble to look at her house. Her door wasn't locked; she might have stepped out just for a moment. Inside, everything was undisturbed. If she went to live elsewhere of her own choice, she didn't take much luggage with her.

'Others of my team of enquirers have reported that, also last August, the captain of a team of tin miners disappeared and so did a potter – a man with a successful business, making fine tableware to an exceptional standard. Again, last August, a young fisherman disappeared from Mawnan, a village near the Helford inlet, and not because of an accident at sea. His boat was found still at its mooring. A girl from St Anthony, across the Carrick Roads from Falmouth, vanished at the same time. There was nothing special about those two except that both of them had vivid red hair.'

'Which you think may be significant?' enquired Sir Robert.

'All the other cases, sir,' said Sir Francis, 'had something special about them. The scholar who speaks so many tongues, the embroideress who is so skilled in her craft and the potter the same. Petroc here speaks of fair-haired twins – well, they are just a little unusual. The innkeeper's daughter is apparently spectacularly handsome, not to mention untamed. Even the family that so abruptly vanished from their smallholding – Mr Poole says they had done wonders with it. And we have two redheads snatched as well.'

'So, what are you saying?' enquired Sir Robert.

'I am saying, sir – at least, I *think* I am saying,' Sir Francis told him, 'that someone, and it seems that a Turkish vessel or at least a Middle Eastern corsair vessel is involved, is snatching selected victims from along the Cornish coast. In every case, the victim lived near the sea. We have constant trouble with slavers from the Mediterranean. They make sudden raids and grab anyone they can get hold of. But this is different. It looks as if these individuals are chosen because they are exceptional or unusual in this way or that. There was a flurry of disappearances last August and now again in spring. As if the chosen ones are collected together to be carried off on a ship that is specially sent to collect them. But if so . . .'

'Yes, Sir Francis?'

'It seems to me, sir, that there must be someone here – I mean in Cornwall – who receives the requests for various slaves with special abilities or exceptional looks, seeks out suitable ones and seizes them in readiness. He snatches them shortly before the ship is expected; whoever it is probably doesn't want to feed and house reluctant captives for too long! He apparently stores his human merchandise in a cave until the ship arrives. I have some suspicions, I'm sorry to say, of my own in-laws. My wife was born a Killigrew and the Killigrew family, whose family home – it's a magnificent place called Arwenack House, not far from Falmouth and about ten miles away from my home at Helston – well, they're notorious. They're a power in the county, but the truth is that they have been buccaneers – pirates! – for generations. And not only out at sea, either. If ever a ship runs into trouble on the rocks of the Lizard peninsula, so it's said, they're down there like the plague of locusts in the Bible, and according to my wife, there are tales that at least in the past, they didn't only grab the cargo, they sometimes murdered the crew. She doesn't know all that much for certain; as a girl at home, she didn't witness such things and wasn't told about them but of course she got to know the tales. Servants' talk! I think that many of the rumours are true. My wife says that her mother – my own mother-in-law – was as keen a pirate as her menfolk only—'

'You *married* one of them?' enquired Sir Robert.

'We were in love, and her dowry was very good indeed. They liked the match, too. Sheriff of Cornwall – I was a catch. Also, my gentle wife was glad to be taken from her birth family.'

'I daresay. And no doubt they were glad to plant her into yours,' said Sir Robert grimly. 'They probably hoped to put law and order in their pockets. I wonder where the dowry came from. Did you ask?'

'No. But I said from the start that I would arrest an in-law just as I would anyone else. I have never had to do so yet. They make a joke of it when we meet,' said Sir Francis ruefully.

'Humph,' said Sir Robert, 'they say that love is a strange thing. The Killigrews are buccaneers and have been for generations father to son. They remain at large because the queen turns a blind eye to buccaneers provided they pay tax on their takings. The Killigrews do. They can probably afford to. Treasure ships sometimes carry emeralds in bags of convenient size for a child to carry.'

He leant back in his seat where there were cushions to keep pressure away from his humped back, and sighed. 'Her Majesty had thought, this year, to make a Progress into Cornwall. She has never done so before. This state of affairs means that no such Progress can now take place.'

Sir Robert shook his head impatiently. 'I suppose that here in Cornwall, whoever is receiving the instructions about who or what kind of people are wanted, and is seeing that they are abducted, has an opposite number in Constantinople, someone collecting the orders – my God, like a servant setting out to the market with a housewife's list of things to buy – and sending them to the agent in Cornwall. We'll never lay hands on *him*. But the fellow at this end *must* be caught. What an appalling situation! The queen can't go on a Progress to a county that is part of her realm!'

Sir Francis looked puzzled. 'But surely just because the corsair ships – I suppose that's really what we're dealing with – have changed the way they work, that's no reason for cancelling a Progress. The corsair raiders have always been there, one way or another.'

'You are not using your imagination, Sir Francis!' said Robert Cecil and unexpectedly revealed a resemblance to his father, who on occasion had a decidedly wayward imagination.

'Sir Francis, you say that people who are unusual in some way are chosen, I suppose to enhance the standing and to inspire envy of the Turkish or Algerian gentry to whom they are sold. The captives are taken apparently in response to requests, but would you put it past their captors to snatch someone who hadn't been, as it were, on the . . . *shopping* list! . . . but who would surely have great appeal when offered for sale? And is therefore worth taking a chance on. If I were a wealthy lady in those lands, my tongue would hang out, I would *dribble*, at the idea of having my dishes washed or my hair brushed, by the unbeliever queen of England.'

We were all silent. Aghast, I think. But after a moment or two, we realized that we were relieved. The danger had been recognized in time. Our sovereign lady would not come to harm. She wouldn't come anywhere near Cornwall. Then Sir Robert said, 'There is one more thing is there not? Sir Francis?'

'There is, but no one can be sure that it – or they – are connected to the disappearances. There have been two killings.' Sir Francis spoke sombrely. 'One was a young woman, Beryon Lander, a servant in the house of a lady of some substance, a widow called Mistress Juniper Penberthy. She lives just outside Penzance, on the Land's End side, in Juniper House. It has juniper trees in the garden. Mistress Penberthy planted them when she came there as a bride. They reminded her of home, apparently. Her parents had such trees in their garden and even named her for them. The girl Beryon was Mistress Juniper's laundress. She was found drowned in a washtub. It was a big one; she used to soak things in it before putting them into a smaller tub where she could really work on them. She was found hanging over the side with her head in the water. It may not have been murder; Beryon might have fainted for some reason and fallen if it happened while she was leaning into the tub. Only, there was an inquest, and it was said that anyone who fainted while working at the tub would surely have fallen to the floor, not into the water, that it was most unlikely that enough of their weight would have been over the edge of the tub for that. Also, there was bruising on her ankles as though someone had upended her and held her head down in the tub, and there was water splashed about as though there had been a struggle. The verdict was murder, but the finger hasn't been pointed at anyone.

'The other was the son of a fisherman called Jago. Just that – he has no other name. He has, or had, four grown sons; they're all fishermen too. The youngest, aged twenty, was found lying in his own rowing boat, with his throat cut. There was no doubt about whether that was murder. But the boy had been quite a lad among the girls. A cut-throat could have been the wrath of an outraged husband or father. There is no certainty. It's just that these sorry events have happened now, when the disappearances are taking place.'

Sir Robert nodded gravely. 'It does seem that Cornwall is just now a place of perilous mystery, shall we put it that way? For myself, my first concern is the safety of the queen. The idea of a Progress into Cornwall must certainly be forgotten. She is now considering a Progress through the counties around London. Her Majesty has in any case never cared to make Progresses through the country very far from London. She has been hesitant from the first about travelling to Cornwall. It was her own idea to begin with, but she has changed her mind now.'

There was a silence, until Sir Francis said, 'Our quarry may well be someone who has a good position in life. It could even be me.'

Everyone laughed politely.

Sir Robert smiled thinly and then said, 'What is plain is that something must be done. Her Majesty's subjects are under her protection; this can't go on.'

John Poole said unhappily, 'Along the Cornish coasts, yes, and along the Somerset and Devon coasts as well, there have been raids by slavers ever since anyone can remember. It's been impossible to stop them.'

'I was caught in one of them once,' I said. It was a hateful memory.

'This is . . . selective,' said Sir Robert. 'It seems certain that there is an agent in Cornwall who takes the orders, finds people who fit with them and has them captured and waiting when the ship arrives to take them to the Mediterranean. He would need to be based in Cornwall in order to be able to find and catch his prey. Once we have him, this loathsome trade, this betrayal of the queen's people from within, will naturally cease. In the Tower of London,' said Sir Robert, in a tone now as soft and deadly as the slither of an adder, 'there is a cell prepared for him. We must make sure he claims his reservation.'

There was another silence, before Sir Francis said, 'I would undertake the investigation willingly but I am too prominent and my Killigrew in-laws are an embarrassment. We need an invisible enquirer.'

Without glancing at me, he added, 'The house on the Lizard, where the scholar Edmund Wells dwelt, now stands empty. As far as anyone has been able to ascertain, he had no kin. But what if, after all, he had? What if someone came along to take charge of his house and settle there? His sole heir, a distant cousin, perhaps. Who would question it?'

I clasped my hands in my brocade lap and stared down at them. I didn't want to catch Sir Francis' eye and certainly not Robert Cecil's.

'It would need to be someone who appeared quite harmless,' said Sir Robert. I interpreted his tone as silky and menacing. 'A middle-aged lady, maybe, with one or two servants brought from her former home. Perhaps a widow who had previously just had a small house and a small income. Such a lady might be very glad to take over a good-sized house on the Lizard and a number of rents from property.'

'I wasn't going to suggest a lady,' said Sir Francis, visibly disconcerted. 'Surely, this isn't a task for a woman.'

Sir Robert ignored him and smiled at me. I knew he was smiling even though I was still staring into my lap. I could not go on avoiding his eyes. I raised my head and looked at him. I said the first thing I could think of. 'Sir Robert, I am past middle-age. I shall be sixty this year.'

'But you are seemingly in good health.' He showed no surprise because I had read his mind. 'And no physical effort would be required of you. The house is furnished, just as Master Wells left it. All you would have to do would be just to go there and take up residence. Yes, I am considering you. You are experienced. You would make acquaintances, talk to people, talk to womenfolk, perhaps learn things that a man, even one not burdened with inconvenient in-laws, could not.'

'Have you thought, sir, that I could be a target myself?' I was cold inside. I wondered what on earth the Brockleys would think of this. 'Perhaps some fine Turkish lady would like to have a queen's sister washing her dishes or her linen, even a sister born out of wedlock.'

'You would not be there as yourself,' said Sir Robert soothingly. 'We will give you a name, a history, that will protect you. You can be . . . yes . . . Mistress Archer. Mistress Catherine Archer. Every other lady in the realm is a Catherine. No one in Cornwall knows you by sight. We would give you all the information we can, to help you. I believe that Sir Francis has a written list of the disappearances, and the places from which they vanished.'

'I can hardly believe this!' said Sir Francis, shocked.

'You needn't believe it if you don't want to,' said Robert Cecil, 'though surely you wondered what Mistress Stannard was here for. If you have that list with you, please hand it to her.'

'I assumed that she was representing her sister, the queen,' said Sir Francis stiffly. 'Yes, I have a copy here.' Eyeing me with frank disapproval, he handed me a folded paper.

'Thank you,' I said. Nervously, I stowed it away in my hidden pouch. Life as a secret agent had caused me to adopt the fashion of open skirts with pretty kirtles beneath. Within these skirts I stitched pouches where I could carry such things as a small dagger in a sheath, a set of picklocks and some money in a little purse. It had become a habit. I had hoped never to undertake any more assignments but I still maintained the pouches.

'Can I refuse, or is this an order from the queen?' I asked bluntly.

'I have naturally consulted Her Majesty,' said Sir Robert. 'She says that you should undertake this task only of your own free will. But I think she also assumes your consent. As far as I am concerned,' said that silky, silky voice, 'it is a command.'

In strangled tones, I said, 'Then naturally, I consent.'

Back in my rooms, I sent Dale to fetch Brockley from the stables where he was tending our horses. When she came back with him, I told them what had passed in the pleasant little study with the linenfold panelling. They were silent, horrified.

I sat there on the cushioned settle in the little parlour and, irrelevantly – I think because I didn't want to think, let alone talk, about Sir Robert's frightening assignment – I said, 'Sir Francis Godolphin was wearing his hair in this new fashion, long and curled and hanging down on each side of his face. I wonder if he wears his hair like that when he's aboard ship.'

'Can you see a man with hair like that standing on a deck and shouting *ready about*?' Brockley said. 'I've already noticed a good few courtiers with that hairstyle but I think most of them are wigs.' He smiled mischievously at Dale. 'How do you think I would look in such a wig, Fran? There's a good wigmaker in Guildford, I know.'

'Brockley,' I said, 'I will not have you going about looking like a spaniel. Oh, dear God,' I added, giving way, 'how can I face pretending to be Mistress Catherine Archer, widow of limited means, happy to be the heir to a house on the Lizard!'

'What *is* the Lizard?' asked Dale.

'Master Hugh had a lot of maps,' I said. 'I've often looked at them. I brought them to Faldene with me from Hawkswood. There isn't one of Cornwall on its own but there's a fair-sized map of England that includes Cornwall, shows the main towns and the shape of the county, anyway. We went to Cornwall once, remember? Years ago. We went almost to the tip of it. But I don't think we bothered too much about its geography. From Hugh's map, it's a very long county, and near its tip it splits into two, like huge claws. One is called Land's End and the other is called the Lizard. There's a bay in between, with an island in it. I believe that in the last century, when the pretender Perkin Warbeck tried to raise an army in the west of England, he made a stay on that island. St Michael's Mount, I think it's called. Sir Robert Cecil owns it, I think, but there's only a caretaker staff there. The Lizard looks big enough to have farms on it, but Sir Francis said that the Wells' house overlooked the sea. I fancy it's a lonely place.'

'And we're going there,' said Dale, not very enthusiastically.

'I rather think we are,' I said.

FOUR
The Queen's Burden

T hat was the point at which Brockley cleared his throat
and said, 'Are we? I must say, madam, that I have something to say in the matter.'

I looked at him enquiringly. Dear Brockley. He must be over
sixty now but he hadn't changed much through the years. His
high, gold-freckled forehead was the same as ever and his steady
blue-grey eyes met mine with the same old concern and assurance.
Brockley had always had assurance. Before becoming my
personal manservant and sharing in my sometimes uncomfortable
way of life, he had been a groom employed by an aristocratic
house and then a soldier, following King Henry into France. He
knew the world.

He also longed to protect me from it. He didn't really approve
of my curious career as a secret agent any more than Sir Francis
Godolphin did, although he had a latent streak of adventurousness
and when necessary, he had proved to be a stalwart and resourceful
colleague. However, just now, his protective instincts were to the
fore.

'This could very well be a dangerous assignment,' he said.

'I know,' I said. I was all too well aware of it. I wanted with
all my heart to refuse it. I wanted with all my heart to complete
my attendance on the queen and then go home to dear, safe
Faldene and ask how my maidservant Bess was faring in her first
pregnancy, see how my corn was growing and whether my orchard
was promising well. I didn't want to go to Cornwall, which I
remembered as though it were a foreign land, with an atmosphere
all its own. Least of all did I want to step into the path of slavers,
to risk . . .

The thought of that risk made my stomach twist. Only, I knew
well enough that this order did not come from Sir Robert Cecil
or even from his bedridden father.

It came from the queen. These orders always did and how could I refuse them? I was a lady of the bedchamber, I was her servant, I was her sister and her blood kin. I could not say no.

Brockley was still talking. 'Whoever is organizing these snatches is surely being well-paid for his trouble. Trouble it must be! He has to work through a shopping list, as Sir Robert Cecil so feelingly puts it. He has to seek out victims who match the orders he has been given, find ways of abducting them and getting away with it. He is betraying and selling the queen's subjects and if he is caught, he will die a traitor's death. Difficulties and risks like that command high fees. If he once realizes that you are intruding into his affairs, he – or they, for surely this isn't a one-man business – will resent it fiercely. He will also be alarmed. And if he, or they, do guess that Mistress Catherine Archer is really Mistress Stannard, half-sister to the queen, well, she would from his point of view be a suspect, she would also . . .'

'I would be a prize myself,' I said. 'Yes, I know.'

'I would rather use the word *victim*. We've been told of two murders that may or may not be linked to this business. If they are, in all probability, those two, the laundress and the young fisherman, they knew too much and were got rid of, both to silence them and warn off others. You would run a double risk, madam, of being either murdered or sold. I can't let you do this.'

'I agree!' Poor Dale dreaded danger and I had dragged her into it so many times. The marks of her childhood smallpox always seemed to stand out more when she was upset and they were standing out now. Her slightly protuberant blue eyes were full of worry. 'This isn't right for you, ma'am. It's *too* dangerous. That man Robert Cecil ought to be ashamed of himself, wanting to send you into such peril. Ma'am, you could end up dead, or else scrubbing floors in Turkey. And so might I!'

'I don't like it either,' I said. 'But it's an order. And . . .'

'No one has ordered me,' said Brockley. 'I can't prevent you from going, madam, but I can refuse to accompany you. And I will, unless you have better protection than just myself. And I don't suggest Miller, by the way. Miller may be the guardian Cecil appointed for you but he's not an experienced agent or all that handy with weapons. You don't like him much anyway and besides that, he has duties at home.'

There was a silence.

The little parlour was a pleasant place. The fire crackled softly in its hearth and the colours of the cushions were bright; the leaded window gave a view of a courtyard with a fountain in the middle. I could also see a stretch of rosy brick wall trimmed with pale stone at the top, and in the centre of it, the lofty entrance to an inner courtyard. My lodgings were a place to be comfortable; to talk of agreeable things such as the latest fashions in hairstyles, yesterday's hunt, tomorrow's card party, the latest dance, the latest song, the weather. It was no setting in which to talk of slavery and murder.

Eventually I said, 'What do you mean by protection, Brockley?'

'It's hard to be certain, madam. I think I mean at least one man experienced in dangerous affairs and accomplished in arms. *At least one man.* I can't take on such a responsibility alone.'

'I see.' I thought about it. At last, I said, 'I agree about Miller. I would rather he went home to Withysham, kept a protective eye on Faldene, and was ready to help if the stud groom at Hawkswood wants to consult him. At this season, there is young stock to train and prepare for sale, foals soon to be born and mares to be mated. He's likely to be called upon to advise. I would rather he was there to answer the call. We must find someone else. If we do, will you then agree to come?'

'I suppose I must,' said Brockley grimly. I could see he was realizing that although I was reluctant, I was also resigned. He knew me very well. 'If you won't heed my warning and insist upon going, then I suggest you ask for Christopher Spelton,' he said.

Christopher Spelton, one of my most longstanding friends, a man I had once almost married, who was now married to Mildred Atbrigge, a young widow and a former ward of mine. He had been a Queen's Messenger and also an agent. Christopher met the requirements, certainly. I had once seen him whisk his sword out of its scabbard and take a man's head off, all in one smooth and unbelievably swift movement. But . . .

'Christopher is a married man with a family of children to rear and provide for. I don't want to put him at risk. I wouldn't wish to see Mildred widowed for a second time. She has had trouble enough in her life.'

'Master Spelton came to see us when we were at Hawkswood,

madam. While you ladies were all attending on Mistress Margaret, the men talked. Well, Master Harry was too worried about his wife to talk to us much, but Master Spelton and I had a long conversation. He has money troubles, madam. West Leys never has been so very productive, as you know, and from time to time Master Spelton goes back to acting as a Queen's Messenger and – now and then – as a queen's agent. Yes, he has a family, of four little girls. The eldest, his stepdaughter Susanna, is nearly thirteen. In a few years' time she will be ready for marriage, and she will need a dowry if she is to marry well. That means a man who can offer her a comfortable and secure way of life, who can afford to bring up their children in comfort, educate them and give them a position in life. It's a ruthless world, madam. The kind of man we would all want for Susanna would take it for granted that his bride would have a dowry. Even when it's a love match, which is what we would all hope for.'

'Lord Burghley recommends early betrothals, to prevent girls from making imprudent matches just because they've fallen in love,' I said. 'But yes, even in a love match, I expect a dowry would be needed. I can see that providing for four wenches could be a . . . challenge.'

'And Master Spelton must somehow meet it. I don't think that Sir Robert would grudge the cost of hiring him to help you – to help us. If he hesitates, you can prize his coffers open just by saying you won't undertake the task unless you have more assistance. Your own payment, in view of the risk, ought to be substantial and if – let's face it, madam – if Christopher were killed in the course of his duty, I think Sir Robert would have to see that his family were cared for. If you can't be persuaded to refuse this assignment, then you should arrange in advance for a suitable agreement to be drawn up. I would like Fran to be similarly cared for if anything happened to me. I would wish the terms to be set out in writing, signed and witnessed. Then Christopher's family would be secure and Fran here would be a well-off widow in her own right . . .'

'Please don't!' Dale protested.

'It would be almost worth Master Spelton's while,' said Brockley thoughtfully, 'to get himself killed, or taken. His family could do well out of it. Even I . . .'

'*Brockley!*'

Brockley gave me that occasional, mischievous grin of his. 'On the whole, I would rather go on living, madam and living free, at that. If I have to go to Cornwall because you insist, then, I repeat, we must have at least one more experienced agent and experienced swordsman at your side. I would like you to have a private army of them but it would attract too much attention.'

Brockley, as ever, was talking sense. 'I will put it to Sir Robert,' I said. 'For a moment, I feared you would say that you wouldn't come with me at all, under any circumstances.'

'I considered it, madam,' Brockley said candidly. 'But – I know you. This is an order from the queen and therefore there can be no more argument!'

'If Christopher is willing,' I said, 'I would be glad to have him. I know this will be dangerous. Not to mention difficult! I can't imagine where we can start! I will negotiate for you and Christopher. I'll push your rates of pay and compensation up as high as I can get them.'

Sir Robert, as it turned out, was agreeable. In fact, he was ahead of me. Yes, he did think I should be better protected than I would be with just the Brockleys at my side, and yes, Christopher Spelton was a good choice, and yes, if either of them were 'lost', as he carefully put it, meaning killed, disabled or snatched into slavery, then the futures of Christopher's family, and also of Dale, must be safeguarded.

This time, my attendance on the queen was cut short. I stayed with her for only two weeks, instead of the six that was usual. I had one private talk with her before I went. She always did have such a talk with me when I was at court but over time, these had grown more and more formal. These days, instead of a loose gown and slippers, she usually wore court dress, with a mighty ruff and farthingale and long ropes of pearls, and she would be seated on a throne-like chair in an audience chamber, not casually at the desk in her study, or on a settle in the ante-room to her bedchamber. These days I, as often as not, had to remain standing throughout. It was a long time since she had asked me to address her as Sister.

This time, however, she summoned me to the anteroom, and

it was as though time had run backwards, for she was in a loose peach-coloured gown with neither ruff nor farthingale and she invited me to sit beside her on a cushioned settle. She bade me call her Sister and several times called me so in return. After a few pleasantries, she said abruptly, 'So, Sister, you are once more going into danger for my sake.'

'I am going to Cornwall, Sister, yes. I shall make a brief call at Faldene to set all in order for a long absence, and then I shall go on to Cornwall and to the house on the Lizard.'

'You can refuse if you wish. Sir Robert says you are the best person to make what he calls these enquiries and Lord Burghley, my dear Cecil, agrees with him but Cecil warns me that there are serious dangers. There have been suspicious deaths. I gather that his son has virtually ordered you to undertake this enquiry, but I countermand that. You are free to say no. I understand that if you do go, Christopher Spelton will go with you. For my part I would let him perform the task on his own. He is more than capable.'

'Sister, the arrival of a stranger is sure to be noted and talked about and a man, of mature years and considerable dignity, just might arouse suspicion if he appeared on his own. Whoever is organizing these kidnappings, will be on the alert for . . . enquirers. When Sir Francis first began to be suspicious, he sent a few men around to ask questions. Whoever is doing this will be no fool; by now he has realized that the mysterious disappearances have been linked up and are attracting attention. He will be watching for investigators. Master Spelton will be safer in the guise of Mistress Archer's manservant.'

'And Mistress Catherine Archer, a middle-aged widow with a modest household in the form of a maidservant, a manservant and a groom, taking over the home of a man who is not likely to come back to it, that won't be so suspicious?'

'I think not,' I said. I felt heavy at heart, as though I were planning my own funeral. 'I shall let it be known that I am Wells' cousin and his only relative and that in any case I do but care for the property and will relinquish it if ever he returns. I shall say I hope that he would in that case let me stay, continue to look after it and look after him. I shall live quietly and appear to have only a little natural interest in my neighbours.'

'You will have some lively ones. You have heard of the Killigrews, I gather. They have their family home at Falmouth, not so very far from you. They are more of a tribe than a family and nearly all of them, according to Sir Francis Godolphin, have at times engaged in piracy. Some of them are still buccaneers, swelling my treasury with treasure seized from Spanish shipping. Sir Francis himself has a wife who was born a Killigrew and his mother-in-law was once an enthusiastic pirate in her own right! She's dead now but the Killigrews are a dangerous family. Beware of them, Ursula.'

Elizabeth shook her head at me. She had suffered a loss of hair after an attack of smallpox and had resorted to wigs. The one she was wearing gave her waves of a magnificent red-gold, with pearls entwined in it. 'I don't know how you can set about your task,' she said frankly. 'You will have to seek information without seeming to do so. Ladies living quietly, without showing an undue interest in their neighbours, rarely ask the kind of questions you will need to ask.'

'I know,' I said and hoped that I didn't sound as sombre as I felt. 'However, I hope I shall think of ways around that.'

'Well, I can believe that. You have never lacked resourcefulness. Learn what you can but take no risks. You are *not* ordered to go. It is your decision.'

Elizabeth sighed a little and stirred on the settle. Despite the fine jewelled wig, she was wearing no cosmetics and as she moved, the light from a window fell upon her face and showed me how lined she had become. Where was the beautiful young queen I had known when first I entered her service? Elizabeth was growing old.

She was one year older than I was. I too was feeling my years. I was past the age for dangerous adventures. But . . .

Suddenly she burst out, 'It's intolerable, Ursula! I will not have my people picked over and picked up and the best of them taken away as though they were the plumpest chickens, or the leafiest cabbages on a market stall, or pieces on a chessboard, taken by an opponent. It is bad enough that there are raids along those south-western coasts. I have ships always there, trying to prevent it, but it still happens, again and again. But this . . . this *choosing* . . . of this person and that . . . it's outrageous. There is – there must be – someone in Cornwall with greater knowledge and power than my own, who buys and sells individuals as a dealer might buy and sell horses. It's hateful. I thought of making a Progress through Cornwall this year. I was uncertain, however, and now I know that I cannot. My council wouldn't allow it even if I myself were willing to take the chance.'

She shuddered. I saw it. 'I know now,' she said, 'because my spies in Spain have confirmed it, that Philip of Spain is creating a new *armada*, to attack these shores again. But Philip I could face, as a queen and an equal. His army I could face! If they landed and I knew that all was lost, I would put on armour and ride out to meet them, sword in hand, to die in the field. But this is different. My council are right. I must not go to Cornwall. Slavery! To be taken from my people, taken away from England, the country to which I am espoused, to which I have sworn to be a lifelong servant – that would be intolerable. My coronation ring is my wedding ring. I have a duty to England. I will not endure slavery and I will not see my people sold like chattels either. I want whoever is behind this monstrous business taken, clapped into the Tower and brought to the scaffold.'

'I will do my best to put them there,' I said, and I finished the sentence with the words 'Your Majesty,' addressing her by her full rank, to indicate how seriously I took this latest mission.

She sighed again. 'I am losing my old companions. Time is taking them from me. Walsingham has gone, so has my sweet Robin of Leicester; Cecil keeps to his bed most of the time. Essex, my Robin's handsome stepson, is good company but there is a waywardness in him that I find wearisome at times. Come back to me safely, Ursula. You are not to lose your life or your freedom. Be wary. Be cautious.'

Before she sent me away, she kissed me and for a moment she held me as though she didn't want me to leave her. Then she let me go and as I went, there were tears in my eyes. Hers was a burdensome life and she must carry that burden until the end. I at least had the alternative of running away from mine.

Before I left the court, I had more than one private interview with Sir Robert Cecil, as we settled details of my prospective journey. He knew that I was going into danger but, quite simply, he considered me the best person for the task. He was quite as ruthless as Walsingham had ever been.

At the time of his death, Sir Francis Walsingham had been Secretary of State and also the queen's spymaster. A tall figure, always dressed in black, he had been as formidable to look at as he was ruthless in rooting out treason. Elizabeth had disliked him to the point, at times, of throwing things at him, but she had trusted him utterly. I think she now trusted Sir Robert Cecil in the same way. She had told me that I could choose not to go but she hadn't vetoed it, either. To me, that was the same as a royal command. I asked Sir Robert to supply me with a really good map of Cornwall and a really good sufficiency of funds as well. I said that if I or any of my companions should be captured but could be rescued if a ransom were paid, then I would expect it to be paid. Sir Robert agreed without argument, and the agreement that was finally signed included a clause about that.

During that final two weeks at court, I also had a visit from Sir Francis Godolphin.

He came unexpectedly, one afternoon. He asked to talk to me in private, so I sent Dale and Brockley out of hearing and poured wine for the two of us. I had by then bought a keg of good wine for myself, rather than have to buy whatever the court cellars had to offer. I handed his glass to him and said, 'So, what is this private matter?'

By now it was April. The day was warm so the fire wasn't lit but there was a full wood basket beside it and Dale had laid it just in case. Sir Francis sat down opposite to me. He crossed his sleekly stockinged legs, adjusted his curly spaniel's ears of a wig, and remarked that my choice of wine was admirable.

Then he said, 'I am here to tell you that I am not at all happy about this proposed mission of yours. I don't think women should be employed in such a way. If you wish to withdraw, and I certainly urge you to do so, I will support you. This is no task for a lady. You risk being killed; you risk being enslaved. I don't like it.'

'Neither do I,' I admitted. 'But I understand how Sir Robert is thinking. I am the most suitable choice because I am the least obvious. My . . . quarry may well have the same view of women as you have, Sir Francis. I haven't undertaken any assignments for the queen now for years. My reputation has dwindled. No one will expect me to be caught up in this and of course I am not going under my own name. I hope to be just Edmund Wells' cousin, come to take over his home unless or until he returns to it. I suppose he really doesn't have any relatives, by the way? You said that you know him a little.'

'Yes, I do, or did. But I never asked him about his family and he never mentioned having one, even in the sense of having distant cousins. He once had a sister but she died some years ago. If anyone suddenly appears, claiming to be his heir, well, we will deal with that when it happens.'

'Very well. I shall be Mistress Catherine Archer, cousin to Edmund Wells, and not reclusive as he was but wishful to make acquaintances in the district, naturally interested in local gossip, concerning disappearances and two murders. Her servants will be just the same. By the way, what about Master Wells' servants? Surely they have been questioned?'

'Yes, we managed to trace them all but none of them knew anything and there's nothing whatever against any of them. One of his women servants, a girl named Tamzin – only about eighteen and betrothed to a young man in Penzance – was away from the house that day, attending a christening service. Her father is a builder, quite well-off and just as well, as his wife never stops breeding and all the children so far have survived. Tamzin went to Penzance the day before the christening and wasn't expected back until the day after. The same applies to the boatman, Griffin Brown, who ferried her across the bay to Penzance. His wife is a distant cousin of Tamzin and they were going to attend the christening as well. On the actual morning of the christening, Master Wells was seen by a farmer's wife who delivered eggs and butter to him. It would seem that Tamzin and Griffin are clear of suspicion and they don't look like suspicious characters anyway.'

'Well, Mistress Archer and her companions can only do their best,' I said. 'We *may* pick up useful information – who knows? A snippet here and a snippet there and suddenly, the snippets may come together in a pattern. At least we can try.'

'So, you are willing to go and intend to go?'

'The queen is distressed and very angry at the way her subjects are apparently being picked off like pieces being taken from a chessboard, as she puts it. She dares not make a Progress through what is after all part of her realm, and this outrages her. Something must be done.'

'You didn't answer my question.'

'My mission as you have called it, is for the queen. She is my sister and the victims of this ugly trade are her subjects, her care.'

'I see, I think.' Godolphin's expression, though, was one of exasperation and he emptied his wineglass with a single impatient swallow. 'I leave for my Cornish home tomorrow,' he said. 'I shall be there when you arrive; Helston, where I live, is ten miles from Cliff House, as Wells' home is called, but there's a direct track. Do please call on me for help if you need it. We will meet socially, of course. My wife would like to meet you, I know, though I shall not tell her who you really are. You will be Catherine Archer to her. I shall pray, Mistress Stannard, not only for your success but for your safety. Women should *not* be involved in things of this kind – but when the queen orders, there is of course, no more to be said. I will see that there is someone at Cliff House to welcome you when you arrive and see that you are comfortable. That list of disappearances that I gave you – you have it safe?'

'Yes, indeed, Sir Francis.' I gently pressed my skirt and heard the list rustle in my pouch.

'And you truly mean to undertake this task?'

'Yes, I do.'

Sir Francis went away, shaking his head in sorrow.

FIVE

The House on The Cliff

Cliff House, once the home of Edmund Wells, master of languages, was well named, for it stood high on a cliff, overlooking a wide bay. According to my vague memories of the visit I had made to Cornwall long ago, and also according to the map I had asked for, this was Mount's Bay and the island in the midst of it was St Michael's Mount, where Perkin Warbeck had once lurked. Across the bay was the town of Penzance. Its clustered roofs were visible from the path we were following, along the western side of the Lizard promontory.

Christopher had joined us at Hampton Court, where he had more than one interview with Sir Robert Cecil 'to receive the instructions that you have had already, Ursula,' he told me. On leaving the court, I needed to make a brief visit to Faldene, to prepare my household for an absence of unknown length. Christopher came with me. Then we all set out for Cornwall together: myself, Christopher and the Brockleys.

Dale as usual travelled in the carriage with the luggage. Christopher and Brockley shared the driving. When not driving, they rode their horses which otherwise were tethered behind, along with Dale's ambler. I rode or used the carriage if the weather was bad.

We made the best speed we could but what with the carriage and the tethered horses, all of which slowed us down, and a good many days of bad weather, we were travelling for over a fortnight. On one occasion, the carriage became bogged down in mud so badly that it took half a day and the help of a big horse borrowed from a nearby farm before we could get its wheels free.

We made use of the time by getting accustomed to our new names. We addressed each other by them. I was Mistress Catherine Archer. Brockley and Dale were Mark and Mary Smith. Christopher kept his Christian name but adopted the surname of

Wood. We were fairly used to our new identities before the afternoon when we reached our destination. It was Friday, the thirteenth of May. Dale said it was a bad omen.

The track to Cliff House left the main road onto Penzance and Land's End and took us, always in sight of the sea, along the huge headland that according to my map, stretched its claw far southwards. Away to our left, on the broad back of the Lizard, we caught sight of villages and farmland, glimpsed grazing animals and the hearth smoke of cottages. On our right was the bay. There was a wind, tossing our horses' manes about and bringing us the smell of the sea.

The light had an astonishing clarity that I didn't recall from my earlier visit. We could see the harbour and the roofs of Penzance so well that it seemed as though anyone capable of taking a running jump could get there with a single leap. There were numerous small vessels dotted about in the bay, and further out, in the open sea, were a couple of big ships with billowing sails. They were made small by distance, and yet we could see details: one ship had a sail with a patch, the other had what looked like a dragon for a figurehead. Then, at last, we came in view of Cliff House.

It wasn't actually on top of the cliff but on what I can best describe as a deep shelf, about three quarters of the way up. A right-hand branch from our track went towards it, down a gentle incline. It was quite broad enough for the carriage. At the foot we came to a weathered wooden fence with a gate. Brockley, who was riding, dismounted to open it. We passed through, on to a wide paved space in front of an oaken front door. Here we stopped.

The journey along the Lizard had been quite exhilarating but the sight of the house was not.

'Is this it?' said Dale disparagingly as she clambered stiffly out of the carriage. Her ambler, Blue Gentle, who had made the entire journey on a tether behind the carriage, snorted loudly as though agreeing.

Master Wells had lived in a tall, narrow house, four storeys of it, built of dark stone; bleak, stark and uncompromising. It was almost a tower, protected from the north wind by the cliff though it seemed plain enough that if north winds couldn't get at it, then south-westerly gales could. I looked about me and at once, I found that I knew all too well how south-westerlies would howl around this building as though trying to take possession of it, warping window frames, pouring draughts through every room, penetrating every crevice, so that floors and doors and timber staircases would creak as if the place were full of ghostly presences. It was not inviting.

Seen close up, the shelf where the house stood was much broader than it had looked at first and extended a good way to our left. There was a stone archway on that side and before we tried the front door we went through the arch to see where it led. We found ourselves in a combined courtyard and stable yard, very much the arrangement that Hawkswood had.

On our left, stretching away from us, the place was bounded by a wall, which caught my attention at once because a blackbird was on top of it, apparently pecking for worms. Worms don't as a rule live on the tops of walls, so I turned my head as we rode in and was surprised. Beauty wasn't a word I would have associated with that forlorn tower of a house, but I had never seen a wall as beautiful as this. It was very thick and quite high, and its lower levels consisted of three layers of flat stones, laid horizontally. Above them were three more layers of similar stones but this time standing on end like books packed tight on a shelf. The effect was an attractive pattern and at the very top, like marchpane icing on a cake, was a layer of earth thick enough for grass to grow from it. The blackbird evidently regarded it as a natural haunt of worms.

I could not, however, spend long admiring even the most beautiful of walls. Facing us was a long run of stabling, along with a tack room and an open-fronted barn where we could see a stack of hay bales and to our right, opposite to the remarkable wall was a square stone building that – judging by the slender chimney – was probably a wash-house. Next to this was a little edifice that looked encouragingly like a well-head. Next to that was a large shed and beyond all these we glimpsed a garden with flowers and shrubs and what I thought might be a vegetable patch.

All this was much friendlier than the house itself. I felt more hopeful. Brockley handed me down while Christopher, who had been driving, climbed down as well and helped Dale out of the carriage. Brockley passed his reins to me and went to look into the barn. He came back to say that he had found bales of straw as well as hay, and a barrel with oats in it. At least we could feed our horses and the well promised a supply of fresh water. These were hopeful signs.

We were working together to unsaddle our mounts and release Red and Rufus from the shafts when, from a side door into the house, a small, plump woman came hurrying. She had a white apron over a brown fustian dress, a white cap from which just a few strands of greying hair had strayed, and a harried expression.

'You're here at last! You will be Mistress Archer? I am so glad to see you, so very glad. These are your people? I am so *thankful* that you're here!'

'Have you had to wait long for us?' I asked. 'I mean, have you been here for many days? Were you living in the house? What is your name?'

'I'm Nessa Penrose, may it please you, madam, in service with Sir Francis Godolphin, and I've been here for nigh on two weeks, just after Sir Francis came home from London way, on a lathered hireling and said someone got to be at the house on the cliff to meet a lady, a kinswoman, seemingly of the scholar Edmund Wells who'd vanished, likely taken by pirates and not like to come back. The house must be set right, supplies bought in and beds made ready. I've been here alone because the maids Master Wells had have both gone home and so have his other servants and it's such a place! How it creaks in the night when the wind blows off the sea and wails and screams all around like the voices of fiends from hell; I've scarcely slept for the fear of them . . .'

As a hostess whose duty it was to make newcomers feel at home, Nessa Penrose had some shortcomings. Dale was looking at the house with renewed alarm.

'We are here now,' I said firmly, heaving my saddle off Jaunty's back.

Christopher took it from me and said, 'You go in, Ursula. Leave us men to see to the horses and bring the baggage inside.'

'Thank you,' I said, and turned to Nessa. 'My maid and I

would like to go straight indoors and perhaps you would show us round the house.'

I had a vague hope that the inside of the house would be more hospitable than the outside, but I was wrong. The lively wind certainly did make the place creak. It might as well have been a ship at sea. The kitchen was fairly encouraging for it was large, and there was a good fire complete with a trivet and a simmering stockpot. But there were only three small windows, and two of them were shuttered. The lucid light outside didn't penetrate far. I opened one pair of shutters, whereupon the window began to rattle in its frame. I closed the shutters in haste.

'Do all these windows rattle like that?' I asked Nessa.

'Seems so, madam.' Doing anything about it clearly hadn't occurred to Nessa.

'They need to be repaired,' said Dale disapprovingly.

'They will be,' I promised her. 'Nessa, may we see the rest of our new home?'

We found that the kitchen and some smaller rooms, comprising one for stores and another for butchery, occupied the whole of the ground floor. I looked at the stores and decided that they needed a good deal of replenishing. The cold room and dairy combined was a little better. This was not on the ground floor but under it, reached through a trapdoor in the floor of the butchery. Beneath that was a steep wooden staircase into a cave. I mean, a real cave, with uneven, rocky walls and a cavemouth, taller than its width, overlooking the sea. Light flooded in through this, though it was a shimmering, tremulous light because a waterfall poured past the opening. The place was certainly cold. It was a practical arrangement in its way, but Dale looked horrified.

Nevertheless, the cold room contained a long marble-topped table on which were two big round cheeses, a basket of eggs and two crocks full of milk standing in basins full of cold water. Hooks had been driven into the wall, from which two mutton carcasses and some chickens were hanging. I was relieved to see these. We could at least eat.

I suggested that we should go back upstairs. Nessa led the way. From the kitchen floor, a flight of steep and creaky wooden stairs with a sharp bend in it took us into a long, narrow room or passage inadequately lit by a lancet window at each end. There were doors to either side. It was furnished with a couple of wooden settles – there were no cushions – and two stands carrying branched candlesticks, essential even in the brightest daylight. There was a set of shelves with some books and papers on them.

The two doors led respectively to a parlour and a dining chamber. The latter looked as though it had never been used. A long walnut table was flanked by four chairs on one side and a long bench on the other; there was a sideboard and a window seat with a view inland, and not much else. Everything was clean; Nessa had been meticulously busy with dusters and polish but the place was somehow stiff, as though human society had never warmed it.

The parlour was better. It still had an unused air but there was nothing really amiss with it. It was furnished with tapestries depicting classical scenes, including one of Julius Caesar, in silvery armour, setting foot on, presumably, an English beach. The words *veni, vidi, vici* were woven in large letters along the top and there were some cowering Britons, dressed in primitive looking tunics, at the top of what I thought were meant to be sand dunes. The parlour also held chairs and two settles, this time with cushions. Three small tables were scattered about. There were more bookshelves and a small spinet stood in a corner. I would find out if that was in tune, I thought.

A further staircase brought us to three bedchambers, all furnished alike. One four-poster and one truckle bed; a dressing table with a small looking glass on it, a sizeable clothes press, a couple of woollen rugs on the floor.

As we stood in the one on the seaward side of the house, Nessa said, 'This one was the master's, or so I was given to believe. Sir Francis' steward, who brought me here, knows Master Wells quite well. I don't want to stop here now you've come but I will if it'll be an inconvenience if I go.'

'No, no,' I said soothingly. In other circumstances I would have wanted her to stay, but our mission must be kept secret and here on our own premises we must be free to talk about it and not be overheard. 'Where do you live?'

'The Godolphin place, near Helston, back at the root of the Lizard, where it parts from the mainland. I'm in service there, like I said. It's only ten miles,' said Nessa hardily. 'I can walk it in two hours.'

That wouldn't do. The final leg of our journey had only taken half a day and as Christopher had been driving, his horse, Jet, hadn't had to carry him, but had merely trotted behind, tethered to the carriage. Jet was a big, strong animal and after a rub down and feed, probably wouldn't be too tired. I hoped that Christopher would be willing to take Nessa home.

SIX
Red Chalk

Nessa, clearly anxious to finish and return to her home, made short work of showing us the rest of the house. On the floor above the master bedchamber we were shown a well-stocked linen cupboard and four more rooms – small ones. Three had rush strewn floors and two of these had wide beds in them with straw mattresses. They had no hangings and were not made up.

'Servants' rooms,' said Nessa. 'Well, that do be the three with the beds in. The fourth one be the master's study. He preferred it high up, so I was told. He liked looking at the stars.'

The study had a forlorn atmosphere. It was as though the very walls and furnishings missed their master. There were shelves with books – bookshelves were a kind of motif throughout the whole house – a big jar full of ink, supplies of paper, a glass for peering into distances. There was also a desk, littered. On it stood an inkpot, quills in a pottery holder, scrolls in another, a couple of paperweights in the form of little lead figurines, one of a soldier and one of a horse. A book lay open, with the two paper-weights holding it firm. It seemed to have Arabic on the left-hand pages, and Latin on the right-hand ones. There were illustrations which suggested that the subject matter concerned the movements of stars and planets. Another book on the desk was all in an unfamiliar script and beside it, held open not by a paperweight but by a smooth grey stone, was a set of handwritten pages roughly stitched together and covered with words in Latin. It looked as though Master Wells had been translating something.

The ink in the desk inkpot had dried up and the quill Master Wells had presumably been using when last he was here had been carelessly left lying and had stained the desktop. Other such stains here and there suggested that he was habitually careless with his quills. The scrolls in the holder turned out to be maps. I pulled one out and opened it up and it proved to be a map of Cornwall, which I thought could be useful. It was more detailed than the map Sir Robert had found for me and much more detailed than Hugh's map but it was very complicated, dotted with lettering and small pictures. Dale picked up a thick book from the shelf behind the desk and we found that it was a ledger, containing household accounts. Its entries stopped in March.

We went downstairs to the kitchen and met Christopher and Brockley, just coming in. A moment later, a voice hailed us from outside. Nessa went to see who it was and came back accompanied by a lad who was carrying a rod over his shoulder, with fish dangling from it.

His Cornish accent was so dense that we could hardly make sense of him, but Nessa translated. He was a fisher lad from a village at the foot of the cliff. From one bedchamber window I had already glimpsed the village. It was not immediately below us, but close enough and I had glimpsed a zigzag track leading down towards it. The boy had caught sight of us as we arrived and thought we might like some fresh fish, all cleaned and ready to cook.

We did. The fish was mackerel, and we could have a whole one each. We paid the boy, who went away very happy, and I hunted for frying pans. Christopher, somewhat resignedly but with perfect courtesy, agreed to take Nessa back to her Helston home, saddled Jet again and took our hostess away. We didn't have a pillion saddle but Nessa, unconcerned, kilted her skirts and sat astride behind him, holding on to him as he set off.

We waved them goodbye and Brockley told us that he had looked into the garden and found a vegetable and herb patch, in need of weeding but fairly well-stocked. He had also examined the shed beside the wash-house.

'There's a supply of firewood in there though it won't last long. We'll have to do something about that. When we were coming here, I never saw a single patch of woodland on this Lizard and I'd wager there's no firewood here either to buy or to forage for. Still, there's enough for the meantime. We can have fires in our bedchambers, where you can air some sheets.'

'And I've looked at the stores,' I said. 'There's a flour bin with not much flour in it, and a big box of candles with not enough

candles in it, and no raisins at all. I would like a bag of raisins.
We shall have to do some marketing soon. Just now, we have to
think about supper.'

We had spent the previous night at an inn not far from Helston.
I hadn't wanted to seek lodgings with Sir Francis Godolphin. He
would probably have tried to persuade me to go home to Faldene.
He had had Cliff House tidied for us, but he had clearly given
no orders about getting stores in. Well, I thought, if he hoped to
discourage us, he would not succeed. The effect on me was to
stiffen my determination to stay here and carry out my assignment. Sir Francis didn't know me very well.

The inn had given us noon-pieces of cold meat, fresh bread
and almond tarts which had sustained us on the road, but now
we were becoming hungry and fretful because of course we must
wait until Christopher came back. Meanwhile we set about
unpacking, lighting fires, deciding who should have which
bedchambers and setting sheets to air but it was three hours before
Christopher returned and by then, we were all ravenous. However,
cheese omelettes, fried mackerel and some Canary wine that
Brockley found in the storeroom made a satisfactory supper.

We ate together at the kitchen table rather than in that uninviting dining room. We had finished the meal and were sitting
back, replete, when Christopher said, 'Now that we are here and
have seen to our meals and beds, we had better consider our
business here.'

Dale was very tired. I could see it in her face, and it was
probably because of this that she let herself make an outburst.
She was usually restrained, respecting her position. Not this time.

'I don't clearly understand what we're supposed to be doing
here. I've been thinking about it all the way on the road and I
still can't make sense of it. We're supposed to find out who is
behind these kidnappings but how can we? We know no one
hereabouts. Where are we supposed to start? And this house is
too big for just us. That poor woman Nessa must have been
running up and down these endless stairs all day every day,
dusting things. If we've really got to stay here, can't we find the
servants who were here before and get them back? And there
are six horses to tend. I don't see how Roger and Master Spelton
– I'm sorry, Mark and Master Wood – can look after all those,

while we two women, ma'am, look after the house, and make the meals and yet we've got to find time to go about finding out things and . . . and . . .'

She stopped, as much for breath as anything else, stared defiantly round the table at the rest of us, mumbled an apology and lapsed into silence.

'As a matter of fact,' Christopher said, 'I have been thinking about Wells' servants. I agree that we should get them back if we can. We do need help with the horses. You are right about that, Dale. Also, former servants and grooms may know some useful things – no, Dale, I don't know what kind of things; we'll have to wait and see. We were told, I think, that Wells had a manservant and an outdoor man, a groom and two maids. I can have it cried in Penzance that Cliff House is occupied again and that the former servants are invited to apply for their old jobs. We should get results in some cases, I think. Now, Brockley?'

Brockley was also wanting to say something. 'That last inn we stayed at,' he said. 'While we were waiting for them to get our food ready for the last part of our journey here, I got to chatting with the landlord. I reckoned that we were probably not so far from the Lizard and its fishing villages by then so I pretended that by chance, we had heard of the death of Jago's son. I said what a shocking thing and I hoped he wasn't one of their parish. He said no, but they knew all about it through a pedlar who'd slept at the inn just after it happened. The pedlar travels Cornwall – rather like that man Petroc – and he knew the Lizard well. He said that Jago, the father of the murdered boy was – is – a fisherman at St Aidan's. That's a fishing village on the other side of the Lizard from here. I think I saw the name when you and I were looking at the map that Sir Robert gave you, madam. I asked if the killer had been caught and the landlord shook his head and then he said: *that Jago boy that was killed, well, he was a lad and no doubt about it. Got a baby daughter in Penzance and a toddler son somewhere near Zennor. Asking for trouble, seems to me.*

'I listened and didn't say much else,' said Brockley. 'I said what a dreadful thing and I hoped the killer would be found and then I talked about fish and the kinds that are caught in Mount's

Bay and then the landlord's wife came out of the kitchen with our noon-pieces.'

'You didn't mention this before,' I said, annoyed.

'We couldn't confer much while we were on the road,' said Brockley. 'Not with two of us riding, one in the carriage and another one driving! But now seems to be the right moment. I think we must find out more about this man Jago. That's one place where we can start.'

'We have two names,' said Christopher. 'Jago and Mistress Juniper Penberthy, whose laundress died so strangely. This business,' he added, 'has a bad smell. I wish it didn't concern you, Ursula. Sir Francis had a point. This affair reeks of ruthlessness and it reeks of money. I keep thinking of the big sums that must be behind it. Whoever is doing this has a very lucrative business indeed – as long as he doesn't get caught. He's taking enormous risks for the sake of the pay.'

'Why do people do such things?' Dale asked. 'Why aren't they afraid of the danger? I would be!'

'You would think so but believe me,' said Christopher, 'where money is being dangled like a golden bait, there will always be fish ready to bite. Few things can beat money as a reason for crime – or for murder. I am not sure that even religious fervour, the desire to rid the world of unbelievers – the way the Spanish do – really outdoes money. Some of our spies have reported that when the Inquisition take people in, it's surprising how often they pick on wealthy victims, and what good pickings there are for unscrupulous informers!'

'But this – this snatching of the people who've been singled out! It's so wicked! *Think* of the danger!' said Dale.

'Money opens the door to so much,' Christopher said, soberly. 'It means freedom! To do what you like without asking anyone's permission. To ride a fine horse and pay a groom to look after it, to drink good wine, to sleep in a four-poster bed with smooth linen sheets. We're fortunate. We're all used to such things without having to commit crimes to get them, but many folk hardly ever eat meat though they long to eat it every day, and they shiver round a few spluttering twigs on winter nights when they yearn for good log fires, and they long to exchange a straw pallet on the floor for the comfort of a four-poster bed. Many would kill for such things.'

Brockley nodded. 'They know they would find themselves on the gallows if they are caught but the longing outdoes the fear. And I suspect that the determination to avoid capture is very strong. Those responsible are gambling with their lives. I did say *lives* – more than one man is running this business.'

'And so,' said Christopher, 'I want us all to carry one of these.' He fumbled at his belt pouch and now drew out a small brass box which he put on the table and opened. It contained a number of small red chalks. He tipped them out and gave one to each of us.

'Your secret sign!' I exclaimed.

'Yes. You all know about it. I and other agents like me use red chalk to leave signs in places where we feel endangered and want any of our friends who come in search of us to know that we've been there. It's a way of leaving a trail. My sign is a circle quartered by a cross.'

He demonstrated, on the tabletop. I said, 'It helped us to trace you once, a few years ago. We found it in a place where other people had said you'd never been.'

'Yes. So take them and keep them handy,' said Christopher. He watched us pick them up and then said, 'The day after tomorrow is Sunday. Tomorrow, I think we'll have to do some settling in. There's a lot to find out – we need to introduce ourselves to the villagers where that fisher-boy came from – and look round for what farms are within easy reach and so on. But on Monday, I will go into Penzance and hire the services of a crier in the hope of finding some services and I would like Brockley to come too. Will you, Brockley – Master Smith – undertake to replenish the stores? I take it, Ursula – no, Catherine, we must remember our new names – that you have a list?'

'Flour, candles, firewood, raisins,' I said. 'And sugar too, I think.'

'Thank you,' said Christopher. 'Now, Br— Mark Smith's task will be quite a lengthy business as he will have to go to several different vendors. On the other hand, I doubt if I'll take long to find the criers' office. Criers are never difficult to find, in any town. I should have some spare time. While I am in Penzance, after I've seen the criers, I think I shall find out where Mistress Penberthy lives and maybe learn of any gossip there is about her.

I hope that . . . what is it, Mary? That's you, Mistress Brockley! You've cocked your head – what can you hear?'

'That noise!' gasped Dale. 'Can't you hear it? Am I losing my senses all alone? That booming noise from somewhere down below!'

'Yes, what is it?' I said. 'I can hear it too.'

'It's the sea. There's probably a cave beneath us,' said Brockley. 'And at high tide the sea gets into the cave and makes that noise. When we were on our way here, there was a place where the cliffs bent round a little and gave a view of the cliff face ahead. I saw caves, several of them. Our cold room cave mouth is one of the little ones. It must be fairly high up. Some of the caves lower down looked as though high tides might get into them.'

'That's so,' said Christopher. 'I've heard the waves echo like that in other places. There's nothing to be afraid of, Mary.'

'Perhaps not, but I don't like it,' said Dale.

That council of war had cleared our minds, which was a good thing. The journey to Cornwall had been long but on the way, as Brockley had pointed out, it had hardly been possible to do any conferring. Trying to imagine it made me want to laugh. We would have been calling remarks from one horse to another, up to the driving seat, in at the carriage window . . . and it was true that at the end of each day we mostly just wanted to take supper and sleep. Only now could we begin to make plans.

Though Dale and I, at least, were far too tired to do much planning. We all had a last glass of wine, then Brockley and Christopher went to the stable to make sure that all was well and I went with them because I had a habit of saying goodnight to Jaunty. Then we all retired to bed.

Our first full day at Cliff House was very much taken up with finding our feet, as it were. Christopher was right about that. In any case, if I were to establish myself as Mistress Catherine Archer, cousin to Master Wells, then I ought to behave as such a person naturally would. Mistress Archer would not be concerned with gossip but with filling up her stores. After a night's rest, Jet was full of energy again and Christopher went out, as he called it, to explore. He left at a canter but came back at a walk, accompanied by a small boy pushing a hand cart laden with a big can of milk, a lidded bowl containing cream, four slabs of butter wrapped in cloths, two capons, plucked and drawn, a box of twelve eggs, three pots of honey and a keg of ale.

'I found a farm only a mile away,' Christopher said. 'It's called Hollow Farm – it stands in a sort of wide hollow, not a valley exactly. It's just a small place. The farmer, Master Grove, wasn't there but his wife, Ellie Grove, says they rear capons, and Master Wells had a regular order for things like this and would we like to do the same. I said yes and arranged it then and there. This is Ellie's son Hamnet.'

Hamnet, who was sturdy and freckled and happy to help, chopped up some of our small store of firewood for us and was refreshed with bread and honey and ale before we sent him home. Brockley meanwhile investigated the track leading down to the fishing village below us. This proved to be called Polgillan and the people there were happy to sell fish to us; they had made a good start with the mackerel. Brockley had arranged for regular deliveries of fish and also found Griffin Brown, the boatman who had taken Tamzin to Penzance the day before the christening and had stayed until the next day, when he brought her home.

'He says he's getting too old for much fishing nowadays,' Brockley said, 'but he always did the ferrying for Mr Wells. Mr Wells had no boat of his own; he was no waterman. Landsman all the way, was Mr Wells, according to the locals. There's a cargo boat plying out of Penzance that regularly delivers orders to people on the Lizard, too. Again, we can inherit arrangements made by Wells. Also, the Polgillan villagers own a pair of mules – owned in common by everyone, apparently – that they use for dragging boats up out of the way of high tides and apparently Wells used to hire them sometimes. When he ordered loads of firewood or barrels of this and that, the mules would haul them up the cliff for him. There's a small cart belonging to him that was used for that. It's still down there. The village has a church too. I think we had better attend. I feel sure that Mistress Catherine Archer would.'

Cliff House, I thought, wasn't quite as lonely as it appeared.

The next day was a Sunday so we dutifully went down to Polgillan to the church. The track down the cliff wasn't at all precipitous, just long. It zigzagged a couple of times and descended the cliff in a series of easy slopes.

I was interested to see the village. A fold in the cliff had created an inlet where boats could be safely moored. The cottages of the village were strung out along another shelf, like the one where Cliff House stood. They were well above the high tide level and the dwellings had small gardens. There was a track round the curve of the cliff, leading down to where the boats were moored. Some boats were moored close together to form a bridge so that anyone wanting to reach a boat moored on the further side could cross by stepping from deck to deck, as casually as if they were on a good stone packhorse bridge. We saw them doing it.

The church was crowded. It seemed that there were other small villages along the edge of the Lizard that had no churches of their own. They shared this one, and on Sunday mornings arrived, some on foot, some by boat, to attend the service.

The vicar was a small and slightly harried man, who apparently did not live in Polgillan but had a home some way off, to be within easy reach of his other parishioners as well. We had hoped to make ourselves known to him but we had no opportunity, for the moment the service was over, he climbed into a small boat and rowed off, apparently to dine elsewhere. Brockley hired the mules so that Dale and I could ride home up the cliff path. The fisher lad who had brought us the mackerel came with us, to lead the animals back. At the top, I paid the fee for their use. Dale was thankful for the ride. The cliff path wasn't really steep yet Dale had nevertheless found it so.

Once home, however, she tackled the stairs with the rest of us as we went up to the study to examine Wells' map of Cornwall and compare it with the ones we already had.

One piece of information that the maps gave us was that to reach Penzance on horseback would involve a ride of about twenty-five miles. Fifty miles there and back. 'No wonder Wells always hired a ferry!' I said.

That night, we all had tinderboxes at our bedsides and candles in useful candlesticks which we discovered dotted about the house. I had seen such candlesticks before. They had copper hoods which meant that the flame could be shielded from the wind, and the polished copper of the hood would reflect and enhance the candlelight.

I hadn't slept very well on the previous night and I didn't

sleep well this time, either. The wind had become blustery and the house creaked so badly that on the Saturday night I twice started up in bed, thinking that I could hear someone creeping up the stairs. Once I actually got up, lit a candle and crept to the door to peer out. There was moonlight to help me see and there was no one on the stairs. It was only the wind.

On Monday morning, as soon as they had tended the horses and taken a little breakfast, Christopher and Brockley went off down the cliff. They had already arranged to hire Griffin Brown and get across the bay to Penzance and Brockley was equipped with a large basket. They expected to be away for most of the day. Dale and I occupied ourselves with household affairs and in due course began to plan dinner. On the previous evening, Dale had set some bread to rise and the house was full of pleasant baking odours when Brockley and Christopher reappeared, sooner than expected but full of news.

'Griffin Brown took us across the bay in his little boat. She has red sails and Griffin told us that her name was *Sunrise*,' Christopher said. 'While we were out in the bay, we looked back, up to the cliffs and believe me they're fairly riddled with caves. I fancy there may be ways into them from this house; we'll have to explore more thoroughly.'

'Meanwhile,' Brockley said, 'I have ordered all the stores we need and brought a few things back – raisins for you, Mistress Archer – and some sugar and a keg of cider and some more eggs. I also found the fellow who runs stores across to the Lizard. He transports goods along the coast and over to this side of the Lizard as a regular business. He'll collect our orders and bring everything across tomorrow. Firewood, a big barrel of flour, a huge supply of candles – enough to light Hampton Court Palace. Now you, Christopher.'

'I saw the crier,' said Christopher. 'He'll be announcing our need for Master Wells' servants this very day. And I found where Juniper Penberthy lives. Look, is there any dinner? We're both ravenous. It's the sea air. I'll talk better across a good meal.'

Dale and I were ready. In the course of the morning, a man carrying a mass of oranges in a net slung over his shoulder had come to the house and we had bought a supply. We had also made good use of the supplies we already had. We sat down to a dinner of fried mutton chops, fresh bread made by Dale, with butter and honey, asparagus from the garden, fried in butter and orange sections in cream.

'And now,' I said as I set it all out on the kitchen table, which we still preferred to the uninviting dining chamber, 'what else have you to tell us, Christopher?'

SEVEN
Cautious Steps

' I saw the crier, as I told you,' said Christopher, through a mouthful of mutton. 'We'd set a time when we were to meet Griffin to go home and I had plenty of time to spare so I went to find out something about this Penberthy woman. I had a drink in an inn called The Good Catch and asked the way from the landlord. He knew where her house was. Most of Penzance knows, apparently, because it's a talking point. It's surrounded by juniper trees, queer looking things, the landlord said, the sort of things folk stare at. It's easy to find, he told me. The market's *that* way, when you get there, turn left and keep walking. You'll come out at the south side of the town, more or less and the house is there.

'I found it easily. It's a fine-looking place, quite modern, half-timbered above rosy brick and it has wide grounds which certainly are dotted with junipers. I've never seen them before. They're like stunted trees with greyish green leaves and they grow in all manner of weird shapes. I was standing and staring at them when a dear plump soul with a basket over her arm came by and I asked who lived there.'

Christopher, mopping up meat juices with a piece of bread, began to laugh. 'She was a darling. She wasn't surprised that I was interested in the place, everyone was who set eyes on all those funny twisted trees. *That's where Mistress Penberthy lives – she's a widow now – she was born in the north of England; it's said there were them trees all round the place she lived in as a child; she was named after them. She come here and missed them so and had them planted here as well. A great lady though nothing to look at, but did I know, a terrible thing happened lately – her laundress got drowned in her washtub and everyone's saying it was murder!* The last few words were in a kind of whisper, with wide, stretched eyes.

'I said how dreadful, has it been found out yet who did it? She said no, but all Penzance is buzzing and there are laundresses who won't work alone but must have some trusted fellow servant with them in case this is a madman with a hatred of laundresses. But we know now where to find the lady. And this afternoon . . .'

'We're going after Jago,' said Brockley.

'We'll have to be cautious,' said Christopher warningly. 'If we move too fast we will draw attention to ourselves. In Penzance today, I just made myself look like a mildly nosy passer-by. Yes, we do plan to go to St Aidan's village this afternoon, but we've got to be careful. We did risk asking a few questions of Griffin Brown. We said we'd heard about the shocking murder at St Aidan's on the other side of the Lizard, and I asked if the killer had been caught. Griffin said no and more or less repeated what we've already heard, that the Jago boy had a bad reputation with the girls. He reckons – everyone seems to reckon – that some outraged father or husband did it.'

'We also found out,' said Brockley, 'that the fisher folk in Polgillan think that Wells' disappearance was due to an accident. These cliffs are perilous. Wells most likely had a fall on the cliffs and went to his death among the rocks and the seething waters round the foot of the cliff below his home.'

'In other words, no one has really been looking for him,' Christopher said. 'Well, Mark Smith, we'd better have a last look at those maps and make sure we know where to find St Aidan's. From my last glance at Wells' map, I got the impression that the Lizard is crisscrossed with little paths. We wouldn't want to get lost, now, would we?'

'My name is Tamzin Grigg, if it please you, madam,' said the very pretty wench with the wide grey eyes and the dark hair coiled in braids behind her shapely head. 'I was second maid here when Mr Wells was here. I had to go home when he vanished but I've been looking for work; my mam and my da they do have so many children in the house to see to. I heard it being cried in Penzance that the old servants of the House on the Cliff were wanted again, so . . .'

The crier had clearly set to work at once, to produce results on the very same day. Come in, Tamzin,' I said, standing back from the door to make way for her.

It was a beautiful afternoon. In the clear air, the wheeling gulls were more than just white; the sun on their wings turned them into flakes of white fire. It was the kind of day to lift one's spirits and it seemed to be going well. Tamzin wasn't the only former employee of Master Wells to respond to the crier. A young man called Thomas Tremaine had arrived half an hour before, declaring that he had been Wells' groom. His arrival had coincided with the return of Brockley and Christopher from their expedition to St Aidan's. They were unsaddling at that very moment. I had at once presented Tremaine to them and the three of them were still in the stables, where Tremaine was being put to the test.

Meanwhile, I took Tamzin to the kitchen and asked how well she knew the house. The answer was very well indeed except that the master never let anyone into his study and if it ever got dusted, it wasn't by her. Otherwise, she could do all that was needed.

'There was me and Mistress Isa; she was older than me and she did most of the cooking. But I beat eggs and chopped onions and I could fry and boil things anyhow, like Ma taught me. Isa taught me how to make pastry and said I had a light hand. Isa's name is really Isolde but she said it weren't suitable for her station in life and she often wondered what her parents had been thinking of. I'm used to cleaning here and if Isa doesn't come back, I reckon I can manage the cooking.'

'Do you know where she went?' I asked.

'To her brother in Devon, I think. She said she was looking forward to it. It seems she and her brother were brought up on a farm near Bodmin but it was a dismal place, all amid the open moors and it never grew much. She went into service, her parents died and her brother and his wife stayed on the farm, but then he got the chance to buy a place in Devon where the ground's more fertile. Anyway, she's visited her brother in Devon and it's a good place and she can help with the children. I think she won't want to come back to Cornwall. Though her name will attract attention.'

She gave us an almost mischievous smile. 'Not many wenches in Devon are baptized as Isolde. Vicars don't like it. But there,

Cornwall's different. In England did you ever see a hedgerow like that patterned wall in the courtyard?'

I shook my head and she added, 'In Cornwall we call those walls hedgerows, even though they're mostly stone. You'll see many of them on our side of the River Tamar. Cornwall's a country all of its own.'

I nodded. I was sensing that more and more strongly. I had begun to sense it as soon as we crossed the River Tamar that separated Cornwall from England. On my one previous visit to Cornwall I had been less aware of it, but then there had been immediate and pressing things to do and so many people round me. Today, in this strange tower-like house, in this astonishing light and with the sea booming beneath us, I was very aware of it indeed.

I asked Tamzin where she had slept and she said in one of the bedchambers on the floor below the study. Mr Wells – 'he liked to be called Mr instead of Master' said Tamzin – had said that the bigger bedchambers on the lower floor might as well be used.

Just then, the back door clicked and in came Brockley and Christopher. 'We've left Tremaine cleaning harness,' Brockley said. 'He's good enough except that he tried to get tangles out of Jet's mane with a curry comb!'

'Dreadful,' said Christopher. 'And he was surprised when we told him to stop. He said what of it, it wouldn't touch the horse's skin but curry combs are for cleaning the dandy brush and nothing else and so I told him. Otherwise, he's capable enough, knows how to prepare the right feeds and look after the hooves. He'll do, as long as we keep an eye on him.'

'I am sure we both hope we'll please you, madam,' said Tamzin, smiling round at us. 'And be let to stay.'

Dale took her off to see to the bedlinen and explain her duties to her more fully and I looked at Christopher and Brockley. Brockley grinned broadly and said, 'Once more, we have news.'

EIGHT
Pictorial Maps

I called to Dale to join us. Tamzin knew the house; she could choose her bedchamber and find her sheets for herself. We all sat down round the kitchen table, like a committee. 'Tell us!' I said.

'As the maps show, there are paths all over the Lizard,' said Brockley. 'They go this way and that and it's very easy to get on to the wrong one. Would you believe it,' he said solemnly, 'the two of us were going home after exercising our horses and we found ourselves going down completely the wrong side of the Lizard and do you know where we ended up?'

'St Aidan's, presumably!' I said.

'As you say. We arrived all puzzled and bewildered and found some fishermen mending nets,' said Christopher. 'I asked where we were. I explained that we were trying to get to Cliff House – that we're in service with Mistress Catherine Archer, who has just moved in. People have to know where you are, madam, if anyone ever wants to bring information to you. This was a chance to inform a few people in a harmless way.'

Brockley took the tale up again. 'When they told us where we were, my eyebrows went up and I told them about the tale we'd heard on the way here and again from Griffin, about the murder of a St Aidan's lad, not so long ago. Was it true? The tale came out in a flood and one of the fishermen called out to another who was working at his nets some distance off and fetched him over. This is the boy's father, Jago, he said.'

'What was he like?' I asked.

'Huge, hairy and surly,' said Brockley, 'but has an air about him. He's a fellow who gives orders and expects to be obeyed. The other fishermen respect him and I think they're even rather scared of him. We couldn't see any signs of grief for his son. The boy was his youngest, going by the name of Arthur Jago.

The father's got no first name of his own but I suppose he had to give his children first names, so as to tell one from another. According to his father, Arthur was a fool of a boy, nineteen years old, big for his age and crazy for the girls. Couldn't keep it in his breeches, that's how Jago put it, begging your pardon, madam.'

'I've heard worse things at court, Brockley.'

'Jago said there'd been trouble already, with angry fathers who didn't care for his . . . er . . . influence over their daughters. Fool of a boy, got what he was asking for, that's how he described finding his son – his own son! – lying in a rowing boat in a pool of blood with his throat cut right through the jugular.'

'Ugh!' I said, shuddering.

'He's got three sons left,' said Brockley. 'The eldest two, Clemo and Bryok, he says they're good boys. We saw them. Madam, when you were a girl sharing your cousins' tutor, did you study Roman history at all?'

'Yes, why?' I was intrigued.

'The sons appeared from somewhere and stood behind their father, one at each shoulder. They made me think of tales I have heard about the Pretorian guards who protected the Roman emperors.'

'And murdered some of them,' I said.

'I don't see that happening here,' Christopher said. 'To judge from the expressions on the faces of the other fishermen around us, the sons are cut from the same pattern as their dad. They certainly look like him. The third, Pascoe, according to his loving father, is quite different, a silly weakling, won't do this, won't do that, doesn't even like cleaning fish. Prefers clean hands. Wanted to go to school, so Jago's let him go to a school in Penzance. Jago's got no time for book learning – his own words – but if he's got a son as can add up profits and maybe write a letter or two, perhaps the boy will turn out useful in the end. A practical man is Jago.'

'Do you think . . .?' I began. Brockley began to nod before I finished the sentence and I saw that Christopher wanted to speak. I stopped and gave way to them.

'I'd say that Jago could be in it, yes,' Christopher said. 'He's impressive. There's a fleet of fishing boats that ply out of St

Aidan's and we found out that he owns all but two of them. The young fisherman who told us that – in a low voice – described them as the two who have kept out of his clutches. Jago's bought up the others bit by bit – taken advantage of the odd lean year when the fish shoals don't arrive on time or the weather's too stormy to put out. He has money, you see. There's no mystery about that. Jago told us himself. His father and grandfather were pirates – in with the Killigrews, bringing treasure home in their holds.

'He told us, grinning – though it looked more like baring his teeth; he's got a fine mouthful of them – that he'd decided that piracy was too dangerous for him. His forebears left him well provided for. Now, most of the St Aidan's fishermen run the vessels that were once their own but have to hand over the greater part of their catches. He sells the fish and pockets the proceeds. He does very well without fighting for it. The St Aidan's fisher-men don't like him much.'

'I'm not surprised,' I said.

'There's a little inn in the village,' said Brockley, 'and after Jago turned his back on us and he and his bodyguard of sons walked off – the sons never said a word, throughout – one of the men who still owns his own vessel, invited us to join him in a mug of ale. He told us that the whole village wonders where Jago keeps his wealth. They know it isn't in a locked box under his bed from which I suspect that someone has had a look, but wealth he certainly does possess.'

'That's as far as we got, though,' said Christopher. 'We can say, yes, Jago could be in it, but there's no proof and the mystery of Arthur's death remains a mystery. Angry menfolk don't sound right to me, though. They would usually come demanding that a seducer should marry the girl. Or else they'd just start a fist fight. I can imagine two or three of them going for him together and half accidentally drowning him in the sea, but cutting throats – that isn't natural, somehow. But again, where's the proof?'

'So,' said Brockley, 'what next?'

All through the day, while with half my mind I attended to such things as trying to make the parlour and dining room a little more inviting, with the other half of it, I had been thinking. I said, 'I suggest that we put Jago aside for a moment and get out

the maps and look to see where the various victims were taken
from. There might be a pattern. It might tell us something. I have
a list of the known victims and where they were snatched. Sir
Francis Godolphin gave it to me.' I felt inside my hidden pouch
and brought the folded paper out. 'It's here. Can we go up to
the study?'

We adjourned up the stairs. Brockley, when we were all at the
top and most of us breathless, said that he doubted if Master
Wells ever bothered to climb down them at all most of the time.
'I expect he made his servants bring his meals up here. Whew!'

Once in the study, we settled ourselves around the desk and
Christopher unrolled our various maps. They were all lacking in
various respects. Hugh's map only gave a small space to Cornwall
and there was little detail. The map that Sir Robert had given
me didn't mark houses. Wells' maps – he had three of them – all
had detail but were almost pictorial. The numerous little pictures
of important features such as hills and large houses and their
accompanying labels created much confusion. Christopher
selected the simplest and spread it out, keeping it flat with the
aid of the paperweights and the inkpot. He equipped himself
with a quill and put fresh ink into the pot. I put my list out beside
it and Christopher prepared to mark the places where victims
had been seized.

'Cliff House – presumably Wells disappeared from here, not
from anywhere else. Petroc was taken somewhere between Land's
End and Penzance . . .'

'He thought that the dark girl he saw on board the corsair ship
was probably the daughter of an innkeeper in Penzance,' I said.
'Was the inn The Good Catch?'

'Yes, it was,' said Christopher. 'I said to the landlord there
that I'd heard a rumour and had it been his daughter and he said
yes it was, grimly and almost tearfully, as well. I was wary of
showing too much interest. I'm Mistress Archer's manservant,
not one of Sir Robert Cecil's agents. The landlord just said that
his daughter went out one day to bring in some fresh fish for the
kitchen and never came back. The weather had turned a little
squally while she was gone and he expected that she'd be back
quite quickly. It was the sort of thing that had happened before.
She never came and her little boat was found drifting, empty.

That's when I saw tears in his eyes. He's a widower. He said he was glad his wife never knew about their girl disappearing.'

'It's a heartbreaking story,' said Brockley.

'It is,' Christopher agreed, making a mark on Penzance. 'All these vanishings cause heartbreak, the hearts of the people whose lives are stolen by slavers, and those they leave behind. Finding out who's doing it is the best way to avenge them. Now, who's next on the list?'

We worked busily for a few moments. One thing emerged at once. 'They're all in one general area,' Christopher said. 'The embroideress was teaching girls in Penzance. The two redheads came from St Mawes and Portloe – they're up the coast on this side of Cornwall. Do you see? Everyone was taken, roughly, from along the easternmost edges of the two claws, as you call them, Mistress Archer – the Lizard and Land's End. That suggests that whoever is conducting this unpleasant trade knows this area well and probably lives here.'

'There's still a fair amount of it,' I said despondently. 'And a fair few people on it.' I picked up a ruler and demonstrated. 'The Lizard alone is between nine and ten miles long and about eight miles across at one point. It's a mighty fat Lizard by the look of it.'

'Probably because of all the ships it's swallowed down the centuries,' said Christopher. 'Its coast is a death trap. And that still leaves the Land's End claw. Yes, it is a big area.' He sat back, frowning.

I said, 'Well, so far, who do we have as possible suspects? Jago, who may be the murderer of his own son – because the boy knew too much and intended to reveal it? Those sons that you saw – well, they don't sound as though they're ever likely to tell of anything they know. I can't see us making much progress there. Then there's this Mistress Penberthy who we haven't yet met, but whose laundress somehow came to be drowned in her own washtub. Possibly because *she* had found out something she wasn't supposed to know?'

'Sir Francis Godolphin,' said Brockley. 'Who married into a family of pirates, the Killigrews. What about him – and them?'

'Yes, he's possible. I agree,' I said. 'He tried to discourage me from coming here. As for his in-laws, well, if they aren't likely suspects, I can't imagine who is. The Killigrews, Mistress Penberthy and Jago are all close enough to the area that people have been disappearing from. I would call them all suspects.'

'Could Godolphin *really* be part of this nasty business?' said Dale. 'He's the County Sheriff! Ma'am, was he not there when you were summoned to speak with Robert Cecil? I am sure you told me so, and you said that he was open about being married to a Killigrew and that he said he was as willing to arrest an in-law as anyone else.'

'I want an introduction to the Killigrews,' I said. I quaked as I said it. I didn't at all like the sound of them. Nevertheless, it was an obvious move. I said, 'Whichever side Sir Francis is on, he will expect me to be interested in the Killigrews. We don't have to hide our intentions from him; he already knows them. I shall oblige him.'

'You may walk into their lair and never reappear,' said Christopher.

'I shall visit them, if I can, well attended as a lady should be.' I smiled round at them and tried to sound confident. 'Catherine Archer will have her maid and two menservants and Thomas the groom.'

I looked at the map again. 'Sir Francis told me the name of their house and I wrote it down afterwards. They live somewhere called Arwenack House and it's marked here. It's a good way off. We had better use the carriage for Dale and myself. It will give some exercise to Rufus and Red.'

'How do we get ourselves invited to this Arwenack House?' asked Brockley.

'I expect that Sir Francis can see to that,' I said. 'I shall send him a note today, requesting his help. He'll be expecting such a move. Though we must indeed step warily.' With determination, I smiled round at them and made a joke. 'I suggest that if and when we reach Arwenack House, we all have our red chalks handy.'

NINE

Dining With Buccaneers

My note to Sir Francis was despatched that very day, by the hand of Thomas Tremaine. He returned bringing polite salutations and a promise that the arrangement I wished to make would be forthcoming; leave the matter in his hands.

He kept his word and on the Saturday, only a week after our arrival at Cliff House, the invitation arrived, brought by a smart young lad in livery. Would Mistress Catherine Archer do the Killigrew family the honour of dining with them at their home, Arwenack House, on the following Wednesday, the twenty-fifth day of May. They customarily dined at two o'clock but would be happy to welcome me and such attendants as I wished to accompany me, at any time after ten in the morning. They understood that I was a friend of Sir Francis Godolphin, who would also be present, with his wife Lady Alice. Would I indicate whether I wished to accept or decline, by way of their messenger.

'I shall be delighted to accept,' I said graciously. 'Do you wish for that in writing?'

The lad said there was no need; my word of mouth was good enough. How many attendants would be with me?'

'Don't leave me out of this,' muttered Christopher, who was standing at my shoulder in the doorway.

'Three,' I said. 'My manservants Christopher Wood and Mark Smith and Mark's wife Mary who is my maid.'

When the boy had gone, I said apologetically, 'All three of you may end up eating in the kitchen. If I insist on treating you as equals, it could make the Killigrews think. Ursula Stannard is known to have that foible.'

'We will eat in the kitchen and gossip with the servants,' said Brockley. 'We may learn something – who knows?'

* * *

During the days before the Wednesday, life at Cliff House was without incident. I concentrated on making further arrangements for food supplies and Brockley formed friendships in Polgillan village. On the Saturday night there was a gale, during which the wind howled round the house and the cliffs with a voice that sometimes sounded almost like human wailing. Dale said as much the following morning, and Tamzin said that there was a legend that the wind and sea between them were haunted by the many sailors who had lost their lives in the many shipwrecks round the rocky coasts of Cornwall.

'They say you can hear their ghosts crying in the wind,' Tamzin said earnestly, blue eyes stretched with the horror of it.

On Sunday night, Dale had a nightmare in which drowned men were rising out of the sea and trying to break into Cliff House. She woke Brockley with her cries of fear and he in turn had to wake her up and comfort her. In the morning he told Tamzin, quite curtly, never to speak of such unpleasant legends again. 'They are all nonsense, anyway. Drowned sailors are in the arms of God, like all other Christian souls,' he said.

Brockley himself wasn't very much of a Christian soul. Like me, he had few beliefs. But he did put an end to the talk of ghosts.

On Monday, Sir Francis paid a call on us, to say that it was a fair way to Arwenack House and that it would be best if I and my attendants came to his house on Tuesday evening and stayed the night. Then we all would set out together for Arwenack House in the morning. He would have the pleasure of introducing us to his wife, Alice and by the time we reached Arwenack, he said, we would all be close friends.

'I arranged for you to be invited,' he said, 'by describing you as friends, people I had met in London. Not that it would matter all that much if you were known to my in-laws by your real names. None of the Killigrews are involved in this business, of that I am convinced. In fact, one of them has lost a highly valued groom and is very angry about it.' He looked at me with an air of sadness. 'I wish you were not caught up in this matter, Mistress Stannard. I know I have said it before but it is *not* a business for women. Alice knows nothing about it at all, not even that there have been odd disappearances. I protect her from such things. I tell you this so that you won't mention the disappearances to her. To her too, you are people I have met by chance. She isn't always with me when I go to London; she won't think it odd that she doesn't know you. And I have to say that I don't think you will learn much if anything at Arwenack.'

I smiled and thanked him for his help and agreed that it would be a good idea for us to spend a night at his home and meet his wife before we were fellow guests at Arwenack. When he had gone, I asked Brockley and Christopher what they thought of Sir Francis.

'He's supposed to be a brilliant seaman and a danger to all Her Majesty's enemies,' said Brockley. I found that much out while we were all still at Hampton Court. 'But after meeting him, all I can say is that as far as women are concerned, he's as innocent as the babe born last week.'

Christopher said, 'Well, he can hardly be innocent about his in-laws, but he says, with an air of assurance, that we won't gather any information from them. Is he sure of their virtue or just sure that they won't let anything out by mistake? The Killigrews have a grim reputation. I found *that* out when I was in Penzance. When I was having my glass of ale at The Good Catch and cautiously finding out that the kidnapped girl was the landlord's daughter, I gossiped about other things as well. We had all better be careful.'

Sir Francis' plans were followed. We spent Tuesday night at his beautiful house and met his wife. Lady Alice Godolphin, formerly Killigrew, was beautiful too. She was a gentle lady, brown-haired, with soft brown eyes to match and a quiet voice, though I noticed that when she gave orders to her servants, they were clearcut and she was instantly obeyed. I thought that they loved her but also respected her. Well, she was a Killigrew.

In the morning, we set out early. If it was roughly ten miles from Cliff House to Helston, it was the same distance from Helston to Falmouth, where Arwenack House and Dale and I must arrive well-dressed and tidy. As I had suggested, we took the carriage, leaving the horses for the menfolk.

Neither Sir Francis nor any of Wells' maps told us anything of what Arwenack House was like, and the approach to it startled me. Sir Francis had said that the Killigrews were a power in the county but somehow, in view of their dire reputation, I had instinctively expected their home to be somehow furtive. Concealed in a grove of dark trees, perhaps, or poised on a cliff edge like my own current home, or maybe a house backed into a hillside, probably with a network of tunnels behind it and a secret exit into a cove.

What I found was firstly, a lodge, with a keeper who at once despatched a young assistant on a pony, to announce us. Once past the lodge, we found ourselves in an avenue of trees, in full leaf now, casting sun and shadow patterns on a cobbled track which went on for a long way before bringing us to the frontage of a handsome manor house. Though it was a fortified one. My instinct had been sound up to a point. There were crenellations round the roof and the windows of the floor below them were a set of arrow slits.

Elsewhere, the windows were wide enough, most of them mullions with lead patterned casements, and anyone gazing out of the northern ones would have plenty to look at, for on that side of the house, I could see what was surely a field for arms practice. Archery targets were set up there and some tiered seating had been built for the benefit of audiences. This was a place where the skills of battle were polished and applauded. For all its gracious beauty, Arwenack lived in readiness for war. Backed up by wealth, of course. House and arms field were surrounded by meadows where crops grew and sheep and cows, in considerable numbers, were grazing.

We drew up at the door and as if by magic, grooms materialized from an archway at one side, coming straight to our horses' heads, and from the front door came a dignified butler, in a suit of black velvet with a gold chain of office. It was like being welcomed into a royal residence. I was glad I had made sure that Dale and I were dressed well and had travelled by carriage, with our finery uncrushed. Sir Francis had likewise provided a small carriage for Lady Alice and her maid, and both he and Lady Alice were marvels of elegance, he in crimson velvet with gold slashings; she in a pink over-gown over a silver kirtle, with a pearl pendant and matching earrings.

I was in cream and tawny, a favourite colour scheme of mine, with jewellery of gold and amber. Dale was in dark blue as usual on such occasions, but her gown was velvet, and she had a silver pendant and earrings. Dale's ruff and farthingale were moderate, but I, like Lady Alice, had enormous ones. Christopher and Brockley had chosen to match and were both in soldierly buff with dark blue slashings. They looked like a bodyguard. I found them reassuring.

We hardly had time to dismount before our carriages and riding horses were being led away. Brockley always liked to see that our horses were properly looked after and tried to go with them but was courteously prevented. The butler escorted us all up the front steps and into a vestibule, long and shadowy, for the day was overcast. Our hosts were there to greet us, a good-looking man in a summer doublet and hose of light grey silk and a fashionably curled wig, accompanied by a slender and most graceful lady in a gown of dark red silk, who announced themselves as Sir John and Lady Dorothy Killigrew. They welcomed me with kisses, as though we were friends of long standing.

Dale took my travelling cloak and my hat but after that, she and my two menfolk were taken away by a housekeeper, a lady in a black dress and neat ruff, who swept them off into the rear of the house. Sir John showed me through a door on the left, into an immense reception room where there was already quite a crowd of people.

I looked about me with interest. All round the walls there were fluted pilasters with gilded tops and between them were frescoes of scenes from classical history. There was a tinge here of violent tastes. What I felt sure was the assassination of Julius Caesar involved a good deal of blood, and the destruction of Troy – according to the Latin across the top – burned with a savage gusto. I found Sir Francis by my side and commented on them.

'You have to admit that the work is well done,' he said. 'Did the avenue of trees impress you?'

'Yes, it did. Very much so.'

Sir Francis grinned. 'I take it that the avenue wasn't what you expected in view of your host's reputation?'

'Well, no. This is a remarkable house altogether.'

'You must meet our other guests,' Dorothy Killigrew was saying, as she led me forward into the throng. 'Nicholas, come here. This is Mistress Archer, who has just taken up residence in Cliff House. Nicholas . . .'

'Good day to you, Mistress Stannard,' said the brown-bearded Master Rowe, whom I had last encountered in the stable yard at Hampton Court, arguing with Brockley over where to stable a vicious grey gelding.

So much for Mistress Catherine Archer and her entourage. I can't imagine what my face looked like, but I well remember how I felt, which was as though the very earth had given way beneath my feet. I couldn't breathe. I stood still, speechless.

Then Sir John said, 'It's all right, Mrs Stannard. I know who you are, as well. Come, Nicholas. Let us withdraw into privacy for a moment or two, for some explanations. There is a parlour here.'

He guided us quickly to a door at the far end of the reception room, and took us into a parlour, quiet after the buzz of talk in the reception chamber. It looked out onto a meadow where cows were grazing or chewing the cud, and it was furnished with cushioned settles and chairs, little tables and also with a small fire in the hearth. The day was cool as well as cloudy.

Sir John settled me in a softly cushioned chair. He was a dark man; at least, his eyebrows and beard were black. His dark wig concealed his hair. He had handsome features and a beguiling smile. As I arranged my skirts, he directed the smile at Master Rowe. 'You had better explain yourself, Nicholas,' he said.

'I'm a member of the Killigrew family,' said Rowe, casting himself into one end of a settle and relaxing with one forearm along its arm, and his fingers fondling the lion's head carved into the end of it. 'Well, more or less. My mother was the daughter of Sir John's cousin Frank, who lived at Helford, close to Sir Francis' house. My father was a sadly attractive young Helford fisherman. My mother, poor lass, died in producing me, and my father, I believe, met with a sailing accident shortly before I was born. Or perhaps it wasn't an accident; I shall never know. My Killigrew grandparents brought me up. Their two sons both died as infants and they couldn't have any more, so they were childless. Perhaps they adopted me to fill an empty gap. They gave me my father's surname, though. I am a Rowe, not a Killigrew. But I was kindly treated and they had me educated. I am qualified as a lawyer. As you know, Mrs Stannard, I attend at court from time to time; I have undertaken duties for the crown on occasion.'

'It's helpful that one or two of the family should have the entrée to the court,' observed Sir Francis dryly. 'The Killigrew activities are occasionally, er, misunderstood.'

'Be quiet, Francis!' said Sir John, and for a moment there was nothing beguiling at all about his expression. The dark eyes had a warning glitter, like the sharp edge of a sword. Beneath the amiable host, I thought, lurked a different kind of man. One who didn't always wear curled wigs; one who might well wear sword and dagger and stride about on the decks of pirate vessels.

I had my usual pouch concealed within my open-fronted gown. It no longer held Sir Francis' list of disappearances but its other usual occupants were there: the little purse of coins, the small, sharp dagger in its sheath (I had killed a man once, with that dagger), and a set of picklocks. For a moment I let my fingers stray over my tawny velvet gown to find their outlines. I was glad to have them.

'The other day,' Rowe was saying, 'I saw Mr Brockley in Penzance. He didn't see me but I was intrigued to find him here in Cornwall so I followed him to see where he was going. He went to a wood-yard on the edge of the town and ordered fire-wood to be delivered to Mrs Catherine Archer at Cliff House. Mrs Archer? I said to myself. But that man works for Mrs Stannard. So, I paid a call on my distant cousin, Lady Alice Godolphin and had a pleasant talk with her and Sir Francis and . . . yes, Francis?'

'Since we met at Hampton Court,' Sir Francis said, 'there have been developments. For that reason, I felt free to tell Nicholas Rowe that you were indeed here, Mrs Stannard, and why you are here. Together, we came to talk to Sir John. John, will you take up the tale?'

'It isn't much of a tale,' said Sir John. 'I believe, Mrs Stannard, that when you met Nicholas at Hampton Court, it was during a disagreement about stabling for a horse called Grey Cornish. In fact, he belongs to me. I bought him despite his history and his temperament, because Nicholas here had in his employ a groom with exceptional gifts when it came to calming difficult horses. Robbie – the groom – has for some years had a sideline in breaking in young horses for anyone who wants to use his skills. He did well out of it. Horses seem to trust him. When he's in charge of them, most colts accept the saddle and then the rider quite quickly.'

I nodded. 'Robbie was there when we met, Mr Rowe. He was holding Grey Cornish. The horse tried to bite him and had apparently tried to kick him too.'

'Robbie would have overcome that before long,' said Nicholas. 'In fact, he was beginning to. But I'm getting ahead of myself. John here had seen the animal at a dealer's premises in Hampton village, been taken with its looks, bought and paid for it but because it was so fractious, didn't want to cope with it all the way to Cornwall. He had it put out to grass until he could send Robbie to fetch it. When he came home to Cornwall, he despatched both Robbie and me – I was in Cornwall at the time – to bring it home for him. When Mr Brockley and I had our wrangle about stabling, we had just collected it from the dealer, who was glad to be rid of it. We brought the horse to Cornwall, here to Arwenack – I live here, with my Killigrew kinfolk. With Robbie handling it, its temperament was already improving before we arrived here. The improvement continued – until, a week after we arrived, Robbie disappeared.'

I caught my breath. Sir John heard and nodded to me. 'We know all about the disappearances. Francis has told us. We had heard of some of them, but they were so scattered that until he talked to us about them, we hadn't realized they were connected. Now, we understand them all too well. Nicholas has lost his groom, most likely because of Robbie's unusual skill. Someone in the Ottoman world wants the use of him.'

'He wasn't in the consignment that Petroc escaped from,' said Rowe. 'It looks as though a new one is being assembled. There has been a report of an apothecary vanishing from Penzance.'

'Well, Mrs Stannard,' said Sir John, 'we have to tell you that we know what your purpose here is. We have no wish to hinder it. Our ancestors were pirates, true enough, but today, we are honest buccaneers, which means that our victims are Spanish galleons and we pay our taxes to the Treasury. This appalling business of abducting people is none of our doing. We are victims, not perpetrators. We will tell no one of your identity or your intentions. As far as the rest of the world is concerned you are Mrs Catherine Archer, and your companions are Mr and Mrs Mark Smith, and Mr Christopher Wood. We know that Mr Wood is really Christopher Spelton and we are aware that he too is one of the queen's agents. He is a good man to have beside you. You must let us know if in any way, we can help.'

'I want Robbie back,' said Nicholas grimly. 'I want this whole thing exposed and stopped before his ship sails. We are all at your service, Mrs Stannard.'

We went back into the reception room, where introductions continued. Apart from Sir Francis and Lady Alice and myself, there were more than a dozen guests – several men without wives, three with and one couple with a son and daughter, both in their twenties. I met several members of what I can only call the Killigrew tribe. I was introduced as Catherine Archer.

Knowing what the Killigrews' reputation was, I wondered if they all trusted each other and doubted it. Everyone to whom I was introduced *seemed* frank and straightforward, but I thought of their villainous ancestry and wondered more and more. There was one man I distrusted at once. He was about forty, good-looking but with not enough lines on his face though there was something knowing about his dark eyes. By the age of forty, a man should have just a line or two, evidence that he has at times been worried or had to make difficult decisions.

His name was Alexander Killigrew and he had the same effect on me as a jay's warning call has when it tells everything in its surroundings that a pine marten or a fox is on the prowl. He appeared to be a third cousin of John Killigrew. He too lived in Arwenack House, which was extensive, and by the sound of it he was of a studious rather than a violent nature. He was interested in family history and was writing a book about it.

There must have been some gruesome episodes in this family's history. I wondered if he would include them.

Another third cousin, a Captain Jerome Killigrew, looked unreliable for a different reason. He was quite clearly a drunk. He was already drunk when he bowed and greeted me, for he nearly fell over and his speech was slurred. He gave off a powerful alcoholic smell and he had the reddened nose and broken veins of a habitual drunkard, as well. Sir John apologized for him, whispering information in my ear as we turned away.

'He likes his wine a little too much. He sometimes has night-mares about being pursued by sharks or serpents.'

'Oh, dear.'

'Alexander runs a ship called *Serpent* and Nicholas calls his *The Shark.* I expect Jerome's nightmares come from that. He calls his own ship *Cormorant.* He's not married – lives in a house about a mile away and has women friends who come and go. Now, I want you to meet Mr Adrian Killigrew, my young nephew, and his wife Jane. They were recently married, and they're a real pair of turtle doves, always cooing. Adrian, this is Mrs Catherine Archer . . .'

In due course we were led out of the reception chamber and across the dim vestibule into a splendid dining hall. Here the walls were lined with tapestries, telling the story of a stag hunt. The tale began to the left of the door. Against a leafy background, huntsmen were setting out with leashed hounds, accompanied by ladies and gentlemen on fine horses. One man carried a goshawk and the lady beside him, mounted on a prancing white palfrey, carried a merlin. During the meal that followed, I followed the story all the way round the walls. Various stages of the hunt were depicted. Opposite to the vestibule door, the background changed from leafy to open sky and the two riders with hawks flew their birds. They had a spaniel which retrieved a rabbit. The hunt ended to the right of the door. It showed the stag goring a hound with his antlers and then being speared by a huntsman. Once more, there was plenty of blood.

The dining chamber was well-lit despite the dull weather, for it had elaborate candle chandeliers. There was a lower table for attendants and I saw my own friends among them. I, however, was seated at the top table and had been placed next to Sir John.

The meal was enormous. I can hardly recall the list of dishes. I know that for the first time in my life I tasted the delicate white flesh of a shark and was surprised because I would have expected that such a fierce creature would yield much harder meat. After the shark, I partook of roast mutton, and then there were calves' feet pies and small bird pies, stewed capons in a spicy sauce, the fashionable new vegetable, potatoes, sliced and boiled, glazed with honey and served with a spiced dip, an array of vegetables in various sauces: asparagus, radish, cabbage. There was a huge salad platter, too. To go with it all, was a red wine that I did not recognize. There were sweet dishes, too: cream pies, almond tarts, wondrous confections of marchpane and honey and spun sugar. Somewhere in the depths of this great house, I thought, there must be an army of cooks. I was careful not to gorge myself. It wasn't long before there were people belching loudly and I didn't want to be one of them.

Sir John's wife was on his other side, and she spoke across him to tell me that the spices used for the potato dip were black pepper, ginger, cardamom and a red pepper that was a rare and expensive import from the central isthmus of the New World. She called it paprika, and said that it was the reason why the dip was coloured red.

I said I would remember that and asked where I might obtain it. I also looked at the tapestries and did some thinking. No doubt, successful buccaneers could afford an army of cooks. They could probably afford an army of soldiers and investigators, too. Now that they knew about the unpleasant traffic going on under their noses, did they intend to investigate? I asked Sir John what steps he himself proposed to take.

'I have taken a few already,' he said ruefully. 'But it's like trying to catch a ghost. There's nothing to get hold of. Someone is being given a . . . shopping list, as it were. There is much contact between merchant ships from the Mediterranean and the Cornish folk. Who knows how or where a list is passed from one hand to another? And the snatches are so stealthy. A man, a woman, two little girls – even, I understand, a whole family on a remote smallholding – are just going about their ordinary business when they are seized or enticed and appear to vanish. Because whoever took them chose his moment carefully. Knowing where to begin is the problem.'

I thought, well, we do have Jago and Juniper Penberthy and the two murders that they just might have committed to protect their lucrative crimes from discovery. But though Brockley and Christopher think Jago could be in on it, they've found nothing to confirm that and I am learning nothing here. So, next, I must inspect Mistress Penberthy. I shan't share my ideas with Sir John.

I haven't taken to cousin Alexander at all and as for Captain
Jerome . . .

My musings had got that far, and I was just accepting a sweet
pastry with raisins in it and a marchpane topping, when there
was a disturbance further along the top table. Captain Jerome
had just slid off his seat and collapsed, snoring, onto the floor.

Yes, I must be wary of my new allies, if allies they truly were.

TEN

Playing Chess With Juniper

At that moment, however, Sir John unexpectedly said to me, 'Am I right in thinking that you would like to meet Mistress Juniper Penberthy? Sir Francis has suggested to me that you might be interested in the odd business of her drowned laundrymaid. You have been told about that, so he says. In your place, I would be intrigued by that. And also by the killing of the fisher lad at St Aidan's. Sir Francis has mentioned that to me, too. Am I right?'

'Brockley and Christopher have visited St Aidan's,' I said. 'They came back with theories but nothing further as yet.' I wasn't very happy about discussing my purpose in Cornwall with a Killigrew, but after all, Sir John and also Nicholas Rowe both claimed to be fellow victims, having lost the services of a valued groom. In a quiet voice, I told Sir John that it was true that I wished to meet Mrs Juniper Penberthy.

He was prompt. 'I'm sure it can be arranged,' he said and forthwith beckoned to a servant and told him to fetch Mr Alexander. A moment later, the smooth-faced third cousin with the knowing eyes was beside us, saying, 'You wanted me, Sir John?'

'Yes. You know Mrs Juniper Penberthy, I believe.'

'Indeed, I do. I visit her quite often.'

'Are you courting her?' asked Sir John. He added, 'I have no objection – I just enquire.'

Alexander, however, just shook his head. 'No, indeed. The lady is no beauty and she is no longer of childbearing age either. If and when I marry, I want a pretty face on my pillow, and I shall hope for children. We play chess, that's all.'

'Ah! I have heard about that. It could be the answer. Mrs Stannard here wishes to make the lady's acquaintance. Would Mrs Penberthy object if you brought friends to visit her for a game of chess?'

'I'm sure she wouldn't. There quite often are other people there – sometimes we have little chess tournaments amongst ourselves.'

Sir John turned to me. 'Yes, chess. Do you play, Mrs Stannard? And what about your attendants?' He nodded towards the lower tables, where Christopher and Brockley could be seen in animated conversation. Their matching buff doublets with the dark blue slashings and Christopher's almost bald head, browned by his outdoor life, stood out of the crowd. Beyond them, Dale was leaning forward to talk to the girl sitting opposite.

'I play,' I said. 'My first husband taught me. But my man Br— Mark Smith . . .'

'You can call him Brockley. We don't have secrets within the family.' *I don't like the sound of that, I said to myself though I didn't say it aloud.* 'Does he play?'

'Yes, he does, and better than I do. We play together sometimes and he usually wins. The other man, Christopher Spelton, also plays, I believe very well. I have never shared a chess game with him but Brockley has. My maid knows the moves but isn't really a player.'

'Mrs Penberthy wouldn't expect her guests' maid to play,' said Sir John, amused. 'Alex, will you speak to Mrs Penberthy and tell her that you wish to bring some chess-playing guests to visit her? A lady and two gentlemen. They can be described as her cousins or brothers or upper servants as you think best. I am aware,' he added to me, 'that your attendants are something more than servants but here in my house I preserve the conventions. However, Alex had better know. But the matter isn't for general knowledge, Alex.'

'I quite understand,' said the smooth-faced Alexander, and the knowing look seemed to increase.

On the way home, I asked my friends for their impressions. Of the three of them, Brockley was the most forthright. 'I did a lot of chatting among the servants. They know all the Killigrews well, and they know Sir Francis too. Some of the men have sailed with him. They say what I've already heard; he's a brilliant commander. But in some ways and especially about women, he's an innocent. Oh, not about Lady Alice – she's what she appears to be, sweet and gentle and glad to be rescued from her family, with its bloodthirsty tastes in tapestries. Oh yes, the wall decorations have been avidly discussed among the servants! But in general, they confirm what I've already guessed. In Sir Francis' eyes, women are dear little things to be protected from all the winds of the world and he even criticizes the queen. She should have married, he says, so that her husband could run the country for her. It's improper for a woman to be in power, and not natural to her.'

As an associate in any investigations of mine, Sir Francis certainly didn't look like promising material.

However, my introduction to Juniper Penberthy went smoothly enough. On Monday, I received a note to say that next Saturday we were all invited to join Mr Alexander Killigrew on a visit to Mrs Juniper Penberthy to dine with her and play a few games of chess. We were expected there mid-morning. If we could arrange to be ferried across to Penzance, Mr Alexander would meet us there. It would hardly be possible for us to take our own horses, unless we sent them by land the previous day and left them at The Good Catch. As it was a good twenty-five miles by land from Cliff House to Penzance, he suggested that he should arrange for hired horses to await us at the inn. From there we could ride to Mistress Penberthy's house.

On that Thursday, we received a visit from Mr Arlett, our vicar, who had now heard of our arrival and wished to make our acquaintance. With him, we were careful to maintain our characters as Mistress Catherine Archer, distant cousin of Mr Wells, Mark and Mary Smith, her manservant and maid, and Mr Christopher Wood, her other manservant. Brockley said that when, at Arwenack House, he ate dinner among their servants, he had learned that Mr Arlett was known to them, and was a gossip.

He assured himself that we would all attend church on Sundays, wished us well, took dinner with us and then went away. He was certainly gossipy and one of the things he gossiped about was the Killigrew family. We learned a good deal about their piratical past. We also learned that one of Mr Alexander Killigrew's virtues was a gift for smooth organization.

We boarded *The Sunrise* on Saturday morning at half past nine, leaving Thomas Tremaine and Tamzin Grigg in charge of the premises.

It was another clear day. St Michael's Mount with its castle stood out clearly between us and Penzance, which looked deceptively close. I met Griffin Brown for the first time that morning. He was a short, weather-browned man with dark hair and a fringe of beard, both now going grey. He came up to Cliff House early to say that the wind was contrary so we had better set out as soon as possible. The crossing to Penzance did take time, because *Sunrise* had to beat to and fro across the bay but we reached Penzance at the time we had planned.

Christopher helped Griffin with the sail and watching him, I suddenly wondered how old he was. I had always somehow regarded him as being the same age as myself but now I saw that he was surely a good many years younger. He was still fathering children and the narrow growth of hair round his otherwise bald head was still dark, with only a few grey hairs to be seen. All the same, he certainly wasn't as much as ten years my junior and therefore he must be over fifty.

I then looked at Dale and Brockley and saw that Brockley, who was older than me, seemed strained while Dale, though I knew she was younger than I was, had worry lines etched across her forehead and a good deal of grey in her hair. I was myself about to turn sixty. For the love of heaven, what were we all doing, sitting in this boat in the middle of Mounts Bay, seeking to meet a lady who might, just might, have murdered her laundress and have a stake in a company of slavers?

I tried to comfort myself by remembering that we were all carrying our red chalks but as a source of comfort, it wasn't adequate.

At Penzance, the horses were awaiting us, at The Good Catch inn. There were five horses, two with the promised side saddles. Alexander told the groom to be ready for our return sometime during the afternoon. Then we all mounted and rode off across the town, out to the Land's End side of it, and in due course to Juniper House.

During the ride, Alexander said that for this occasion, we had better go back to being Mrs Catherine Archer, Mary and Mark Smith, and Christopher Wood. I was to be a lady who played chess with her menservants.

'Won't Mrs Penberthy think that odd?' Brockley asked.

'Not at all. She plays chess with her butler. Simmons, his name is.'

'Are you putting them in your book, Mr Killigrew?'

'Yes, indeed I am.'

I decided not to ask if he meant to put us there as well.

I had never seen juniper trees before and looked at them with interest. They dotted the garden in front of Mrs Penberthy's door, small spiky evergreens, some with oddly twisted trunks. They looked half human, and half deformed. There was a weirdness about them. The house too was eye-catching but in a more agreeable way. It was long, which made it seem low, though in fact it had two storeys. It was half-timbered, as Christopher had said, with rosy-red brick walls for the ground floor, matching the brick of the tall, patterned chimneys. The front door and the ground floor windows were outlined in grey brick. Someone, I thought, had taken ideas from Hampton Court. The slate roof had dormer windows poking out of it; the other windows were mullioned. The whole house was most graceful in its proportions.

I didn't have long to stare at it. The chess-playing butler, Simmons presumably, was there at the door to welcome us, smartly clad in black though he didn't wear a chain of office. To our right there was a wall with a wide doorway through which grooms came to take our horses and this time Brockley did succeed in going with them to make sure that all was well in the stables.

The rest of us were taken into a parlour where three small tables with chessboards on them, were awaiting us. There were straight chairs on either side, though these were comfortably cushioned.

Here, we met Mrs Penberthy.

Our hostess had been on one of the settles, sewing, when we came in. She at once rose to her feet and we were impressed though not admiring. Mrs Juniper Penberthy was well into middle-age and even as a girl she could never have been pretty. She was tall for a woman with a barrel of a body. She had clearly given up trying to wear a stomacher and her stomach made a bulge in her brown fustian gown. If she was making money out of slave-trading, she wasn't spending it on dresses.

Her skin was reddened as if she spent a good deal of time out of doors and her heavy features frankly looked as if they had been created by slapping slabs of flesh into place on either side of a broad nose with splayed nostrils. She had some jewellery, though. Round her thick neck, she wore what looked like a double necklace of genuine pearls, and matching bracelets adorned her fat arms. Brown velvet covered the hood on her faded hair.

Her mouth was thick but straight. She smiled in greeting but though the fleshy lips curved a little, nothing reached her eyes, which were small, pale, bright but cold.

Yet her greeting was friendly. She was charmed to meet Mistress Archer. Unlike the Killigrews, Juniper evidently hadn't adopted the modern forms of address. Oh yes, most of Penzance knew about the distant cousin of Master Wells, who had taken charge of Cliff House, until his return. 'And it is greatly feared that he won't return,' said Mistress Penberthy gravely.

Alexander introduced Christopher to her, while Dale stood humbly in the rear and was ignored. At this point, Brockley rejoined us and was also introduced. Juniper rang a bell and a maidservant appeared with glasses of wine on a tray.

'Just one glass, in welcome,' said Juniper Penberthy. 'If we are to play chess, we need clear heads.'

There was a little small talk over the wine. I remarked that Juniper was an unusual Christian name and our hostess, laughing hugely, said that the vicar of the north-country parish where she had been born, and where her father owned a mine for coal, fully agreed.

'My mother loved juniper trees. They were all around our house. My father had died a few months before my birth and so it was up to her to choose my name and she wanted to call me Juniper but the vicar – Dr Hardy, his name was – wouldn't let her; he said it wasn't a name for a Christian child; that no saint or anyone at all in the Bible had been called Juniper and he suggested Mary or Kate. In the end I was christened Kate. But my mother always called me Juniper. She said the vicar couldn't stop her from doing that. As for me, I liked the name and I have kept it. Whatever the Reverend Henry Hardy would have said!'

'What did your husband call you?' I asked.

'Oh, Juniper. He let me have my way over that and he let me plant all my juniper trees in the garden. I loved them so much,

I'm just like my mother. Walter was much older than I was,' said his widow. 'I wasn't pretty and my parents found it hard to marry me off. Finally, Master Walter Penberthy, merchant of Penzance, a friend of my father, took me along with a good big dowry. He was a childless widower and he hoped for children. He brought me here and he did a husband's duty by me until it turned out that I was as barren as his first wife was. After that, well – he no doubt enjoyed the company of pretty ladies elsewhere. I didn't mind too much. I had a good house and he wasn't unkind to me even when he didn't, well, want to bother me any more. I truly mourned Walter when he died of lung congestion a dozen years ago or so.'

I wondered if she always greeted new acquaintances with her life history. Afterwards, when we were back at Cliff House, I said as much to Dale. Dale did not have a brilliant mind but she had flashes now and then of an astonishing acuteness. She said that Mistress Penberthy was probably bitter, because of her poor looks, her childlessness and the loss of her husband's love. 'Telling that story of hers, as if she just accepts her looks and never minded when her husband stopped paying attention to her, is her way of convincing herself that it's the truth.'

Dale was probably right. Those occasional flashes of hers usually were.

Over the wine, I remarked that the other day, by chance, my manservants Smith and Wood had been out exercising our horses and had found their way into a fishing village called St Aidan's. They had come face to face with a remarkable fisherman who apparently owned most of the boats in St Aidan's. Had Mistress Penberthy ever heard of Jago?

'Oh, dear goodness, yes.' Juniper Penberthy was cheerfully open about it. 'Most of this end of Cornwall have heard of him and no doubt beyond. He's a kind of fisherman king. He's a descendent of pirates and doesn't mind who knows it. I haven't actually met him, though. He probably doesn't play.' The ability to play chess was evidently the key to meeting Mistress Penberthy.

I sipped a little more wine and then, cautiously, said that I had heard of the tragedy concerning her laundrymaid and felt that it must have been a serious shock to her. Had nothing more been found out? Yes, said Juniper, it had been a shock, but nothing had been discovered and she for one did not like to talk of it. As a topic, it was cut short.

Conversation only lasted as long as the welcoming wine did. Then a maidservant came to take away the empty glasses and Dale helped her. Dale disappeared into the kitchen and didn't return. In a businesslike way, our hostess set out chess pieces and asked me if I preferred black or red. Simmons came into the room and with a wave of the hand invited Brockley to sit down with him at another of the tables. Alexander sat down too and smiled an invitation to Christopher. I asked to command the warriors in red and prepared for battle with Mistress Juniper.

We had allegedly come to play chess, and play chess we did, except for Dale, who stayed out of sight in the kitchen. The rest of us were practically chained to our chessboards for the whole of the visit except, of course, that we did pause to dine, though not for long. We had small ale to drink, and just a few dishes. Baked fish in a green sauce or crane baked in pastry, salad and then sweet pancakes. After that, the orgy of chess was resumed. We changed partners. I had lost the games I played with Juniper before dinner. In the afternoon, I played against the butler, Simmons and won; against my hostess once more, and lost, against Brockley and won (to my surprise), against Christopher and reached stalemate, against Alexander and lost . . .

By the end of the afternoon, I was exhausted. Christopher was heavy-eyed with tiredness and Brockley looked ready to drop. Juniper and her butler seemed to be enlivened. I caught Alexander's eye and he said that it was time we stopped; Juniper, you know what a long pull it is, across the bay. Their boatman will be waiting at The Good Catch. We had had a wonderful time and must do it again soon.

During our journey home, I became aware that Dale was full of suppressed excitement and I recognized the symptoms. She had something to tell us but the presence first of Alexander Killigrew and then of Griffin Brown, was preventing her. I gave her an understanding nod. We arrived at Polgillan, said farewell to Griffin and made haste to climb the cliff path and get home. Once we were there, we automatically gathered in the kitchen, which had become our normal habitat. It was so much more welcoming than the parlour or the dining room.

'What is it that you're longing to tell me, Dale?' I said. 'What did you find out that I didn't?'

'Yes,' Brockley said. 'Was it about the girl who was drowned in the washtub? Come along, Fran. Tell us!'

'It was nothing about the washtub business,' said Dale. 'I did ask – said what a terrible thing it must have been and one of the maids said it had made her frightened and she said that inside the house, none of them liked being alone and didn't like being only with one person, either. But the housekeeper was sharp with her and said don't talk nonsense, Betty, and remember that the mistress doesn't like us talking about it and that was the end of it. I dared not ask any more. What I noticed, and it wasn't very much, was quite different.'

'Let's hear it,' I said.

'A little while before the kitchen had its dinner,' Dale said, 'the maidservant called Betty asked if I would like to see the house, so I said yes. I was shown a small parlour – much smaller than where I left you, ma'am – and a big formal dining chamber, not the little one where you had dinner, and then she took me upstairs. The mistress and any guests sleep on the first floor. Betty just opened the door of Mistress Penberthy's room and let me peep inside. Then come the attic rooms where the maids sleep. The stairs up to them are as steep as ladders! 'The maids have one big bed. Betty said that Simmons and the other menservants, there were three of them at the servants' dinner table, sleep in the basement. Well away from the maids, you see.'

'Go on,' said Brockley, since Dale seemed to have paused for breath.

'Just then, someone called from below, wanting to ask Betty something – which spices ought to be used with something or other, I think. Betty said *Oh, quick, I must get back, just follow me, take your time on the stairs,* and off she went, bounding down those steep stairs like a goat on a rocky hillside – I suppose she's used to them – and I went down slowly and on the next landing I thought I would like another peep, just a peep, into Mistress Penberthy's bedchamber. What I'd already glimpsed of it did look so luxurious. And so it was when I looked again – brocaded curtains round the bed, a silver basin on the washstand, things like that. Only that second time, was able to take it more slowly and stare around me and on the bedside table I saw a rolled-up document.'

She paused again, doubtfully. 'I don't think I was doing wrong. We are supposed to be finding things out, aren't we?'

'You looked at the rolled-up document, I take it,' said Brockley. 'You did quite right. What was it?'

'It was a map of this end of Cornwall, very like the ones we've been looking at. And there were marks.' We all sat up straighter. 'I only had a few moments to look,' said Dale. 'But lanes were marked very clearly and there were ink lines drawn along some of them. All the lines led to somewhere on top of the Lizard and seemed to stop at the same place, not all that far from here. And I *think* some of them came from places where people have disappeared though I'm not sure. It doesn't prove much but . . . well, it did look as if it could be some sort of guide . . .'

Dale's voice trailed off uncertainly but Brockley looked alert. 'Maybe to show someone the quickest way to get from where they'd snatched a victim, to a central collection point? It could be,' he said.

'I did say it didn't amount to much,' Dale told us. 'But there was something else. Only this is so small and so silly. I wonder if . . .'

'Out with it, Fran,' said Brockley, amused.

'It was that small parlour on the ground floor,' said Dale. 'It was a parlour, not a study, but there was a shelf of books, and in a corner there was one of those tall desks that people stand at to write. That's all, but I *smelt* something. Just faintly, something that made my nose itch. I can't put a name to it. It was sweetish and pleasant and it was only a hint. The perfume that the last visitor was wearing, I should think. Or maybe Mistress Penberthy uses perfume. I can't think what it could mean but it was just . . . odd. I don't know that I should have bothered to tell you.'

'No, you did quite right,' Brockley said. He spoke distractedly though, as if his mind were somewhere else. I looked at him, thinking that he had seemed strained all day and he hadn't been as skilled as usual when I played chess with him and I won. Now, he looked as though he were listening to some small sound far away and there was sweat running down his temples. 'I must say that chess is a tiring game,' he remarked. 'I feel exhausted.'

Then he fainted.

ELEVEN
Crevice

For the next ten days, there were no more attempts to find out who was running the selective slave trade from the tip of Cornwall. I would not have cared if the entire population of Penzance had disappeared overnight. I thought only of Brockley.

A few years earlier, he had fallen victim to a recurrent fever, which had at times made him very ill indeed. However, it seemed since then to have burned itself out. The attacks had become weaker and further apart and now it was over a year since he had had even a minor one. Now, it seemed that his recovery had been an illusion. This attack, though it was short, was also savage. He needed day and night attention. Fever, and inability to take solid food in any form, were the only symptoms but they were so severe that I feared for his life and so did Dale, who was frantic.

Our visit to Mistress Penberthy was on a Saturday. On Monday, the vicar, Mr Arlett, arrived, on a broad-backed skewbald mare. Being a small man, he seemed to be perched on her rather than astride her. He wanted to know why we had not been in church on the Sunday. Did we not know that it was the law that we must attend church?

'Yes, once a month,' said Dale, rapping out an answer before anyone else could. 'And if you want to know why we weren't there yesterday, then please come to my husband's sick room.'

He accepted the invitation and annoyed us all by falling to his knees at Brockley's bedside and bidding us to join him in a lengthy prayer for the patient.

'I wanted to change Roger's sheets and he got in the way,' Dale complained when at last he took his leave. We were to send for him at once if the patient worsened, he told us.

Over the next few days, the patient did worsen but we didn't

send for Mr Arlett. We worked together, taking turns with the
night watches. Now and then we got Brockley to swallow a
spoonful or two of broth, wine, milk, or water from the well.
Liquids were the only things he could keep down. During this
time, our careful pretences about being Mistress Catherine Archer
and Mr and Mrs Smith and Christopher Wood, failed hopelessly.
We kept on using our real names by mistake and finally had to
admit everything to Tamzin. Christopher told her frankly that we
were here to make enquiries because there had been mysterious
disappearances, and Master Wells was one of them, that the queen
herself had sent us and that all this was a secret and that outside
the house, she must refer to us by our pretended names.

Tamzin, mercifully, turned out to be a young woman of sense.
She agreed willingly, though inside the house, she did use our
real names and we couldn't object when we were doing the same
thing. We had to let Tremaine in on the secret too. We had already
made mistakes in his presence and were not surprised, though
chagrined, when he grinned and said he had already realized that
we were all here under pretend names. As Tamzin had done, he
promised to keep the secret.

Dale was more concerned with trying to remember some of
the ingredients of the medicines that had helped Brockley in the
past. She did at length call it all to mind. 'Willow bark, ma'am,
and yarrow and basil.'

'But do they grow here?' I asked wildly. 'I haven't seen willows
hereabouts. There's basil in the garden but who might know
where to find yarrow?' I looked out of the bedchamber window
towards St Michael's Mount, a conical shape in the distance.
Might I find help there?

'You can buy yarrow medicine in Penzance,' Tamzin said.
'And maybe in Helston too but Penzance I know about. There
are two apothecaries there who stock those things. There were
three but one has vanished and may well be bound for faraway
places even now. Griffin will take me across if you wish, madam,
and I will fetch some. I will ask advice about anything else that
might be useful.'

Tamzin was truly anxious to help, but I suspected that she had
her own reasons for wanting to go to Penzance. According to
Thomas Tremaine, who said that he had at first had hopes of

courting her, she had a swain already, in Penzance, a maker of tableware, pewter, pottery and bronze. They hoped to marry before the end of the year, when the young man had built his business up a little more.

However, provided that she brought back what Brockley needed and didn't take an unreasonable time about it, she was welcome. I gave her some money and sent her off, reminding her, however, to remember when in other company, to use our new names. I was in fact thankful to know that Cliff House was not after all impossibly far from help.

Tamzin came back within two hours, bringing the potions I wanted and two others. She was however reluctant ever to do the journey across the bay alone in future, as Griffin had tried to make advances.

'He said he wanted a kiss as payment for the trip, better than money, he said, madam, and would I like to come with him tomorrow on a boat ride over to St Michael's Mount. No one would mind, he said, there were people there, in charge of the place but they never minded a few young lovers coming ashore for a kiss and a cuddle in private . . . my betrothed, Master William Davey, he would be so angry if he knew . . .!'

In the midst of my weariness and fear for Brockley, I had to go down the cliff and make it plain to Griffin that my female employees were not available for lovemaking.

One thing that might well be relevant to our quest, though also more than a little disturbing was found out during those days, more or less by chance. The horses still had to be exercised. Neither Dale nor I were willing to leave Brockley so Tremaine and Christopher took turns at it.

Christopher took Red out one morning, with Rufus on a leading rein, and some distance from Cliff House, he stopped and tethered them to a bent dwarf tree ('The only tree for miles,' he said), and did a little exploring on foot. Dale had said that the map in Mistress Penberthy's bedchamber showed lines marked on lanes that converged on the Lizard, he said, roughly where he had stopped. It wasn't all that far from Cliff House. He was intrigued.

He came back full of excitement and from an unexpected direction. He climbed up from the cold room.

He found me and Dale on duty at Brockley's bedside. He was

dusty, with grazes on the leather of his shoes, and Dale at once fetched some warm water from the kitchen for him so that he could clean his hands. Brockley stirred restlessly but did not wake. Christopher dried his hands with impatience and said to me and Dale, '*Listen!*'

On foot, he had looked around him and found that close by, three tracks, all coming from a westerly direction, did indeed converge, in accordance with Dale's description of Mistress Penberthy's map.

'They all had ink lines drawn along them,' said Dale, nodding.

Christopher had prowled about. It was a bleak area of heathland with rock outcrops. One lump of rock attracted his attention as it didn't seem to be embedded in the ground like the rest. He prodded it with his riding whip and it moved. So, he pushed a lot harder, using hands and arms and it suddenly slid aside and there beneath it was what looked like the head of a shaft to an underground mine. There was a ladder, in good condition.

'You went down?' said Dale, horrified, reading his expression.

'Yes, I did,' Christopher said. 'It was quite easy and at the foot, I found myself in a cave. It wasn't very big. There was light from the shaft I had come down, so I could see that much. I also saw a sort of rock shelf with lanterns on it and a flask of oil and a tinderbox. The place is in use by someone for some purpose and regularly, I would say. But there was no one there so I lit one of the lanterns and looked about and there was a tunnel. I followed it.'

'That was brave,' I said.

Dale exclaimed, 'Foolhardy! That's the sort of exploring best done if you take a couple of well-armed soldiers with you.'

'I didn't have any soldiers on hand,' said Christopher reasonably. 'I just followed the tunnel. It was quite high and fairly wide and there was fresh air in it though I don't know where it came from. It went a long way, fairly level. It forked once but the left-hand fork was narrower than the main tunnel and I didn't like the look of it – narrow, low roofed and it seemed so dark. I kept on along the main tunnel.'

'Christopher, all that was most intrepid of you and I wouldn't have dared to do it,' I said, 'but what is all this about?'

'Wait. I went straight on,' said Christopher. 'After a while

– quite a long while – the tunnel widened out and I found myself in another cave. Bigger than the first one; I held my lantern up and looked about and made out the size of it. There was no shaft there to shed any light from outside so I only had the lantern. I saw a table, though, with more lanterns and oil and so on. I could hear the sea booming away somewhere below the way it does here and then I thought I heard something else. A sort of clinking noise. I began to work my way round the walls. They were rocky and rough. I kept listening, trying to find where the noise came from. Then, it was at a place where the wall swelled out and made – well, it was like a pleat, only it was rock, not fabric – I saw a tiny chink of light. I held the lantern up and I realized that there was a crevice at the back of it. I peered at it and I saw that it was actually a little more than a crevice. I could have got through it. Or into it would be a better way to say it because it was quite deep; a miniature tunnel so to speak. I could still hear the clinking sound and it was nearer. I was wary. I crept through. It was just wide enough for me. There were places where I had to push my way along but it wasn't that difficult. At the far end I just craned forward and what do you think I saw?'

Since Brockley fell ill, no one had made even the feeblest joke. I ventured one now. 'A dragon?' I suggested. 'Or a treasure chest?'

'Nothing so dramatic. I found myself watching Tamzin pressing curds to make cheese. I was looking into the cold room. While I was looking, she finished what she was doing and went away, up the steps to the trapdoor. After a few minutes, I pushed my way out into the cold room and looked up at the trapdoor. It was open. That's all. There is a cave system inside the Lizard, and it connects with our cold room. I came in that way.'

There was a silence. Then Christopher said, 'I have to say that I don't like it. It could very well be part of the business we are here to discover. *Someone* is using those tunnels. In future, I suggest that the trapdoor at the top of the steps down to the cold room should be kept bolted at all times except when the cold room is in use. And especially at night. We would have found that crevice before, except that the cold room walls are so rough and we didn't peer behind every piece of jutting rock. That crevice is a way into this house. We ought to block it up somehow. And

now, could Tremaine take a walk out to the bent and solitary tree
– he knows it – and rescue the horses? I'm tired and I want to
eat and rest before I take my turn in nursing Brockley.'

'I'll stay here for a while,' I said. 'You've done your duty for
the time being, Christopher.'

'I will stay too,' said Dale. My eyes met hers and I knew that
we shared the same fear: that this man whom we both loved,
who was now in this deep sleep that might be not just restfulness
but unconsciousness and might die if he wasn't guarded; that for
all our care, we might lose him yet.

Tamzin arrived then, bringing another pitcher of warm water.
Poor Tamzin, just then, was trying to be kitchen maid and dairy-
maid both at once, and run messages, too. I asked her to take
Christopher's message out to Tremaine in the stables and sent
her away. Then I turned back to Dale and Brockley and saw that
Dale's eyes were wide. She pointed and I saw that Brockley's
eyes were open. I went to him and felt his brow. It was damp
from the sweating he had done earlier but he wasn't sweating
now. His skin was cool.

'Hallo, madam,' he said faintly. 'I've been ill a long time,
haven't I? Is that Fran there? Darling Fran . . .' With some diffi-
culty, he turned onto his back and then heaved himself up into
a sitting position. He was dreadfully pale and thin, too. The points
of his shoulders jutted from beneath his nightshirt and his face
had been pared to the bone. 'I think,' he said, in a voice as thin
as his body was, 'that I'd like something to eat. A beefsteak or
two, and a good red wine, and orange segments in cream to
follow . . .'

Dale, shedding tears of thankfulness, nevertheless replied quite
severely. 'So, you are awake, my love. But you can't have beefsteak yet. We haven't got any, anyway. You shall have chicken
broth, and a little bread and milk with a blob of honey, and well
water to drink. And this evening, perhaps, a little bit of fish
poached in milk. All to be taken slowly and not too much. I *think*
you're going to live. We have been so worried for you . . .'

She sat down and dissolved completely, out of sheer relief. I
patted her shoulder but did not otherwise interfere. She and
Brockley had married long ago because sheer propinquity had
somehow edged them into it but what was between them had

grown and deepened since then. For Dale now, Brockley was her life, the other half of herself.

'I will prepare what you need,' I said to Brockley. 'Dale, you stay here.' I turned to Christopher. 'Come with me,' I said, and then I took us both out of the room, so that Dale could lie down beside Brockley and put her arms about him.

Christopher and I went down to the kitchen where we found that Tamzin had delivered the message to Tremaine about fetching Red and Rufus. 'We'd better get the broth and the bread and milk ready,' I said. 'Christopher, will you fetch a pail of well water for us? What a blessing that broth is always handy.'

Tamzin kept a stockpot always ready, adding leftover vegetables, meat bones and meat juice whenever she could and using the result for soups and gravies. Broth could be created within five minutes. 'I'll add a little barley, madam. Mr Brockley must need food; it's so long since he last ate a meal.'

'I'll see to the bread and milk,' I told her. I knew how to make the easily digestible white manchet bread and I had formed a habit of doing so. I cut some of this into cubes and when Tamzin reappeared, she set about warming some milk. In a very short time, Tamzin and I were able to take Brockley's first real meal up to him. We gave Dale a spoon and then we left her to feed her husband and returned to the kitchen, where Christopher was putting logs onto the fire.

Tamzin said, 'I wonder how long he will take to get better properly. Did you know, madam, that there's to be a midsummer fair in Penzance? And a team of dancers from Helston are coming to dance the Floral Dance – usually it's only performed in Helston early every May. You arrived too late for it but I was there and it was lovely though it ended too soon because it began to rain.'

We had settled round the kitchen table, relaxed into the blessed feeling that the worst of the crisis was past. We were mildly intrigued by this Floral Dance, for none of us had even heard of it. I asked what it was.

'Just a slow dance in a procession, to say goodbye to winter and hallo to summer. It's as old as time itself. It's been danced in Helston since forever.' Tamzin's soft Cornish voice was amused. Clearly she thought that the whole world must know about this Floral Dance. 'But that's no reason not to dance it at midsummer too, and you can see it in Penzance on the twenty-first of June.'

'Shouldn't it be the twenty-fourth?' Christopher said. 'That's where the church puts it. It's the birthday of St John the Baptist.'

'Is it? Well, not here,' said Tamzin. 'We hold to the old ways, here. Midsummer's been the longest day – the twenty-first – as long as anyone remembers. Going away back into our roots, afore the church ever came. Only there isn't usually a midsummer fair at Penzance. Penzance has seven fairs a year but not at midsummer as a rule though some of the villages here on the Lizard hold some jollifications. This one at Penzance has been specially granted by the queen, no one knows why. It's only for two days, not seven like most. There's been some worried talk, people saying that a busy fair is just the place where someone could be snatched. But a fair is a fair and there'll be plenty of folk who'll want to go. But will Mr Brockley be able to?'

'He might,' I said, though doubtfully. 'It's two weeks away but he has been very ill.'

'That's a pity,' said Tamzin. 'The fairs are always so exciting. Craftsmen'll be setting up their stalls – my William will – and as there's always ships from everywhere bringing all kinds of things in, there'll be stalls full of foreign fruits and spices and lengths of silk and gemstones and there'll be fire-eaters and tumblers and mummers too . . .'

Christopher said, 'I expect some of us will go. It might be worth it – there are always things to buy when there's any kind of fair and we would all enjoy the mummers.'

I wondered why the queen had granted Penzance this extra fair, this year. A short one, I thought, licensed only for two days. A *concentrated* two days, during which crowds would gather. A two-day stretch of time during which somebody could indeed be snatched. A fair that could be bait for the snatchers, held while Ursula Stannard and Christopher Spelton, both the queen's agents, happened to be living on the nearby Lizard, trying to catch the said snatchers. I didn't like what I was thinking.

Brockley was basically a strong man but the illness was stronger. Two days later, he relapsed and once more was unable to eat.

He recovered from that within a week and this time his recovery was steady, but he was not well enough to let him go to any kind of fair only one week after first getting out of bed without assistance. Because he had eaten so little, he had lost a great deal of weight and Christopher reported that when Brockley made his first unaided climb out of bed, which was to use his chamber pot, he wavered and shook and nearly fell over.

'Though he waved me away when I went to him, meaning to steady him,' Christopher said. 'He is determined, that one!'

Someone who had been a help to us during this unhappy time, was William Davey, Tamzin's betrothed. When she went into Penzance to call on the apothecary, she also – as I had surmised she would – called on Davey. He twice came over to us with kindly offerings. The first time he brought us half a dozen oranges, which he insisted had healing virtues and also, a pleasing set of a dozen bronze drinking cups that he said would brighten our table when all was well again and we were able to invite company. I wanted to pay him for those but he refused.

The second time he brought sugared biscuits which he said were easy to digest and had given him energy when he was getting over measles. Dale was pleased with those and as Brockley's appetite improved, she began feeding them to him.

He was a pleasant-looking young man, sturdy in build, with dark hair cut tidily short and a fringe of dark beard round a firm jaw. Tamzin would do well with him, I thought.

As the day of the fair approached, Brockley did recover his appetite but he still couldn't cope with strong tasting things. He would heave if he tried to eat onions or beef or anything highly seasoned, and if he forced the food down it was liable to come up again. By Midsummer's Day, he had only just reached the point of being able to put on his clothes and walk about inside the bedchamber. He couldn't travel to Penzance and couldn't be left unattended, either.

However, across the breakfast table the day before, Tamzin volunteered to stay with him if the rest of us wanted to visit the fair. She had been to other fairs and there were several more to come. She would go to those; she didn't mind missing this one. Her William would come over and keep her company.

'He won't want to miss the fair, surely!' I said. 'Won't he

want to have a stall there, and sell his wares?' I had been impressed with the bronze goblets.

'Oh, his sister Gianna is quite capable of running his stall and also, he has an apprentice; a very competent lad, Lambert Trethewy. William says that Lambert is becoming skilled with pewter and will have a chance to sell some of the tankards and dishes he has made himself. Gianna and Lambert can manage without William for once. He says he'll stay with me. He can cook as well as I can; he will help me and it will be good to have a man here, in case Mr Brockley has any kind of bad turn.'

'If you're sure,' I said doubtfully.

'It was William's idea,' Tamzin said. 'He says he will be glad to spend the day here and he made me laugh. He said that if he and I were dining at a great house like Arwenack, their steward wouldn't know where to put him, above the salt or below. William is a qualified craftsman and he should go above the salt, just under family and distinguished guests. I, a maidservant, would certainly be seated below. And yet we are betrothed and should be seated together. How those great folk would scratch their heads, he said. And all the time the answer was simple. We are not yet married, so he would join me below the salt, and once we are married, I would join him above.'

'While in Cliff House we all sit round the kitchen table,' I said, amused. 'The dining room here is enough to destroy your appetite if you just look at it. It's as friendly as a largish prison cell. All right, let your William come.'

'Silk!' said Dale, who had been thinking along different lines. 'Ma'am, the gowns we have to wear at court wear out so fast, and there are these rules that aren't written down but they're always there, about not appearing at any court event in the same gown twice. If we buy some lengths of good silk and some velvet or brocade, we can make ourselves maybe two new gowns each, with a change of kirtles.'

It was a valid argument. I had known after my last court visit that next time we would need new gowns if I was not to be regarded as *Mistress Stannard . . . They say she is sister to the queen but she looks so dowdy now that I reckon she's not so much in favour as she used to be. Maybe I won't ask her to dine after all. You can't be too careful who you're seen with.* I knew the court gossip exchange all too well.

But if we appeared in gleaming new silks and rippling velvets, the whisper would go round that *Mistress Stannard is flourishing, is someone worth cultivating – she just might bring you to the notice of the queen and if you invite her to dinner and she accepts, how your friends will envy you!*

It was an excuse for going to the fair and it might do Dale good. She was very pale and she too had lost weight. Dale never ate properly when she was anxious. Brockley was safe now. We would go to the fair. We would keep together and be watchful; no one would abduct any of us. We would all enjoy a day of relaxation.

TWELVE
Midsummer Fair

We feared that bad weather would ruin the fair, for the night before was windy. The old house creaked so loudly that once again, I kept starting awake, thinking that I heard feet on the stairs, only to remember that the stairs didn't need feet; they could talk to themselves without human help.

But in the morning, the wind had dropped to a moderate breeze and there was sunshine to greet us. We took some breakfast, William Davey arrived and said that the boatman who had brought him was waiting in the Polgillan harbour for us. We set out: Christopher, Dale and me.

We would have known that we were bound for an event of some sort long before we arrived there, by the number of boats making their way across or around the bay towards Penzance, some of them decorated with garlands of flowers or strings of brightly coloured pennants. Many were under sail, and some of the sails were brightly coloured, red and blue being the favourites. The breeze filled them merrily and no doubt called up curses from rowers who had to make headway against it.

We landed and paid our boatman, with an extra gratuity, which he took with a glint in his eye, because he had said that he wanted to berth his boat, *The Merlin*, in the harbour while he went to the fair and would need to pay the harbour dues. The harbour was already crowded; some boatmen were going to be disappointed and would have to land elsewhere and walk into the town. There were three foreign looking ships berthed there and two more anchored outside.

We set off along the track that ran parallel with the shore, lined on the other side with cottages and a few larger houses. Soon we heard the sound of music, slightly ragged, as though the musicians were having trouble in keeping together. It was playing a repetitive little tune. Then, out of a side turning, came a procession of dancers, accompanied by a band of musicians with a variety of instruments: a trumpeter, three lute players and three men respectively playing two tabor drums and a pipe. The dance was slow and the procession seemed to consist of groups of four, dancing together as one.

'This must be the Floral Dance,' said Christopher. We moved aside to let it pass and then, finding a fellow dressed in motley and holding out a hat, we dutifully dropped contributions into it. We had all come with money in our purses. We looked like spending most of it.

We had all dressed plainly. Dale and I were in brown gowns with small ruffs and no farthingales, while Christopher had done what Brockley always did on such occasions and put on a suit of military style buff. Even so, Christopher thought fit to warn us about pickpockets.

'They'll be about, for sure,' he said. 'More likely to get you than the slavers will. At least this kind of slaver. They're choosing individuals. But the corsairs have sacked Penzance before now.'

I hoped that they wouldn't sack it today, and glanced out to sea, half fearing to see a fleet of pirate vessels advancing from the east. The foreign ships we had seen when we landed no doubt had official business in Penzance and the chances were that they were selling, not seizing.

The dance turned back into the town and we followed. Then we found ourselves in the market. It was busy. The stallholders had grabbed their extra opportunity with a will.

Quietly, into my ear, Christopher said, 'This whole affair is bait. Your royal sister is hoping that we are here, with our eyes and ears open.'

We duly kept our eyes open. Our ears were little use to us because the noise, as ever at markets like this, was deafening. Stallholders all have voices like bulls and these were mingled with cheers from various cleared spaces where tumblers were turning cartwheels, building themselves into the human equivalent of card houses and tying their unbelievably double-jointed limbs into unlikely knots, while a fire-eater was gulping down gusts of flame and then giving his wide-eyed audience a delicious fright by emitting fiery streams in their direction. A conjuror with a sweetly smiling wench as an assistant was performing tricks, an enormous man, stripped to the waist, was bellowing invitations to passers-by to wrestle with him and at the edge of the market, a cockfight was going on, with bets being excitedly shouted.

But we heard no cries of alarm or met any bewildered people seeking lost companions. The Floral Dance, having led us into the market, had disappeared beyond it but returned after a time, going very slowly now, until it halted in the centre. The fellow in motley did well with his hat.

We went round the stalls. We had each brought a capacious basket. I bought lengths of silk and velvet cloth and we all made purchases at a glover's stall: soft doeskin for Dale and myself; stout leather for Christopher, who bought two pairs so that Brockley should have one. I also purchased an extra doeskin pair, for Tamzin, hoping I had got the size right. Tamzin was short in stature but sturdy and though her hands were small, in accordance with the rest of her, they were also strong. They were not tiny or childlike.

We found a stall selling hot meat pies and another one offering pomegranates which none of us had heard of before, but which turned out to contain myriads of sweet seeds, like little red jewels. We had to find somewhere to sit in order to eat those without spilling them everywhere so we moved out of the market and found a grassy bank in front of a house. Here, we thought we could sit down and eat meat pies and ruby seeds in peace, but we had hardly begun when a cross old man who had evidently not gone to the fair, came out and told us to go away.

'No one is likely to snatch *him*,' muttered Dale, as we hastily transferred ourselves to a similar bank not far away and there found ourselves undisturbed.

That formed our dinner. In the afternoon, our energies began to flag. It was becoming hot as well. We went to The Good Catch and there sat in a shady room drinking ale and augmenting our peculiar dinner with hot sausages.

'There's a stall out there selling sausages like these,' the innkeeper said morosely. 'Folk like me lose business when there's fairs. I hate fairs. Don't know why we had this extra one forced on us this year.'

We thought it best not to tell him our theory about that and

Christopher politely bought us another sausage each and another tankard of ale. Then Dale and I felt very sleepy so we made ourselves rise and go out and move back into the fair, to shake off the drowsiness and attend to our own business, which was to watch for signs of trouble and should we find any, attempt to trace them to their origin.

There were no such signs and as the afternoon wore on, we decided to make our way back to the harbour and see if there was a boatman willing to take us home. This was easier than we expected, for others besides ourselves had grown tired after hours at the fair, and several boatmen seized the chance of making money instead of spending it. An hour later, we were landing at Polgillan where I hired the mules for me and Dale, for we were both very tired indeed by then and the breeze had dropped. It was hot.

At the top of the cliff, just as we were about to dismount at the front door, it was flung open and Tamzin came running out, followed by Thomas Tremaine. Tamzin was in tears and Tremaine looked frantic. I slipped off my mule at once, saying, '*Tamzin!* What's the matter? Dear God, has Brockley fallen ill again? Whatever . . .'

At that moment, Brockley appeared, walking slowly and leaning on a stick. Tamzin, sobbing, said, 'It's not Master Brockley, no, well, there he be and quite all right only as overset as all of us . . . Madam, it's William! My William! He's vanished!'

When I was a girl at Faldene, because my grandfather insisted, I was allowed to share my cousins' tutor and I was taught to ride. He died before I was five, but in his will, he had put his wishes concerning me into writing and my uncle and aunt had respected them. The groom who instructed me taught me that whenever I came home from riding, even if I was cold, tired, unwell or even injured, I must care for my horse before I cared for myself. Christopher had learned the same rules. He refused, however, to let me or Dale water the mules but sent us indoors to find out what had happened while he and Tremaine saw to the animals and took them into the shady stable. The mules had had a long hot climb up the cliff path and should be rubbed down, Christopher said. Having seen to that, they told Tremaine to take them back later, but meanwhile, to come indoors with them, to hear whatever I had learned.

I had been listening with horror to Tamzin's tale.

'It was just before dinner, madam. I was busy upstairs, dusting. William was here, cleaning the fish for dinner and talking with Thomas, who'd come in for a sup of ale – he'd been exercising the horses, two at a time, he said, riding one and leading another, and he was hot and thirsty. I came down to start on the meal and they'd both gone! The fish were half done, just lying like as if William had gone away for a few minutes. I shouted his name but there was no answer. Just silence! Dear God, that silence!' She stopped, unable to say any more for crying.

Brockley's legs were still weak, so he had seated himself but his eyes were alert. He found a napkin in his belt pouch and gave it to Tamzin. 'Hush now. Cry later. Just now, we need to hear you tell us all about it.'

She wiped her eyes and said, 'Master Brockley heard me calling; he was in the parlour, where it's coolest. He came and asked what was wrong and I said *where's William?* Master Brockley said had he gone out to the stables with Thomas so we went to the stables and found Thomas getting ready to take out the bays. He didn't know where William was; he said he'd left him still cleaning fish. He came back with us to join in the search. Madam, me and him and Master Brockley searched the house all over. We looked outside too, in the garden, even out along the cliff. There was no sign and William isn't one to go climbing down dangerous cliffs, where he could fall; he has sense. He's *vanished.*'

One possibility sprang into my head at once. 'The trapdoor to the cold room,' I said. 'Has it been kept bolted?'

'Yes, madam, it has. I went down before you left, to fetch milk from the cold room so that Master Brockley could have a milk and honey posset later and Master Wood came with me then because I'm scared, down there on my own, knowing about that crevice. You saw us come back and you saw Master Wood bolt the trap. I went down again during the morning for some cheese for a sauce, and that time, William came with me; he was armed, madam, he brought a dagger with him . . . so I've only been down there twice this morning and both times I took care to bolt the trapdoor after me. It's bolted tight and firm now this minute. The cheese was there on the kitchen table. A pan with lard in it was on the trivet, waiting to be swung over the fire, and the half-cleaned fish still lay on the table, beside the cheese.' There was a marked air of sudden interruption.

By whom? And how? 'Go on,' I said to Tamzin.

'That's all, madam.'

'Wait,' I said. I rose and went through into the butchery and looked at the trapdoor. It was bolted securely, just as Tamzin had said. I went back. 'Yes, it's as you say, Tamzin.'

'Could anyone have got into the house, perhaps at night, and been hidden here?' asked Dale, and I saw her shiver at the thought.

Tamzin said grimly, 'Yes. It do be possible. It's a big house and so many rooms not used. Someone could have got into one of the bedchambers perhaps last night and hidden under the bed.'

With a creepy feeling down my spine, I remembered waking in the night and thinking that I had heard feet on the stairs. Perhaps I had. The doors were locked at night. There was a small back door giving on to heathland and that was bolted just like the front entrance. But there were windows . . . one could have been forced . . .

Christopher and Tremaine now joined us and I made Tamzin repeat her story. They looked at each other and at us, appalled. 'Someone got in during the night?' Tremaine said, shocked. 'Well, I sleep over the stables. I heard nothing, just slept. But it could be. It could be.'

'Let's look at all the ground floor windows,' I said.

It was inconclusive. The window frames were all old and some were ill-fitting because they were warped. A man with a small knife could very easily have forced one and then pushed it back into place after him. We went back to the kitchen and stood about, staring at each other.

Thomas said nervously, 'In the end, I finished exercising the horses. Was that the right thing to do? First, I'd ridden out on Firefly, leading Blue Gentle, then when the alarm was raised, I was saddling Red, meaning to lead Rufus. Lovely horses, they are. After all the searching and not finding anything, I saw to Jet and Jaunty. Jet is all right with Jaunty on the leading rein but if it's Firefly, he tries to bite. He's temperamental, is Jet.'

For a foolish moment, that made everyone smile, even Tamzin, a little. Jet was Christopher's big black gelding and temperamental he certainly was. Not as badly as Grey Cornish, but all the same, I had never ridden him and never wanted to. Christopher had once tried to train him to the side saddle, in case Mildred ever needed him, but was bucked off at once, so vigorously and decisively that he never repeated the experiment. For some unknown equine reason, Jet was friendly with my Jaunty but apparently hated the sight of Christopher's dark chestnut Firefly. Firefly, an animal of spirit, appeared to hate Jet in return. They were best kept apart.

Christopher said soberly, 'If there is no news by tomorrow morning we must send word to Helston, to Sir Francis Godolphin. He is the county sheriff. This looks like another disappearance.'

'But who would want to snatch my William?' Tamzin burst out. 'What for?'

'He's highly skilled,' I said. 'A man who creates beautiful tableware in bronze and pewter. A gifted slave who will make such wares for sale and make money for his owner.'

'Aren't there any gifted slaves in Turkey?' Tamzin demanded.

'Plenty, I expect,' Christopher told her. 'But this one would have been imported specially from England, a man of reputation, now harnessed to the interests of his purchaser. I think perhaps this sort of thing is becoming a fashion in some places.'

'Ugh!' said Tamzin, and then sat down and once more began to sob. Dale sat down beside her, putting a comforting arm round her. No one said much. The chances were that she would never see her William again.

'The caves!' I said suddenly. 'The caves that you found, Christopher, when you left the horses and moved a boulder and found a shaft with a ladder. You said that the cave at the bottom looked as if people had been there. You found lanterns and things there. What if that's where he's held?'

We all looked at each other, until Christopher said, 'We must try to find him. We must. There's nothing else we can do. I'll go. Tremaine, you will come with me. We'll take our own lanterns with us and we'll go fully armed. We'll go through the crevice and approach the place that way, retracing the route that I took. Brockley, will you lend Tremaine your sword? Bolt the trapdoor after us. When we come back – if we come back – we will shout and bang on the trap with a sword hilt. Like this.'

He demonstrated by rapping on the table. Three slow taps, a pause, then three rapid ones. 'Only then do you unbolt the trap. If we don't return, report our disappearances along with Davey's. But someone must watch by the trap all night, in case we come back late.'

I wilted but said, 'I'll put a mattress and a pillow beside the trap and sleep there. Bang hard if you come back in the night, so as to wake me.'

'I'll do it. Tamzin can relieve me during the night, say half past two, and I'll take over again at four,' said Brockley.

'You will do no such thing,' Dale and I said in unison.

We finally agreed on leaving the night watch to me. Tremaine looked unhappy but bravely said he would do his best and he had a dagger. 'I've never handled a sword though I'm willing to try.' He and Christopher didn't wait for any supper but went off on their errand, and Tamzin bolted the trap behind them.

While we waited for them to come back, or not, as the case might be, we finished cleaning the fish and fried them. I made the sauce as Tamzin was too upset to be capable. We had bread and honey, and small ale to drink. As usual, we ate together in the kitchen, but the usual conversation was absent. It was a miserable, silent supper.

We finished our meal and washed it up, though we left two mackerel out and placed a lump of lard in a frying pan, acts of hope, like a prayer in physical form. Then we sat in a state of silent anxiety for what felt like a century until we heard the signal taps on the trapdoor and we all sprang up. Tamzin got there first, shouting *who are you?* And at once we heard Christopher's voice below, calling to us. Brockley knelt down and unbolted the trap and our two gallant searchers climbed out.

'We found the cave. It's empty, except for the lanterns and the tinderbox,' Christopher said, sitting down at the table and eyeing the mackerel hungrily. I put the frying pan over the fire. 'Wherever William Davey is,' he said, 'he isn't there. We considered that narrow tunnel that branches off from the main one, but . . .'

'I didn't have the nerve,' said Tremaine candidly. 'I've never been so frit, never, I hate dark shut in places. I ain't never been in a cave before in my life. Down there, where it's dark and knowing how much weight of rocks there is above us – ugh!'

'There's bread and honey and some ale,' said Tamzin unhappily. 'Oh, *William*!'

THIRTEEN
Here Be Dragons

In the morning, Tamzin looked wan and her eyes were ringed with pink. Nevertheless, she was a gallant little thing and before we went to bed, she had begun to make efforts. She had set some dough to rise as she always did, and she had, as usual, risen early and baked bread and rolls for the day. We breakfasted on fresh warm rolls with honey and small ale.

But it was a silent meal except that twice, Tamzin said, 'I wonder what sort of breakfast William is having and *where* he is having it?'

No one answered her.

When we had finished, Christopher left to go to Helston and report William Davey's disappearance to Sir Francis. It was another sunny summer day and once more there was a breeze. Dale said she would like to take Brockley for a walk out of doors. Tamzin cleared the breakfast dishes off the table and said that we could have stew for dinner if we liked and she would make some almond tarts. I helped her for a while and set some manchet dough but after a time I began to feel that she wanted the kitchen to herself and also, her sad face distressed me for there was nothing I could do or say to make things better for her. I went upstairs to the study.

It was pleasant there, with the view in all directions and the sunlight streaming in. I sat down at the desk. I had put all the maps, ours and those left behind by Wells, together in the pottery holder. I began to take them out.

If William hadn't been seized by way of the trapdoor and hadn't been taken to the cave, then where was he now? Was the side tunnel the answer? It was a pity that Tremaine had been too afraid to try it. They hadn't talked about it much, but I suspected that Christopher hadn't wanted to explore it alone and Tremaine hadn't wanted to explore it at all. They probably didn't want to enlarge on this in front of the womenfolk. I stared at Hugh's map, which included Cornwall but on much too small a scale, rolled it up again and tried the one that I had been given at Hampton Court.

This was still not helpful, except that it did show the paths that met where the shaft was. Dear heaven, William could be hidden anywhere. There were many farmhouses on the Lizard; any farmer could be a collaborator who hid captives in his cellar. The fellow victims that Petroc had met, told him that they had originally been held in a cave, though. What cave? The cliffs were riddled with them. Anyway, William could have been loaded straight into a boat and rowed out to any of the foreign ships anchored in the bay.

I hardly knew what I was searching for, but I tried another map, one of Wells' collection, not one we had looked at before. This one was very old indeed and most confusing. Several of his maps had pictures and wording but this one was so extremely full of such things that they obscured the very features they were supposed to interpret. Nor was the scale likely to be useful. Cornwall was there but, as with Hugh's map, it was too small. It was a big map which when unrolled covered half the desk, but that was because it showed most of Europe and the Mediterranean and part of the distant east as well as England and Scotland and whoever drew it hadn't been very accurate. England and Scotland were a most peculiar shape.

The word *Cathay* was written on the right-hand side of the map, set all alone in an otherwise blank patch. There was an uncertain indication of Africa's western flank, just the beginning of it. This too was bounded by a blank space and the words *Here Be Dragons* in a difficult script, accompanied by a drawing of a dragon, with what I supposed were meant to be flames coming from its mouth. The same words and another dragon appeared where I knew Russia to be. The New World wasn't there at all.

I was used to maps; Hugh had been interested in them and from him I had learned a good deal. I put the age of this one at somewhere between the early fourteenth century and the late fifteenth century. Clearly it was made before Columbus crossed the Atlantic, but after Marco Polo had found Cathay. Made by a man with simple ideas, who just assumed that unknown places were inhabited by dragons.

The dragon drawings had a certain charm, but I was not in the right mood to appreciate them. I was inclined to feel that Cornwall was now inhabited by dragons and I knew that I didn't resemble St George. I put the map aside and drew another from the holder. This one looked as if it might well be useful as it looked like a guide to the paths on the Lizard and the Land's End promontory.

But the paths on the Lizard looked wrong. I couldn't trace the long main track that led along the promontory to Cliff House, or the place where three paths converged. I studied that map for a long time, puzzling over it. Cliff House was marked and so were a number of farmhouses and villages. But I now knew the path that led from Cliff House to Hollow Farm where Ellie Grove lived and that wasn't there either. I went on puzzling for some time.

And then I understood. I sat for a good while longer, making sure, until I was aroused by the sound of hooves far below, and what I thought was Christopher's voice, calling to Tremaine about something. I left the map open with its corners weighed down and descended the stairs to find that the Brockleys had returned from their walk and gone to sit in the parlour, and that Christopher, clearly untroubled and probably amused by Sir Francis' opinion of being seated alongside two of my servants, had taken him into the parlour as well.

I had gradually improved the parlour. A few bright cushion covers and some glassware, polished and put on display on a shelf had made a difference. I smiled a welcome to Sir Francis. 'Have you news?' I asked. 'This is a pleasure! I will fetch some wine and—'

'Never mind the wine just now, my dear,' he said, sounding anxious and kindly. He wasn't in court dress, just in plain brown breeches and a matching coat over a linen shirt, with a wide, plain collar. He had no wig and with his dark hair cropped and his eyes very blue in his tanned face, he was very much a seaman. 'I hear you've lost a guest, another of these disappearances.'

He took a seat and waved the Brockleys, who had risen to greet him, to sit down again. 'We're all friends here, I hope,'

he said. 'Mistress . . . er . . . Archer, yours wasn't the only
loss yesterday. During the fair in Penzance, there was another
disappearance. Joseph Dunstan, aged fifty-two, a highly valued
music teacher of that town. I know him because he taught my
daughter Thomasine to play the lute and the virginals. He was
– is – a gifted musician and a fine teacher. He can get a tune
out of almost any instrument, even if it's one he hasn't seen
before. Once in my house, he met a guest of mine who had a
musical instrument with him, something completely new to
me, a big flat thing with strings that were played by a little
hammer; he called it a dulcimer. Master Dunstan was interested
because he'd never seen one before and my guest let him handle
it. He played a few notes and found a scale of sorts and then
began to pick out a melody. It was wonderful! Also, he can
turn even the most unmusical pupil into a reasonable performer.
He managed it with Thomasine, who has no ear at all. Joseph
was a widower – he lived with his married son and two grandchildren and a couple of servants. They all went out to the fair,
but they got separated. The servants went this way, the others
went another and then the grandchildren were apparently
excited by the tumblers and wanted to stay and watch them.
Their parents stayed with them, while their grandfather wanted
to talk to the musicians who were playing for Floral Dancers.
The dance had just ended, and he went off to see them. That's
the last his family saw of him. The musicians say that he did
come to talk to them and they had some ale together at The
Good Catch but an hour later, they left and parted their ways
just outside and Joseph Dunstan vanished into the crowd . . .
and that's it.'

'In the middle of Penzance – in the middle of a fair?' I said,
marvelling.

'His family got the crier to announce his disappearance and
a man has come forward to say that he saw Dunstan with two
other men walking towards the harbour. He knew Dunstan by
sight – most of the Penzance residents do. Dunstan was quite
tall, with a bushy dark beard and dark hair worn to his shoulders
and nearly always in a tangle. The witness who saw him going
towards the harbour, said that the trio seemed quite ordinary,
amicable. He didn't think that Dunstan was being coerced. He

must have been induced somehow . . . *come and see this, it's worth your attention.*'

'And once at the harbour, he'd be persuaded to get into a boat of some sort – and that would be that,' said Brockley grimly.

'Quite,' said Sir Francis. 'And *that* isn't all.' He paused and looked at us gravely. 'You are here,' he said, 'to attempt to find out who is behind these disappearances. Have you made any progress? I understand that you have now seen Mistress Penberthy, whose laundress died so strangely, and the fisherman Jago whose son was murdered. Did you reach any conclusions?'

'I have to say,' I told him, 'that so far I can't claim that we have. However . . .'

He interrupted me. 'I have to say that I am far from happy about this state of affairs. Master Spelton there would be of far more use, just now, in my direct employment and I would be thankful, Mistress Stannard, to see you pack your goods and go home to the safety of your house, Faldene. Will you not consider going?'

'I think the queen would wish me to stay, Sir Francis,' I said.

'You will know best about that, I suppose. But I repeat, I am *not* happy about this. I would never want to see a woman where you are now, Mistress Stannard, living in this forlorn tower of a house on the edge of a cliff, trying to investigate as nasty a form of piracy as I ever heard of. I wish you would go home and leave Master Spelton to me. He would be safer, which would no doubt be a relief to his wife and children, and though I must apologize for saying so, I think he would be more useful.'

No one answered him.

At last, he said, 'Things are happening. Here at Cliff House, you have spare rooms and spare stabling. You'll soon have them packed tight and hard in all your bedchambers, and horses in every stall you have while yours are put outside to graze and lose condition.'

'Sir Francis,' I said, 'what on earth are you talking about?'

'The idea that this year, the queen's Progress should be through Cornwall, has been revived. I was sorry to hear it, but it is true. I have received official information. It will be in July. Her Majesty will go by sea to Exeter and proceed overland from there. I have two of her harbingers in my house at this moment. They arrived yesterday. They have already asked me how many people I can accommodate under my roof. They say there is no question of finding a roof for everyone; the queen's entourage will be much too big for that. A few privileged people will be guests in houses like mine and the rest will sleep in tents. They have decided that one of my fields, because it is well drained and flat, would be ideal for tents. I have corn in that field but according to the harbingers, I am a wealthy man and can sacrifice a field of corn in a good cause. If the weather's good from now on, they say, I might even get the crop in before the Progress arrives as it won't get here till the end of July—'

Christopher broke in. 'The idea of the Progress has been *revived*? It's actually going to happen?'

'Yes. It is. It will reach here six or seven weeks from now.' Sir Francis sounded angry. I think we were all just shocked. He said, 'I will need to provide food for heaven knows how many people for heaven knows how long and I am to get together with the heads of other wealthy households and we must prepare entertainments. The queen would like to see a tournament and other feats of arms; the men of England must always be ready in case of invasion. The threat of Spain remains; after the disaster with his recent *armada*, Philip is said to be licking his wounds and plotting revenge . . . Mistress Archer?'

'I am *horrified*!' I said. 'The queen mustn't come to Cornwall! However well-guarded she is, it still isn't safe! Whoever is snatching people from Cornwall, is cunning and greedy and . . . and . . . dangerous!'

Sir Francis said nothing and I repeated, firmly, '*The queen mustn't come to Cornwall.* Her advisers don't understand!'

'I know.' Sir Francis now shook a despairing head. 'But when the Queen's Messenger arrived with this news, I asked questions. The *queen herself* decided that the Progress must take place. The harbingers arrived yesterday and began asking how many people Arwenack House could accommodate. When they'd finished there, they were coming straight on to me. Sir John's frantic messenger, warning me that the harbingers were coming, reached me an hour before they did.'

'Sir Francis,' I said, 'just now, just before you rode in—'

'Galloped in,' remarked Christopher.

'Won't hurt my horse,' said Sir Francis. 'He's full of life and needs a good gallop every now and then. You were saying, Mistress Archer?'

'Before you arrived,' I said, 'I was up in what was once Wells' study, looking at maps. I found a very old one, the kind that has *Here Be Dragons* written in unexplored places. I am beginning to think that Cornwall is a place with dragons in it. I am afraid of it myself and Her Majesty must, *must*, be kept away from here.

'Dear God,' I said, as the full awfulness of the situation was borne in on me, 'I can imagine very well that somewhere in Turkey or Morocco, there is a man or a woman who would be the social success of their whole country if they had the queen of England dressing my lady's hair or on her knees in the scullery, scrubbing the floor. She would be worth a fortune as a slave.'

'I know,' said Sir Francis grimly. He added, 'You can expect a visit from the harbingers as well. Very soon.'

'What *can* we do?' I said desperately, after Sir Francis, having been refreshed by wine and cakes, had warned us once more to expect a visit from the royal harbingers, taken his leave, collected his Grey Cornish and gone.

'We can talk to those harbingers when they get here, *if* they get here,' said Christopher. 'We can tell them about the cave system that leads to our cold room.'

'We can do better than that,' I said, cutting in. 'We'd better *show* them the crevice in the cold room wall, make them see for themselves how perilous this mad scheme is. I don't suppose they'll want to quarter Her Majesty in this house but anyone who sleeps here would be taking risks of a sort. We're all nervous and protecting ourselves as best we can but the thought of that crevice makes me uneasy all the time. Whoever is organizing this Progress must be made to understand that it had better be unorganized, as soon as possible!

'I fear that that could be difficult,' I added.

'I daresay.' Chrstopher frowned, ruminating. 'If only we could come across real, definite evidence that this or that person is behind it. Or persons. More than one man – or woman, if we consider Mistress Penberthy – is concerned in it. I sense planning, a smooth way of doing things. Transport for the victims and places – caves – where they can be held. The Killigrews could be behind it though there's no actual evidence . . .'

I lifted both hands in a helpless gesture. 'But *how* can we find out? What more can we do? We've followed the leads we have, and they have led us nowhere. The Killigrews are Sir Francis' own in-laws! There's that man Jago – but short of seizing him and holding his feet to a fire and I couldn't agree to that, how can we get a confession from him? He may be innocent anyway. And now it's become urgent. If the queen is coming to Cornwall, then we can't take our time over finding the perpetrator.'

'Could you ride to London and talk her out of it, Ursula?'

'I might not succeed. She knows the risks; she knows them perfectly well. I'd do better to stay here and put my mind to scotching the snake before Her Majesty arrives. And now,' I added, becoming practical, 'we must warn Tamzin about these harbingers.'

We made our way to the kitchen in a body. Custard tarts were being made and a stew was bubbling on the trivet. Tamzin was flushed and this time looked not sad but angry.

'Madam, I beg you, keep that man Tremaine out of my kitchen. He's been in here, making up to me, saying that now William's gone, a fine girl like me can't grieve forever; it won't be long before I'll be looking for a new love and here he is, ready and waiting and then the damned idiot tried to put his arms round me only I was stirring the stew just then and I hit him with a nice hot spoon.'

I stifled a snort of laughter and said, 'Very well, I will deal with him.' I would indeed. Tamzin was an excellent maid and cook but with those dark curls and dark, bright eyes, she was also very pretty. She probably did need protection now that William was gone. I was willing to give it. I said, 'We have things to tell you. Listen . . .'

Brockley was looking out of the window. 'I think they're coming.'

'What? Who?' I said, turning towards him.

'The harbingers. There are horsemen approaching, anyway.'

'Oh, what are we going to *do*?' Dale exclaimed.

'What do you mean? Madam, what are harbingers?' Tamzin was bewildered.

'When they've come and gone,' said Christopher slowly, 'I know what I'm going to do. I don't somehow think Jago is our quarry. I'm going to play chess with Juniper Penberthy again.'

FOURTEEN
Harbingers of Fear

C hristopher's plan was the only one that was laid that day. The harbingers were thoroughly in the way. There were two of them. Their names were Master Reginald Tolling and Master John St Leger. Tolling was short and St Leger was tall; otherwise, they were identical, suave, bewigged, sprucely ruffed gentlemen in black. To my surprise, they had Cornish accents but when I spoke of this, Tolling told me that yes, they were Cornish-born and had been chosen as harbingers just because of that.

'Cornwall is a world to itself,' Tolling told me. 'We are not English. We are from Celtic stock, as are the Welsh and the Irish. It was thought better to use harbingers who would understand this district. Now – to business.'

The business took a long time. They insisted on seeing every room in the house and took notes. Each had a notebook, a quill and a small phial of ink, carried in a belt pouch. They would put the notebook down on any flat surface and write notes wherever they happened to be. When their interminable tour was eventually finished, they had an interview with me in the now tolerable parlour. I shall probably remember their visit on my deathbed. I was left with the feeling that the court of my royal half-sister, Queen Elizabeth of England, had for some reason gone quite mad.

'We observe that you have in total six bedchambers . . .'

'Four are in use . . .'

'We would not drive you out of your own . . .'

'Thank you!'

'But some rearrangements can be made.' Tolling was writing busily. 'Your maidservant can sleep in the kitchen. Many servants do, in other houses. Your own maid can go in with you. Your menservants can join your groom in the attic over the stables.

All the grooms and menservants, except that each gentleman may have one personal valet and one secretary, are to sleep there. All wives may have a maid. There will be enough accommodation here for your two guests. Their names are Sir John Lane and Sir William Hodges. Sir John is bringing a secretary, Sir William is bringing his wife and they will be accompanied by his and her personal maid. These must have a room each. That will fill up all your valet bedchambers. Any other female attendants need only be provided with simple bedrolls that can be spread out in the kitchen, any grooms or other male attendants can sleep over the stables.'

'Just one moment, please . . .!'

'Some extra stabling will be wanted,' said St Leger. 'There are only ten stalls in yours. However, there is a meadow behind the house; your animals can be turned out to graze and a further ten stalls can be erected. It should be easy – what is a stable but just a long shed with divisions inside to make stalls, fitted with mangers and hay racks? There's room in the courtyard for such an extension.'

'Am I to pay for that as well as feeding all these folk?' These men seemed to think that I had a treasure chest under my bed and did they really think that I wouldn't object when the sleeping arrangements for my household were turned upside down?

They did think just that. 'Naturally, Mrs Archer.' St Leger looked up from the notes he was making. 'Is it not a privilege to be housing some of the royal court during an official Progress?' He had a slightly high pitched and maddeningly righteous voice. 'The Edgecumbes of Launceston – we were with them yesterday – are overjoyed, as are the Killigrews of Arwenack, and we hear the same of the Rashleighs, those great merchants of Fowey, and the Whitmeads of Polmawgan House. They are a wealthy tin mining family. Surely you are not going to turn grumpy?'

I already had. I had been involved in Progresses before but this was the first time I had been on the receiving end of the harbingers' demands. They went on ahead of a Progress and arranged for its accommodation at every stage of its stupendous and expensive journey. I knew very well that those on the route of a Progress were often nearly – in some cases quite – bankrupt after it had passed, and I had heard one embittered gentleman say that he had felt as though he and his modest estate had been corn in the path of ruthless reapers wielding enormous scythes. In being merely told to turn my horses out to grass and sleep with my maidservants I supposed I was fortunate. Some people (though not the ones who were actually feeding the queen and were therefore obliged to dine in style) had had to pawn their silver plate to pay their food bills. Others had had their horses requisitioned.

'It puts money into the Treasury,' Christopher said to me after the harbingers and their alarming notebooks had gone. 'For a good few weeks, the queen lives at the expense of her subjects.'

'I can only pray for her safety. I told them about the crevice and the caves but they refused to inspect them; just said keep the trapdoor bolted and after all the queen won't be sleeping in this house. And there's something else.' It had been worrying me. 'They used our assumed names and they clearly don't know who I am. But two important guests are to be billeted on me for three nights, it appears. They're called Sir John Lane and Sir William Hodges and as far as I know I have never met either of them *but* I was given to understand that they are courtiers. In all probability, one or both of them will recognize me. That will wreck my assignment here. It's all madness!'

'I did my best to say so,' said Christopher grimly. 'But they just said that orders were orders.'

Brockley, who had been quietly sizzling ever since he learned that he was not to be allowed to share a bed with his wife, said, '*Whose* orders? That's what I'd like to know. Who's *behind* this? This isn't a normal Progress. It's some sort of sham.'

We were in the parlour. Christopher, having seen the harbingers off the premises, looked as harassed as I was. He said, 'I tried my best to convince them that Cliff House is too remote and uncomfortable to be a suitable place for courtiers to stay in but their minds were fixed. I also pointed out the peril to which the queen will be exposed in Cornwall. All in vain, I fear. Tamzin came out and caught us and had her say but they just seemed amused.'

Tamzin came in with an ale jug for us and caught the last few words. 'Fools, that's what they be. Yes, I had a few words with them. I'm not accustomed to sleeping on any kitchen floor, I said to them. And they just laughed and said I'd get used to it, their own kitchen maids had to. I wouldn't be one of *their* kitchen maids for a whole bag of sovereigns.'

'That damned grey animal tried to bite Thomas and got a clouted nose for it,' said Christopher. 'Thomas is in such a rage about the plans for the stabling and putting our own horses out to grass, that I think I saw steam coming out of his ears.'

There was no escape. I had a dreadful fear that someone, somewhere in Cornwall, was rubbing avaricious palms together and imagining how much he could charge for handing our good Queen Bess into slavery.

When at last, the indignant Thomas Tremaine had quietened down, Christopher gave him a note and sent him off to Penzance.

'I am inviting myself to play chess with Juniper Penberthy,' he said to me.

Tremaine came back with an invitation to Christopher to play chess with Juniper Penberthy, the very next day. It included me, but I had no wish to repeat those interminable hours of play and pleaded that I had too much arranging to do after the visit from the harbingers. There was truth in that. I hated the harbingers intensely. The mysterious kidnappers could abduct *them*, I thought, with my hearty goodwill.

Christopher set off early and didn't return until nearly supper time. We were growing anxious when Tamzin, who had gone for a walk along the cliffs, came back and reported that a fishing boat that looked to her like *The Sunrise*, was making its way towards us from across the bay. She was right. Christopher came up the cliff on foot, a short time later.

'I've nothing to carry,' he said. 'I could walk easily enough. The Polgillan villagers did their best to get me to hire a mule, though. Apparently, Wells used to hire a mule fairly often and the villagers put the payment for it into a kitty for buying fodder. They're so pleased to have Cliff House occupied again.'

'Never mind the mule,' I said. We were once again gathered in the kitchen, this time so that Dale and I could lend Tamzin a hand with supper, while Brockley sat in a basket chair and watched. 'Poached shark in a prawn sauce,' I added, because

Christopher was peering into the pan where I was turning things over with a spatula. 'Accompanied by rice and bread rolls and there are honey cakes to follow. I take it that you played a great deal of chess.'

Christopher sighed and sat down on a stool. 'I played chess. And then some more chess. I lost count of the games. I won about half of them. My brain feels as though it has been wrung out and hung on a line to dry. I learned one or two things, though. During a brief break between games, our Juniper told me that the question of who drowned Beryon in her washtub, is a question no longer. One of her menservants has disappeared but Juniper doesn't think he was a victim of the slavers. Beryon was a flirt and she had encouraged him and then tired of him and rebuffed him. Juniper and most of her servants think that he lost his temper with her, pushed her headfirst into the washtub in a fit of rage and has now run away.'

'You believe that?' I said.

'No, but I couldn't offer you a good reason why I don't. I just don't,' Christopher said. 'I came away feeling very uneasy.'

I left off turning shark steaks and turned to face him. 'Uneasy?'

'Yes. I think – I can't be sure but I *suspect* – she knows who I am, and therefore, quite possibly, who you are as well.'

'What makes you think so? How could she . . . Alexander Killigrew? He knows who we are.'

'Yes. I thought that. But I can't be certain. It was the way she smiled when I said to her – during our few breaks, when we were sipping small ale – what a beautiful house hers is and how I would like to see round it. She smiled as I said it. And her eyes twinkled.'

'They can't,' I said flatly. 'Mistress Penberthy has the kind of eyes that never show feelings. They don't smile. Even her mouth does it in a straight line.'

'Her mouth, I grant you. Straight as an architect's ruler. But her eyes twinkled. And she said *but of course you may see round my house. Simmons and I will go with you and show you everything. Simmons!* And before I knew it, Simmons had answered the call and I was being taken on a tour, though under surveillance, of course. I didn't have much opportunity to open presses or peer into cupboards. Though I manufactured one!'

Christopher grinned. 'I was shown rooms full of fine furniture and wondrous tapestries and I was actually taken into my lady's bedchamber. There's a sumptuous four-poster with brocade curtains that ripple between pink and silver and have little embroidery on them, in pale green. The bed is wide enough for three couples at least. It made me wonder about our Juniper's past or possibly . . . well, she did say that he did his duty by her. Or perhaps she had a wild life for a time after his death, though considering what she looks like . . .'

'Maybe *she* paid *them*,' Dale whispered to Tamzin, who giggled.

I said reprovingly, 'What kind of opportunity did you manufacture, Christopher and did it show you anything?'

'There were tapestries,' said Christopher, not to be hurried. 'And a great bearskin, all black glossy fur, by the side of the bed. A warm place to put your toes on a cold morning. And she had a dressing table, with pots of creams and ointments on it and a bottle of perfume and a silver brush and comb. The view from the window was striking, as well. The next room was supposed to be a dressing room though really it was more like a big clothes press. There were gowns hung all around and rows of shoes below them, and a shelf full of hats. I exclaimed that I must go back to the bedchamber for a moment, because the view over the sea was so remarkable that I must memorize it and describe it to Mrs Archer. It really is a beautiful vista, framed like a painting between two of the tallest juniper trees, and there's a little church in the lower right-hand corner of the frame; it's somehow exactly right, and there's the sea beyond. I fancy that the architect positioned the window like that deliberately.'

Brockley was now becoming restless and suddenly barked, 'Damn you, Christopher, will you stop enthusing and get to the point?'

'When I went back to marvel at the view,' said Christopher, unmoved, 'they didn't come with me. They just stayed in the dressing room, and I went to the window and had a good long stare out of it, and when I turned round, I took just a few moments to look at that bedchamber, to absorb details that I'd only glimpsed before. Our clever smiling lady hasn't been quite clever enough. There was some jewellery on that dressing table: a pair of pearl earrings, a matching bracelet, a little tumble of a thin gold chain. I managed to pass close enough to see that the chain had something on it. A small gold cross, half under the tumble of links. I walked straight on towards the door and this time had a good look at the necklace that was hanging on a hook behind it . . .'

'Dale hangs my long necklaces like that,' I said. 'Then they can't tie themselves into knots as they can if they're left jumbled.'

'I daresay,' said Christopher. His brown eyes were brimming with laughter. 'But this didn't look like an ordinary necklace. I'd caught sight of it earlier and I wanted a closer look. Its stones were shiny but not colourful. Do you know, I think it was a rosary. I fancy that our chess-playing lady is of the Catholic persuasion. In fact, I'm sure. I fancy she is hearing illegal Masses. In the small parlour next to the dining chamber, I smelt incense. It was faint, but it was there.'

'Incense!' Dale clapped her hands in excitement. 'But that's what I smelt! I couldn't put a name to it and I thought it was perfume.'

Christopher shook his head. 'Not perfume, Dale. Incense. I'm sure.'

Christopher said, 'It's not a crime to be a Catholic but the Mass is illegal.' He gazed up at the ceiling, as though thinking. Then he said, 'Our spies in Spain report that it is certain that Philip of Spain is making plans for a second *armada*.'

It was Dale who recognized the connection. 'Then could it mean that the queen is . . . is . . . someone they're after? That they've been scheming to get hold of her? Working to persuade her to undertake this Progress?'

'Very likely,' Christopher said. 'Either to hand over to Philip, at a price, or to sell to a buyer within the Ottoman world, again at a very high price.'

No one had any answer to that, but I was thinking about it, and cringing, asking myself how the queen, once away from the security of London, once away from her protective walls and palaces and her cloud of guardian courtiers, might become vulnerable. A dreadful scene created itself inside my head. I could see them, the enemy, disguised as loyal subjects, bowing to her, offering her . . .

Silks and perfumes from the Orient – may I, a humble merchant of Cornwall, offer them to the queen's ladies? To Queen Elizabeth herself if she should wish to examine any of my modest goods . . . oh, Your Majesty! How glad I am to be in your presence, to have this opportunity of showing Your Majesty the luxuries that our brave seamen bring back from eastern lands. And how happy the people of Cornwall, the sea captains and merchants of that county, would be, how they would rejoice in presenting their wares to you, if Your Majesty were ever to come among them! How they would all vie with each other to see whose stock of wonders appeals to you most . . .

'It would need a cunning mind to plant the idea into Elizabeth's mind,' said Christopher, 'but I fancy that someone has done it. I think the aim now that she has taken the bait, is to capture Elizabeth herself.'

'Those harbingers who are causing us such worry,' said Dale, 'are harbingers of danger. To us, to Her Majesty. What can we *do*?'

'Protect her,' said Christopher. 'Sir Francis is trying to warn her but if she will not heed the warnings and still insists on coming here, she won't move a step without being ringed by guards. I wish to dear heaven that this beastly Progress was over and done with and Elizabeth safely back in Greenwich or Richmond or Hampton Court.'

'To that, amen,' I said.

FIFTEEN
Empty Air

In the morning, restless and worried, I decided to look again at the map of the caves. Christopher said that he would like to look at it as well, and in the end he and I and the Brockleys all made our way up to the study. Tamzin was invited but declined to come. She had things to do, she said. The glassware in the dining chamber could all do with a wash and, well, she was better left on her own, just now. She probably meant that she wanted to do some crying for William and didn't want witnesses.

It was a clear morning but not a sunlit one. The sky was overcast and the sea was grey, with a horizon like a bar of steel. The air was warm but close. Dale was flapping a hand in front of her face, to fan herself, by the time we had climbed all the stairs to the study. I found the map, spread it out on the desk and we all pored over it.

'There's the side tunnel I didn't want to explore,' Christopher said, pointing. 'By the look of it, it passes through the rock behind Cliff House and then to a cave further east. That may be open to the sea, just as the cold room is. It isn't clear. If it does have an open cave mouth, I expect we could identify it from a boat. But knowing that doesn't seem to be useful.'

I had been excited when I discovered the map of the caves but after all, it had nothing to say to us. Regretfully, I rolled it up again and returned it to its holder.

'What next?' I said. 'Christopher, should we not report whatever you learned yesterday, to Sir Francis? I think we have to trust somebody and after all, he is the Sheriff of Cornwall. He may know more about Juniper than we do – he may know that she has Catholic leanings and perhaps there's no harm in them. Quite a number of people have them. Ben Flood, the assistant cook at Hawkswood has! It would be something if we could cross Juniper off our list of suspects.'

'Do you really think we can?' asked Brockley cynically. 'I doubt it. But we might get him to take her in for questioning. I think there's enough evidence to justify that.'

Christopher had paced to the window and was looking out at the expanse of glittering sea that was Mount's Bay. 'St Michael's island looks as though one could reach it in a single leap. It's too clear for my liking.'

'It's always like that,' I said. 'The air here is so clear. I've never seen such light, anywhere else.'

'I know, but this morning it's a little too clear. It could mean bad weather to come.' Christopher turned away from the window. He seemed to reach a decision and he spoke with an air of command, which slightly annoyed me. 'It may not change at once, though. I don't know about Sir Francis. I want to think. I'll give Jet a gallop while the weather stays dry and do my thinking in the saddle. You're probably right, Brockley, but I'd like an hour or two to mull things over. Meanwhile, if you'd like to give your Firefly a gallop as well, you could ride over to St Aidan's.'

'Whatever for?'

'Because of something that kept me awake in the night. Jago is still on our list of suspects. I don't know what you might say or do if you got there, Roger, but perhaps if you tried . . . if you feel strong enough, that is.'

'I feel better every day,' Brockley said. 'I'd like to get back onto Firefly. I'll take it gently, but I think I can get as far as St Aidan's.'

'If you're sure,' said Christopher. 'Don't topple out of your saddle when you're only halfway there. This is the twenty-fourth of June; William vanished on the twenty-first. Where was Jago just then? See if you can find out. Go into the inn for some ale and see if there's any useful gossip to be had.'

He looked seriously at me and Dale, and then smiled. 'You two ladies can exercise your steeds as well, why not? But stay close to home and avoid strangers. I doubt if anyone will attack you now that the harbingers are interested in you. It would attract too much attention. All the same, take care, especially you, Ursula.'

'I hope the weather won't change for the worse while I'm

out,' said Brockley. 'If it catches me when I'm halfway across the Lizard, in either direction, I'll invite myself into the nearest farmhouse. I might be able to bring something edible back with me. Honeycomb or a fine big cheese and what about another bacon joint or even a beef one? I've got some money and I'll take saddlebags.'

'I can't imagine what Christopher intends to think about,' Brockley said crossly, as we stood around the kitchen after Christopher had collected his hat and his riding whip and gone to collect Jet. 'That Juniper woman has had a murder under her roof, and she has Catholic leanings as Christopher so delicately puts it . . . and has probably been hearing unlawful Masses. Isn't that enough to warrant an official investigation?'

I said, 'I think we could all benefit from some fresh air. Let's all go and get our horses saddled and let's go for a ride. I'll remind Tamzin to keep that trapdoor bolted.'

We adopted this plan. We split up, however. Brockley, aiming for St Aidan's, cantered off along a track across the Lizard, while Dale and I stayed quietly on the main track. We were relieved to be free to go out. The harbingers had got on everyone's nerves.

We had gone some distance before I noticed that away beyond the hearth smoke of Penzance, the sky had lost its sharp edges and grown hazy. A breeze had sprung up, too, a chilly breeze for June, and out in the bay there were foam-tipped waves. 'Time we turned for home,' I said to Dale.

We reached Cliff House just in time, barely ahead of the grey rain curtains that had arisen from nowhere and were sweeping over the Lizard. There was no sign of Christopher, so we ate dinner without him. Tamzin fried some duck eggs and bacon in one pan and in another, some asparagus tips in butter and served it along with her fresh rolls. Some plum tarts followed.

'I found some preserves in the stores, madam. Perfectly good ones, pushed behind them boxes of almonds and the spice jars and the big bag of sugar you've bought.'

'You didn't go down into the cold room?' I said anxiously.

'No, madam, I did not. Not alone, I wouldn't, believe me.'

'There are two capons hanging in there, ready to eat,' I said. 'I had to use our only beef joint to feed those confounded harbingers. They took it for granted I would give them dinner, damn them. I didn't mention the capons, though. When we've finished these plum tarts, we'll go down and get them. They can go on the spit for supper. They'll go round nicely.'

'As long as Christopher and Roger are back,' said Dale uneasily. 'I wonder where they are.'

Outside, the rain had begun. 'Brockley is probably having dinner in a farmhouse,' I said. 'Maybe Master Spelton as well.'

Brockley reappeared an hour later. The rain had slackened again but while the downpour was heavy, he had indeed taken refuge in a farmhouse and now had a beef joint and a bag of white flour for manchet bread, in his saddlebags. He brought the bags with him into the kitchen, tossed his leather riding cloak off and emptied the bags onto the table.

He had eaten mutton stew with cabbage and carrots in it, he said, and wouldn't need anything more until the evening. He felt all the better for the outing. Also, he had news. Wasn't Christopher back?

'Not yet,' I said, 'but meanwhile, tell us your news. Did you get to St Aidan's?'

'Yes.' Brockley seated himself. 'There was hardly anyone there except a couple of older men, one of them mending nets and another one doing repairs to a boat that he'd got turned upside down. Otherwise, just the womenfolk and the children. The first person I met was a woman with a basket of washing and I asked her where everyone was. Out deep-sea fishing, she said, and they won't be back for two, maybe three days. The men like to go out as a fleet, she told me. Yes, Jago was among them. Did I specially want to talk to him?

'I said not especially, it was just that I knew him slightly. I'd been out exercising my horse and I'd been near St Aidan's and wondered if I could take a parcel of fish home with me. It was an excuse because I didn't really want to put fish inside my saddlebags and I wasn't at all sorry to learn that fish wasn't available. But I dismounted and asked where I could water Firefly. The woman showed me the spring where they get their own fresh water and I chatted to her while Firefly was drinking. Do the men often go off on these deep-sea expeditions? What kind of catch do they bring back? Are they often away for days? Shark, mackerel, herring, she said. It seems that they've been away a lot this summer. Even missed the midsummer fair at Penzance; they sailed off the day before, would you believe it? That's real devotion to duty, I said and I hoped the expedition would be a success. She laughed and said yes, so did everyone, and now she must get her washing indoors because there was a rainstorm coming up and she'd have to have it all drying on a frame in front of the kitchen fire and a damned old nuisance that were going to be. So, I said goodbye to her and I set off for home, hoping to race the rainstorm, but it caught me so I did have to stop at a farmhouse, as I said. I thought Christopher would be here by the time I arrived myself. I suppose he's obliging another farmhouse to look after him.'

He looked round at us all. 'One thing is clear. Neither Jago nor his fellow fishermen at St Aidan's can have had anything to do with snatching William. They were at sea at the time. There's still the murder of his son, though. Maybe that really was some young woman's infuriated father or brother or husband!'

Dale said discontentedly, 'We aren't getting anywhere, are we? There's nothing to get hold of. And where is Master Spelton? Surely he should be back by now? He can't have . . .'

A clatter of hooves outside and a familiar snort interrupted her. 'There he is,' Brockley said. 'I'll fetch him in and then I'll recite my tale all over again. One moment.'

He picked up his cloak and went out. Tamzin took the bag of flour into the storeroom and said, 'When the men are here, madam, we had better take the beef joint into the cold room. We can fetch the capons then.'

'Yes, of course,' I said. Outside, I could hear Brockley saying something, but I couldn't hear Christopher's voice. Then there came the sound of someone running, and the back door was flung open and Brockley came through it, headlong.

'Jet's come back but without a rider. Christopher isn't there.'

'He must have been thrown! That damned horse . . .' I began, but Brockley was shaking his head.

'No, madam, no, he wasn't thrown. If he had been, the horse would have come back with his reins trailing. The reins are knotted together and looped over the pommel of the saddle, *and* the stirrups have been run up so that they don't flap. He dismounted, or was made to, and the horse was sent home without him. Someone took thought for the horse but Christopher himself has vanished into empty air. I think he's been snatched.'

Dale became hysterical. 'I can't bear it, it's a nightmare, one person after another. William, and the musician that Sir Francis talked about and now Master Spelton, who will it be next? Are we even safe in our beds? I want to go away from here; I'm frightened, I want to go home to Faldene, ma'am, please can't we just go before you or I or Roger . . . oh, dear God, if Roger disappears I shall go out of my mind . . . it could be any of us, one at a time we're being seized and taken the lord alone knows where . . .!'

She broke down into wild weeping. Brockley and I got her to bed somehow and Tamzin brewed what she said was a calming potion. When at last she fell asleep, still with tears on her cheeks and a damp napkin in her hand, the three of us looked gravely at each other. Brockley said, 'She may be right. Should we stay here?'

'I don't want to,' I said with fervour. 'I long to go home!'

How I longed for home. I had begun dreaming about Faldene. Returning to it in my sleep. I didn't want to stay here in Cornwall where the voices of drowned sailors cried in the wind and their bone must still lie on the sea floor all round Cornwall's perilous coast. I yearned for the quiet hills of Surrey, the calm downs of Sussex. I knew well enough that in the past, those hills too had seen warfare and ravaging, bloodshed in plenty. But the hills themselves were not responsible. Cornwall, with its towering cliffs, its caves, its savage rocks, its drowned seamen was another matter. A frightening one.

I looked round at the others and saw my own feelings reflected in their faces. Soberly, I said, 'I wish with all my heart that we could just pack our things and go but we can't. Not while Christopher is missing, and Tamzin's William. Until we're sure that we can do nothing for them, we have to stay and seek for ways to help them.'

'We ought to have a dog!' said Tamzin suddenly. 'A guard dog, to give warnings.'

'Christopher wasn't snatched from here,' I said. 'But a dog might be a protection to some extent, especially at night. Brockley, do you know of a farm that might have some young dog for sale?'

At least it was a practical idea, and it did make the others smile, if faintly.

Brockley went out next morning in search of a dog. Dale was more herself by then but cried when he said that he was going, saying what if he didn't come back, if he just vanished into empty air as Master Spelton had. To make things worse, Jet needed exercise and as Tremaine was afraid of him Brockley had said he would ride him. That made Dale cry even more, certain that Jet would throw him and that he would break his leg or his head and be left lying out on the heath while the horse came home without him . . .

Brockley, to pacify her, gave us a list of the farms he meant to visit. We were all by then fairly familiar with the names of the farms on the Lizard. 'I don't intend to fall off, anyway,' he said firmly. 'That horse is amiable enough if you're firm with him.'

'But you're not properly well yet!' wailed Dale.

'I'm good enough,' said Brockley. 'That ride to St Aidan's helped me. Just as well. With Christopher gone . . .! We seem to have accepted that he has been snatched.'

'What else can we do?' I said. 'Other than be very careful of ourselves and each other.'

'And that's why I don't want you to go out alone!' Dale protested. 'I am coming with you! If you are snatched then I'll be snatched too.'

'We'd be separated once we were brought to Constantinople,' Brockley said. 'But come if you like, my dear. I'll saddle Blue Gentle for you.'

They were not snatched. They came back two hours later with a half-grown mastiff on a long leash. They also brought with them a messenger whom they had met on their way home, who was bringing us a letter from Sir Francis Godolphin. While the messenger was refreshing himself in the kitchen with a jug of ale and Tamzin for company, the rest of us gathered in the parlour and I opened the message.

'It's an invitation,' I said. 'Except that as Sir Francis writes . . .

it's not just an invitation; it's more like a decree. The Royal Progress has begun. Her Majesty crossed the Tamar yesterday. On Saturday the second of July, she will be at Arwenack House and a tournament is to be held in her honour. We are to attend.'

'Who is meant by *we*?' asked Dale.

'Us,' said Brockley, looking over my shoulder. 'Madam and her attendants. That's you and me, Fran.'

'That settles it,' I said. 'We dare not go home. We've been ordered to Arwenack on the second of July.'

I paused, thinking. Below me, the sea thundered and I could hear seabirds crying. In Cliff House, these were normal things. But something wasn't normal. I felt it without understanding it and then it came home to me, like a breaking wave.

'Something's very wrong,' I said. 'I don't mean just Christopher. I have been involved with a Progress before. I know how these things are organized and I know quite well that the harbingers don't arrive and cause their confusion when the Progress is already on its way. They arrive weeks – sometimes months – before. Arrangements have to be just so, and the hosts have to have time to prepare their amusements and buy or borrow enough elegant tableware and embroidered sheets and organize enough supplies of food to satisfy a visitation from a royal court. Or a plague of locusts! Something about this is just not *right*.'

'Perhaps. But by the sound of it the tournament is going to be real,' Brockley said. 'It could be worthwhile. We'll see if the queen is actually there, anyway.'

Tremulously, Dale said, 'We came here to find out things, to go hunting as it were. Now I feel that we're the hunted. I'm so afraid.'

'We'll just have to conquer our fears and our grief,' said Brockley soberly. 'We have to attend this tournament, whether we like it or not. As madam says, this is an order. We had better take Tamzin with us. She'll panic now if she's left here alone, even if she does have a young mastiff to protect her.'

SIXTEEN
Lances Are Lowered

We attended the tournament. During the intervening days, which amounted to little more than a week, we learned nothing of Christopher's fate. Not that we had nothing to do. Despite our fears for Christopher and for ourselves, we were expecting guests and must look after them. They duly arrived. Sir John Lane was a young gallant who said he came from the north of England and was accompanied by a valet and a secretary whose northern accent was so marked that it was hard to understand him, and Sir William Hodges, somewhat older and stern of mien, who came from Norfolk.

Hodges was accompanied by a pretty but subdued wife, her middle-aged maid ('her duenna,' Brockley said. 'Hodges is as jealous as hell; the valet's told me so') and the black-clad valet himself, who spoke of his master so reverently that Hodges might have been God. I had never seen any of them before and if they recognized me, none of them let me know it. They addressed me as Mistress Archer. I was relieved.

Each of them also had a groom and a packhorse. Accommodating and feeding all these people and their horses kept us thoroughly occupied. I think I ran up and down the stairs in Cliff House a dozen times in one day and also had to soothe Sir John's valet, who was horrified by the booming of the sea below us. He turned out to be extremely superstitious and had at first concluded that he could hear the victims of hell, trying to batter their way out.

When we set out for the tournament, therefore, we were a sizeable party. We started the day before, the men on horseback, while I travelled in the carriage with Dale and Tamzin. As Brockley had said, Tamzin couldn't be left alone in the house and neither, I realized, could she be left alone with Thomas Tremaine, who had decided not to come.

Though he wouldn't be remaining on the premises. Thomas had seen tournaments before, he said, the Killigrews held them at least once a year. He had made friends with a lad in Polgillan, who wasn't going to the tournament either and they would like to go fishing. Jet wouldn't need to be exercised and Thomas was afraid of him anyway. He had turned Jet out into the meadow. He could gallop about all he liked in the field and exercise himself, Thomas said.

Sir Francis' guests had now arrived, a whole crowd of them, and what had been his corn field had been hastily harvested, gleaned and mown and covered by tents. We slept under canvas that night. Dale and Tamzin hated it and complained that the mowing hadn't been adequate and their bedding was prickly. However, it was only for the one night and in the morning a much-enlarged party set out, including Sir Francis and his wife and their personal servants. We made a dawn start and reached Arwenack at mid-morning. It was an easy journey, under a sky where harmless fluffy clouds floated in the blue, and a soft breeze countered the July heat. A suitable day for a tournament.

As soon as we arrived, my two guests and their retinues left us. Both, apparently, were to take part in the contests, and their folk had places in a set of special seats for those accompanying the contestants. We wished them luck and then looked about us.

We found ourselves in a line of people at the gate of the archery field that I had noticed at my first visit. We were awaiting attention from mounted marshals whose horses were draped in cloths of red and silver. Facing us across the field, halfway along the upper row of the tiered benches, was something new. A throne-like chair had been installed, under a canopy striped in red and silver, except that in this setting, Brockley remarked, one would have to say gules and argent. The chair seemed to be set on a dais and was presumably the seat the queen would occupy.

Heraldry was everywhere. At one end of the field was a row of tents flying coats of arms and at the other end was a white pavilion with the royal arms on a flag above it and a row of guards in the scarlet livery of the gentlemen who guarded the queen's doors within her palaces. It was all colourful and exciting. For a few moments, I even let myself think of something other than Christopher though I checked myself quickly, feeling ashamed.

The grooms who had come with us had already taken charge of our horses and the carriage, and other grooms, in gules and argent livery, had come to help. Brockley remained with us. 'You're not a groom this time,' I had told him before we set out.

Our turn to be welcomed by a marshal eventually arrived. He asked our names. Sir Francis, somewhat curtly, said, 'Godolphin and party,' and from the marshal's grin, I knew that the two of them were acquainted anyway. We were directed to our seats. There were three tiers, with breaks here and there and wooden steps giving access to the two upper rows. We were sent to sit in the second tier. We would have a good view, I thought, as long as no one in the row just below us had a monstrous hat.

The stands filled up quickly though every seat wasn't occupied; there was room for three people on the bench to my left. A row of standing onlookers, I think mostly from Falmouth town nearby, gathered in front of the tiers. Then from some hidden entrance behind the royal dais opposite, trumpeters appeared. They sounded a fanfare. A line of helmeted soldiers marched out next and dispersed themselves around the dais. The trumpeters sounded another fanfare and then, from the same hidden entrance, came the queen. Magnificently dressed, in a gown of white with Tudor roses all over it, with two ladies behind her to hold up her trailing skirts, and a red wig, studded with jewels, on her head, Elizabeth mounted to her throne and took her seat. Her ladies sank gracefully down to sit on stools at her feet. The trumpets sounded a third time and a marshal rode out into the arena, halted facing the queen, bowed, saluted her with a lowered lance and received a royal nod.

There were more trumpets, and the first competition began. This turned out to be archery. It was only moderately exciting, except, presumably, to the competitors. It took a long time. The winner – his name was announced but the breeze blew it away – was led to stand in front of the queen, who told one of her ladies to present him with a prize.

'It's a purse,' Sir Francis said. 'He'll be celebrating tonight.'

After the archery, there was a break, during which vendors of food and drink wheeled their handcarts round the field and there was a scramble as people from the higher seats jostled down the steps between the lower tiers and through the standing audience to get to them. We supplied ourselves with leather flasks of water and a selection of pies, meat and sweet berry. The empty space on the bench beside me proved useful. We spread out and used it as a table for our picnic. Out in the field, the archery targets were being taken away and three long barriers, brought out in sections, were being set up along the length of the arena, where they were bolted together and draped in more cloths striped gules and argent, which in turn were secured.

'They mustn't flap. It might frighten the horses,' Sir Francis remarked.

Tamzin whispered to me that the bright colours would frighten the horses anyway.

'They won't,' I said. 'The horses know their work. They're trained.'

'What are those long fences for?' Tamzin wanted to know.

'They make sure that the horses won't collide,' Brockley told her. 'You'll see. This is the real business of the day, the tilting.'

The Brockleys and I had seen jousting often enough before, when I was at court, but it was always exciting. To begin with, one of the marshals rode along in front of the seats, pausing now and then to announce the names of the first contestants who would ride into the lists. Or trying to announce them. His efforts weren't very successful. As when he had tried to declare the winner of the archery, he was defeated by distance and the breeze, which had grown gusty as the morning progressed. He had a good stentorian voice but even when he was facing us and thundering his information straight at us, we only heard a little.

Three pairs were to ride in the lists at the same time. We gathered that much. Sir someone or other with *de* in the middle of his name, would ride against My Lord lost-in-a-gust-of-wind. Henry something of somewhere on Thames had challenged Sir Thomas incomprehensible shout. The names of the third pair of contestants were lost altogether. There was more, about the prowess and past successes of the various contestants but we could make little of it.

The six competitors all made a circuit of the field, showing off their horsemanship, and saluted the queen before they took their places. They did this with their faces visible but once they were in position, each facing his opponent at the other end of the lists, they slammed their visors shut in a businesslike fashion, and we could see the horses fretting at their bits, already poised for the charge.

A mounted marshal placed himself facing the centre of the long barrier and used a baton to signal the start. The horses sprang into an instant gallop and tore towards each other, the riders holding their lances at rest until the last moment when they stiffened and took aim across the barriers.

Two pairs survived the onslaught and made ready to ride at each other again, having exchanged ends, as it were. Sir *de* someone or other, however, was thrust straight out of his saddle and crashed to the ground while his horse galloped on without him. He sat up, pulling his helmet off and rubbing his head and a couple of assistants ran out to help him up and lead him away, presumably to tend any injuries, if he had any. He didn't look as though he had. The other two pairs then rode at each other again and this time two competitors were knocked out of their saddles.

That left three competitors in the field. Lots were drawn to decide which two should now ride against each other. One was eliminated and then the last two survivors fought it out, which took some time as they were both determined not to be unhorsed. Eventually a winner did emerge. He rode to face Elizabeth and saluted her with his lance. On her throne, Her Majesty sat motionless except for a small, regal nod.

Another trio of pairs was summoned out and we recognized Sir Willliam Hodges, because we saw his face when he was circling the field before saluting Her Majesty. We didn't recognize his horse. He must have left his charger in readiness in the Killigrew stables for he had arrived at Cliff House on a lightly built Barbary, quite unsuited to this kind of sport. He proved to be an excellent contestant, unseating his opponent at the first attempt.

Sir Francis remarked, 'The lances are blunted, of course. Though they can still leave a good bruise if you're unlucky.'

Tamzin was asking more questions and I explained to her that the winners of the first jousts would ride against each other until a final winner emerged. The queen would honour him by putting a diadem on the point of his lance and then he would ride round the field and present it to the lady in the audience that he considered the most beautiful. By tradition he offered it to the queen first, but she would graciously wave him away and he would ride on to choose someone else. It was a way of finishing a tournament that many a time had caused heartache and resentment among rival court beauties. Elizabeth revelled in the whole business, congratulating winners, declining the diadem with the utmost graciousness, even standing up to shout encouragement at contestants who had kept their seats but only just and were swaying dangerously as they rode to the end of the lists.

So why, this time, was Elizabeth, in her jewelled majesty, so very unresponsive? A nod of acknowledgement here, a polite pattering of palm on palm and when the final winner – we were naturally pleased to see that it was Sir William Hodges – presented his lance, she placed the diadem on it with no more than a small smile as far as I could make out, and no apparent words of congratulation at all. He cantered round the field, offered her the diadem in the usual way, and then cantered off to present it to his pretty wife. There was cheering; this was a popular choice. And still Elizabeth sat motionless. She ought to have given young Mistress Hodges a smile, at least.

Unless, of course, she was afraid. Back in the days of the Babington conspiracy, when Sir Anthony Babington was exchanging letters with Mary of Scotland, planning to assassinate Elizabeth and put Mary in her place, Elizabeth had, I knew, been very afraid. The treasonous correspondence was known, was being watched, but was allowed to continue until such time as Mary declared in so many words that she approved of the plans. In all that time, the fear of assassination had hung over Elizabeth and she had had to live with it. She had agreed to live with it, had been advised to do so by Walsingham, her spymaster. But all that time, I knew that she had been in terror, had suffered from frequent nightmares and once, seeing a suspected man among her attendant courtiers, she had panicked entirely, gathered up her skirts and run for the safety of her rooms and her guards.

Perhaps, now, she was here as bait, like cheese in a mousetrap, to draw the enemy into the open. Perhaps she was here in the hope that an attempt to lay hold of her, would be made.

I wanted to go to her, but I sensed that I wouldn't be allowed near her. That ring of helmeted soldiers was warning enough.

After the tilting, came the closing event, which was meant for simple entertainment. The barriers were removed and a quintain was set up. This consisted of a swivelling pole with two protruding arms. One stuck out parallel to the path of the oncoming contestant and had a bag of flour hanging from it. The other stretched across the path of the contestant and from that, hung a target. This one looked remarkably like a crude representation of King Philip of Spain. Contestants were to ride at it full tilt and try to strike it amidships with their lances. Get it right, the pole would swivel away and the contestant would ride on, unharmed. Get it wrong and the rider would be hindered while the arm with the flour bag would swing round and hit him on the shoulders or the back of his head.

It was hilarious to watch and soon had the onlookers shouting with laughter. But after our picnic, we had resumed our original seats, leaving the three on my right empty once more, and now I was aware of someone moving into them. I turned my head and found that Juniper Penberthy had heaved herself massively onto the bench beside me.

There were shouts of laughter as an inexperienced contestant was thumped on the head with a bag of flour which broke and covered both himself and his horse with flour. Under cover of the delighted uproar, Juniper said, 'My dear Mistress Archer, I'm so glad to have this chance of speaking with you. I have been looking for you. During the pause for refreshments, I walked along the field, right along the stands, seeking you, but you were too busy with your picnic to notice me. But now I can . . .'

Out in the field, another victim had met with disaster at the quintain and was riding off the field looking like a snowman, on a horse that would also need some serious brushing. Mistress Penberthy drew nearer and into my ear, she said, 'I know you have guests just now but when this . . . this *performance* . . . is all over and your guests have gone, may I call upon you? There is something I wish to talk over with you, something I have heard, only I don't know what to make of it. It would be a dreadful thing to point a finger in the wrong direction but it is to do with these mysterious disappearances. I want – need – to talk it over at leisure with someone and, well, I do know who you really are. I won't say your real name out loud but Alexander Killigrew told me what it is.' Silently, I cursed Alexander Killigrew. 'May I come?' Juniper was asking me. 'We could have a game of chess, could we not? Do you have a set or shall I bring one?'

'Master Wells had one,' I said. 'We found it in his sideboard. My guests are leaving on Tuesday, the fifth day of July. Shall we say Thursday the seventh? As you say, we can play chess together, and perhaps discuss other matters across the chessboard. You will dine with me? I warn you that the Brockleys always share my dining table; indeed, when there are no guests, we take dinner in the kitchen and Tamzin and our groom, Thomas Tremaine, eats with us. They don't join us when guests are present but you may still think us an unconventional household. You will not object?'

'As long as I have a chance of private talk with you, Mistress, I won't object to anything.'

'That's agreed then. I'll see that there is a roast dinner.' I smiled at her and she smiled back, before withdrawing and going away, presumably to her own seat. There was one item still to come, a parade of winners round the field. Then I was to go with Sir Francis and join the Killigrews for dinner in the house. Sir William Hodges and Sir John Lane would be present as well; their attendants and mine, which meant the Brockleys and Tamzin, would eat with the Killigrews' servants. Whether or not they were pirates, in private life the Killigrews were not in the least unconventional.

SEVENTEEN
Shock Wave

'Is Mistress Penberthy coming alone, madam?' Tamzin wanted to know. 'How many will there be for dinner?'

'She may bring her maid,' I said. 'A lady of her standing rarely travels alone, not even just across Mount's Bay.' I had myself dressed suitably for a social occasion, in a brocade of rose and pale green, with matching slippers. In the summer warmth, my freshly starched ruff prickled and where the steep staircase was also narrow, my farthingale brushed the walls. 'She might even bring two! Cater for four and make it something we can finish up for supper if after all we have leftovers.'

'I have made plenty of fresh bread, madam, and there were some more capons delivered yesterday. Could someone ask Thomas to go down to Polgillan and see if there's a catch in, so that we can have a fish course? I can make egg and butter tarts for afterwards, and some redcurrants in jelly.'

'That will do very well, thank you, Tamzin. I don't know when she will arrive but she was hoping for a game of chess before dinner, I think. She could be here at any time. Have some raisin pastries or some honey cakes ready for welcome refreshments. I think she would rather have small ale before a chess game – nothing likely to blur one's concentration.'

I left these arrangements in hand and went to the parlour, to set out a couple of tables, in case Juniper brought a partner for Brockley, who grumbled at the thought of it but finally agreed to oblige if asked. Dale went to help Tamzin while Tremaine went down the cliff in search of fish. He shortly returned with a bagful of mackerel and herring, which he brought straight into the kitchen.

Brockley had been setting out chess tables in the parlour, but now left them and came to help with cleaning the fish. His nose wrinkled when he came near Tremaine. 'You reek of herrings,' he said. 'You ought to wash. Help yourself to some hot water but take it to the stables. These rooms are too crowded.'

Tremaine did so, though he looked annoyed. 'You were rather brusque with him,' I said to Brockley.

'I know. But I can't take to him somehow,' Brockley said. 'He's fairly good with the horses – I mean, he knows what to do, only he'll skimp if I don't watch him. Now let me get at those fish. Why did God put so many bones into them?'

I made a few rearrangements in the parlour and then looked out of the window. A small boat was coming purposefully across the bay, pointing straight towards Polgillan. Mistress Penberthy was on her way, bringing, I hoped, news of some interest; perhaps, at last, a clue to the hidden name behind the hateful events in Cornwall. My guests had left; they had gone on to Penzance ahead of the Progress to see to some final arrangements for the queen's visit there. Apparently she was to stay at The Good Catch. For today, I understood that the queen was still at Arwenack, where she was to be entertained by a masque, followed by a ball. Yesterday she had gone hunting. She would travel on to Penzance tomorrow.

It was all wrong, I thought restively. Elizabeth shouldn't be anywhere near Cornwall. She shouldn't be confronted by such an exhausting programme of events and in spite of the guards she had brought with her, she was surely afraid. It was *wrong*, hopelessly wrong, and now the prospect of Mistress Penberthy's secrets had become alarming. Did they concern knowledge of a definite threat to Her Majesty? I should have asked Sir Francis to join us today. Except that his presence might well have silenced her until another time; she had been so very secretive when she spoke to me at the tournament.

That boat would be tying up at Polgillan at any moment. It was too late to change the arrangements now.

Mistress Penberthy did not bring a maid with her but she did bring a partner for Brockley. Most unexpectedly, she brought the brown-bearded Nicholas Rowe, the man whose valued groom Robbie had been snatched.

'I thought, if we were to be playing chess, your Brockley might like to join in, so I brought him someone,' said Juniper, sounding almost bright. She slid down from the mule on which she had climbed the cliff path, while Nicholas led it. Tremaine took its bridle and led it to the stable. Juniper would want it when she was ready for the trudge down to the village.

I took my guests inside. I felt overdressed as they had dressed quite simply. Juniper's gown was of elegant cut but only made of thin blue cotton. She had no farthingale and her ruff was unfashionably small. Nicholas was in a summer-weight black doublet and had no ruff at all. He was wearing his shirt with its neck open.

However, I showed them into the parlour, Dale brought honey cakes and small ale and we partook of these refreshments and talked about the weather, which looked as though it meant to be hot and clear. Brockley joined us, in shirtsleeves because the heat was increasing. The shirt was clean and white but he too was wearing it open at the neck.

Dale withdrew to go on helping Tamzin with dinner and the rest of us played chess, Brockley against Nicholas while I played against Juniper. Once I said, 'Mistress Penberthy, I think you have something to tell me.' But she murmured, 'After dinner, I think. Do you agree, Nick?' and Nicholas nodded.

After two hours of unadulterated chess, dinner was served. The Brockleys ate with us, in the bleak dining room, but if the surroundings were bleak, the meal was not. Tamzin had excelled herself. When the meal ended, Brockley fetched her into the dining room to receive our congratulations.

'Thank you, Tamzin,' I said, and saw the shy pleasure in her face.

Unexpectedly Mistress Penberthy said, 'Stay here for a moment, Tamzin.'

Surprised, I said, 'We are all replete. Shall we go back to the parlour? I take it, Mistress Penberthy, that you are about to give me your mysterious message. Does it concern Tamzin in any way?'

'It concerns you all, and I prefer to tell it here and now.' Juniper's smile had in it something disconcerting. I didn't know what to make of it. Then Nicholas suddenly moved, rising from his seat, stepping behind Tamzin and then seizing hold of her

and setting a knife edge against her throat and for me, understanding came, breaking over me in a huge, cold wave. My whole
body clenched in disbelief, in horror, in readiness to fight and
the awful knowledge that I dared not move.

Nicholas said, 'You will all obey the orders given by me or
by Mistress Penberthy. The latter, brushing a few crumbs off her
skirts, as though everything was completely normal, said, 'Our
friends are unsuitably dressed and we have had trouble with that
kind of thing on other occasions. Let us improve matters this
time. The man Brockley must have a doublet and a cloak, hooded
for preference. He may also bring a spare set of under-linen. He
can fetch them himself. We will stay here with his wife and the
woman he serves and is known to value. Go and fetch the clothing
I have told you, man. Try no tricks. Bring a change of under-
linen and a cloak for your wife, also.'

'What is all this?' I demanded, more because the question
seemed natural than because I wanted to know the answer. I
knew that already though I didn't want to believe it and inside
me there was a voice screaming *no, no, NO!'*

'I am sure you have already guessed,' said Nicholas, and his
face suddenly crinkled with amusement. 'You especially, Mrs
Archer, or should I say Mrs Stannard? You are half-sister to
Queen Elizabeth of England. I never thought to find such valuable
merchandise in my possession.'

Merchandise! But I looked at him and I saw that he really did
regard me – and presumably the Brockleys as well – as merchandise. To him, we were not people, individuals with
responsibilities, with loves, hopes, fears, friendships of our own.
We were something for sale, like the calves we took from their
mothers and sold to be turned into veal. I choked back an outburst
of abuse. He would take no notice. Why should he? A valuable
bull may gore you if it gets the chance but if it promises well
as a sire, it remains valuable and you just keep out of its reach
and make sure its nose ring is secure.

Brockley went upstairs and presently came back with the
clothing he had been told to bring. Juniper inspected it and
demanded a bag to put it in. In a trembling voice, Dale said that
we had some leather bags we used for bringing stores home.
'Get two!' snapped Juniper.

Dale fetched them. Juniper then turned her attention to me. 'That brocade you're wearing is too fashionable. Go to your chamber, change into something plainer and don't put on a farthingale or bother with a ruff. Put on stout shoes as well, not those pretty slippers you're wearing. Also bring a change of underclothing and a hooded cloak.'

I went upstairs without a word. There was nothing to be done. I could perhaps climb out of an upper window and hope to drop to the ground without hurting myself and if I managed that (which I probably wouldn't), I could then run down to Polgillan to fetch help. But our captors would find out what I had done long before help could arrive and then they might take vengeance on the others. Therefore, I did not climb out of any windows. I went in docile fashion to my bedchamber and changed my pretty brocade gown for a brown everyday one in a thin wool and cotton mixture.

Then I smiled secretly, for here there was one thing our captors didn't know about. They didn't know about the pouches hidden inside my open-fronted skirts. Even when I was dressed for company, I still had a pouch, and I transferred the contents whenever I changed my dress. I did so now. Purse of money. Small sharp dagger in its sheath. Picklocks. A piece of red chalk, as requested by Christopher.

I collected the cloak and under-linen and went downstairs. As I stepped into the dining room, I heard our dog barking. For one glorious moment, I thought, help is coming. But I was wrong. Tremaine came in, remarking, 'I have fed the dog. He's quite valuable; we can make a penny or two from him, I should think.'

So, Tremaine was part of this, too. Brockley's instincts about him had been all too sound. He obviously had more concern for the dog than he had for us. Looking at him now, I saw that he had changed, become suddenly older, more authoritative. Colder. And his voice was different. He had lost his Cornish accent.

'You know what to do, Tom,' Nicholas was saying. 'You must stay here still we return and be ready to answer questions if anyone calls. Mistress Archer has been suddenly called away, that's what you have to say. When we come back, we will stay here until our cargo has sailed. Then we'll sell the place. You must take good care of the dog and the horses, they'll be sold as well, next time there's a fair in Penzance. The horses won't be recognized once they're away from here. I trust you have made the preparations downstairs, as I asked you to do?'

'Yes, Father. I have done everything as you told me.'

Father! I suppose I gaped. Anyway, Nicholas turned to me and said, 'Yes, Thomas is my son. My natural son and therefore doesn't have the name of Rowe. Any more than I, because I too am a natural son, can claim the name of Killigrew. But the blood in his veins and his heart, like mine, is Killigrew.'

Bemusedly, I let Dale put my cloak and linen into the bag she was holding. Nicholas was talking to Juniper, referring, I thought, to some earlier disagreement. 'Tamzin is young and strong and now we have seen that she can cook. She's well worth taking and though I know you don't agree about the Brockleys, I still say why not turn an extra penny while we have the chance? The man is good with horses and his wife is a tirewoman. She can sew and embroider. They may not be young but they'll still be worth something. Thomas, we'll be back soon. You are sure you can manage meanwhile?'

'Of course.' Affronted, Thomas resumed his local accent. 'I am only the groom. Them as I work for don't tell me all their business. The mistress has been called away and off she's gone, taking the Brockleys with her. *I* don't know when she'll be back or even if. I just look sullen.' He grinned.

'Good boy. Now,' said Nicholas, 'we had best start off. Lead the way, Juniper. I'll come last, holding Tamzin and with my knife at the ready. Remember, all of you, I can do her considerable damage without actually cutting her throat. She's a pretty piece of merchandise and I don't *want* to damage her; scars would take too much off her selling price. But there are times when one has to cut one's losses. I will do what I must to enforce obedience for the rest of you. If I'm forced to injure her too much, well, she is expendable.'

Tamzin, who so far had been all distended eyes and trembles but had been silent, now opened her mouth and screamed, and he shook her. 'That won't help you, my girl.'

Gaping, tears running down her face, Tamzin subsided.

'Save your breath,' said Nicholas. 'Come along, everyone, get in line.'

We did get in line. Juniper walked majestically ahead. Brockley and Dale were behind her. Dale was shaking and Brockley's arm was round her. I walked behind them, wishing that I could have that strong arm round me but knowing that I never would. Gerald, Matthew, Hugh, all my lawful husbands were dead. I was alone and must make the best of it. Nicholas was behind me, with a sobbing Tamzin in his grasp. As our horrid little procession marched out of the dining room, he remarked, with sickening cheerfulness, that in my brocade dress I had been a picture.

'Quite delightful; it breaks my heart to make you leave that gown behind, dear Mrs Stannard, but for you, I fear, the days of silk and satin and exquisite brocades are over. Forward!'

There was no escape. Juniper led us into the kitchen and then into the butchery, which was now just another storeroom, and there we saw that the trapdoor was open, flung back, with the downward steps revealed.

'We go down, one at a time,' said Juniper. 'Try any tricks and Tamzin will pay for them.'

We went down, one at a time. Nobody tried any tricks. We arrived in the cold room and, as we all by now expected, were invited to proceed through the hidden crevice into the adjacent cave. Lit candles awaited us on a table and beside it there were lanterns. These were presumably the preparations that Thomas had been bidden to make. Juniper lit a lantern, remarking that in the tunnels, lanterns were better than candles; there was a current of air that could blow out a candle flame. She led the way onwards, holding the lantern up so that we would find it easy to follow.

I thought at first that we were going to the entrance out in the middle of the Lizard, so that no one would witness us leaving the house. But after a while, Juniper turned right, leading us into a narrow side turning.

It forked once but the left-hand fork was narrower than the main tunnel and I didn't like the look of it – narrow, low-roofed and it seemed so dark. I kept on along the main tunnel.

Christopher's voice spoke in my head. I stopped short and Tamzin bumped into me. Nicholas snapped, 'What is it? If you don't like underground tunnels, Mistress Stannard, that is your misfortune. You will enter this one or Tamzin will have to encourage you.'

From behind me, I heard a sob. Whether or not he had actually hurt Tamzin, I didn't know. But an idea had caught hold of me. 'I'm sorry,' I said, with what I hoped was a slight gasp in my voice, 'but I ate too much at dinner. I've got the gripes, I've got to squat down, I must . . . Brockley, come behind me so that that man Rowe can't watch, and Dale, block Juniper's view as well. This is so humiliating . . . It has happened before; it's a weakness of mine . . .'

The Brockleys had never heard me complain of such a thing before but they responded nobly, Dale planting herself in front of me, turning her back, facing Juniper and folding her arms while Brockley stepped past me and took up a position behind me, saying, 'Leave Tamzin alone. We are trying no tricks. The mistress needs to ease herself. It can be a problem for those who are ageing.'

I crouched down. I managed to produce a fairly convincing motion. I also whisked my red chalk out of my pouch and low down on the rocky wall just inside the narrow side passage, in haste, I drew a circle and quartered it with a cross inside. I had to do it in virtual darkness and could only hope that I had done it right. I did some groaning, to cover any grating from the chalk though I don't think there was any to speak of. Then I stood up, saying again that I was sorry; I was better now. Brockley went back to Dale. Juniper held the lantern up higher as they took their places. This passage was too narrow to let them walk side by side, so Brockley placed himself behind Dale, with a hand on her shoulder.

Our procession set off again. It was a long trudge, slightly upwards at first and then changing direction and going somewhat downwards. Then we saw a gleam of light ahead and the passage widened out into a cave. Here too there was a table with lanterns and a tinderbox on it, and there was also a charcoal brazier with a sack of charcoal beside it. Straight ahead was a tall door, its hinges fastened somehow to the rock. The light came through a small square aperture in the middle of it, and between this and Juniper's lantern I made out bolts, one at the top of the door and one at the foot. Halfway up, there was also a stout, shining, brass lock.

Juniper produced a key, unlocked the door and undid the bolts while Nicholas stood guard with his knife caressing Tamzin's throat. She was still crying, silently, but crying nonetheless, and when the lantern light swung her way it showed not only her tears, but a streak or two of red. She had suffered for my chalk symbol, I thought, contritely and probably for nothing. We would be very lucky indeed if anyone with knowledge of that symbol ever found it. If such a miracle should happen, it would no doubt be long after we had all been exported to purchasers in Mediterranean countries.

The rocky walls on either side of us were rough and uneven, with cavities here and there and tin lodes, which I had seen on my previous visit to Cornwall and now recognized, running along them like streaks of dark blue ink. Having released the lock and the bolts, Juniper reached into one of the cavities and dragged a box out. It was evidently heavy, for she nearly dropped it. She positioned it more safely on one hip and pushed the door open. She led us through, and then we were out into a cave that was open on one side, letting in a bright light that made us blink after our walk in the near dark. It also let in the sound of the sea. The cave had an open mouth, overlooking the bay.

It was a deep cave, running well back from its mouth. Near the mouth, there had at some time been a fall of rock for lumps of it were lying about. Along its back wall, four people were sitting.

They were sitting on what looked like straw pallets. Behind them, stretching along the wall and somehow fixed at both ends, was an iron bar. They were chained to it. Their chains were fairly long; evidently they could stand or sit, or lie down on the pallets, at will, but the chains ended in the gyves that each had round one wrist. They had blankets, wrapped round them, for the cave was cold. In practical fashion, a small two-tiered table stood beside each pallet. The lower shelves held what looked like chamber pots and the top ones each held a jug and a glass. There were no other furnishings except a pile of spare pallets and blankets and in the middle of the floor, one small table with a couple of large ewers on it. I looked at all this and then looked towards the cave mouth. I saw a few fronds of dried seaweed there.

The quartet of prisoners consisted of one middle-aged man, a handsome but haughty-looking middle-aged woman, a nondescript girl and a young man. They were all in ordinary clothes and only the two men had ruffs on. Three of the quartet looked utterly miserable. The fourth was the young man, who just looked furious. They stared at us as we were brought in but did not speak. They left that to our captors, who did.

'We have brought you some more company,' said Nicholas breezily. I had originally seen him as an ordinary man who had been given the charge of a difficult horse and had now lost the groom who was going to tame it. He had turned into a pirate with an air of jolly enthusiasm for his odious calling.

'It will still be three or four days before we can move you to your ship,' he said kindly, as though we were all waiting with impatience for the ship that would take us away from our homes and our normal ways of life for ever. 'She has berthed at Penzance and she has cargo to unload and repairs to make. The Bay of Biscay lived up to its wild reputation when she came through it. But soon she will set sail, and then she'll drop anchor out near the horizon and at the first high tide, we will have a boat ready to take you out to her.'

Juniper put the heavy box down on the table and in reassuring tones, said, 'High tides make it possible for boats to come within reach of this cave mouth. Of course, when there are storms, the sea sometimes does splash in. But you will notice that the cave goes well back and that the floor of it slopes upwards a little. We have never drowned any of our merchandise yet. Now, let us secure our new friends.'

While we stood in a group, not daring to stir because Tamzin was still in Nicholas' pitiless grasp, Juniper went to the pile of pallets and pulled out four, which she placed at the end of the existing row. Then she went back to the box. This should have been a handsome thing, since it was made of what looked like mahogany, and had brass corners and a big brass lock. It was however, badly scratched. Being stored in a rock crevice had done it no good. Juniper produced a key and unlocked it. Out of it, she took some chains and padlocks. 'Each of you sit down on a pallet,' she said.

Nicholas dragged Tamzin over to one of them and with a jerk of his head commanded the rest of us to do as Juniper had said. Helplessly, our eyes on poor Tamzin, we obeyed. Juniper came over to us and one at a time we were secured to the iron bar behind us. The gyves round our wrists were fastened with padlocks and I now saw that the long bar had stout brackets at intervals all along its length, through which chains could be slipped. Each chain had a square iron block at one end, so that it could not be pulled back through its bracket, and it had a large final link that could be slipped onto the gyve when it was open. The hapless wearer could sit, stand, use the equipment we had been given, lie down to sleep, but not move more than a step or two from our pallets. Once we were all safely chained, Nicholas let go of Tamzin. She was shivering and Juniper went to fetch us some blankets.

'There, there.' It was a horrid imitation of a solicitous hostess. 'You'll soon be warm again. Though supper will be late this evening, I fear. We won't be bringing it to you ourselves. You will be taken off by boat as soon as the tide is high enough and taken out to your transport ship. You'll have supper there. The cook on board is excellent; you'll be hungry before you get your meal but it will be worth the wait.'

'Well, there you are. We will now leave you to become acquainted,' said Nicholas, smiling facetiously, as though we were all guests at some grand social occasion. No one answered him. We all sat still. The chains were not very heavy but the feel of the cold iron round my left wrist was terrifying.

Juniper locked the box, picked it up and walked out of the cave. Nicholas, maddeningly, bowed to us all and the young man snarled, audibly. Then our captors were gone and we could hear bolts sliding home and a key turning in that shiny brass lock. We heard feet and voices receding.

'I suppose,' said the middle-aged man, 'that we had better all introduce ourselves.'

'One word from me, please,' I said softly. I cocked my head. 'I think I heard them talking as they went away and I don't think they have their ears to the door, but I will keep my voice low just the same. I am Mistress Ursula Stannard, natural half-sister to the queen. I have had an unusually adventurous life for a lady. I have picklocks.'

EIGHTEEN
Ifs And Buts

I t takes quite a long time to undo eight padlocks with the aid of picklocks. My hands were cold and inclined to shake and I had to begin by undoing my own with just my right hand. Once I had released myself, I got on better. At last, it was done. We were all free.

At the end of all this, as people sat rubbing abraded wrists and expressing grateful thanks, the middle-aged man said, 'I still think we all ought to know who we are. I am Joseph Dunstan, musician, tempted into a secluded lane at the midsummer fair by a promise of seeing a wonderful new design of spinet, then grabbed, gagged and bundled onto a cart, bounced and jounced for miles till I thought every bone in my body would break, and finally tumbled out on top of the Lizard, to find those two ready to march me down here at knifepoint.

'Apparently I'm needed as a music teacher in Turkey some-where. I said to them, don't they have any music teachers of their own, but it seems that there is some kind of pride in having one specially imported from Albion. That's what they call it. I think it refers to the white cliffs of Dover though we're a good long way from Dover here. These ladies will speak for them-selves.'

The haughty-looking woman was Mistress Eleanor Pentreath, a distant relative of the famous merchant family, the Rashleighs, and the wife of a sea captain, at present on a voyage to the New World. 'What he would say – what he will say when he learns of this, I don't like to imagine. Our family will be dishonoured. He will be so angry!'

I received the impression that the absent Captain Pentreath was an angry man and also that his wife was in agreement with this. She did not fear him herself but was proud of his ability to inspire fear in others. 'That accursed woman Juniper Penberthy,'

Eleanor said, 'told me that there's a buyer who longs to make a housemaid of a well-bred unbeliever from England! This sort of thing is becoming a fashion in Constantinople, she has told me.'

Her voice was lofty, like her appearance. The haughtiness was an intrinsic part of her, I thought. She perfectly fitted the specification that her captors had been given.

The nondescript girl was called Anna Clay and she was a singer. She obliged us with a verse or two of a well-known song. Her voice was beautiful, strong, melodious and with a glorious range. She had been one of a group of travelling minstrels. They would miss her, she said, as a fact, not with any special pride.

The young man was Gervase Pearce, and he had once been a manservant in the Penberthy household. 'I am supposed to have murdered Beryon Lander by drowning the little bitch in her own washtub,' he informed us. 'I didn't, and I don't know who did but I fancy it was Mrs Penberthy herself. Beryon hinted to me that she knew something about the mistress of the house that Mrs Penberthy would pay her to keep quiet about. She was a nasty little girl, was Beryon. I reckon that Mrs Penberthy did pay her, or maybe I should say pay her out. Headfirst into a washtub. I tell you, I'd have loved to be the one who drowned her, but I wasn't.'

Tamzin, when I introduced her, wanted to know if any of them had heard anything of William. He had been taken on the same day as Joseph Dunstan and Gervase Pearce, but he was not here among us. Anna enlightened us, however.

'I heard them talking when I was brought here. Saying it was a nuisance, that Master Dunstan and Master Pearce had just missed a ship. That Juniper woman said she'd wanted the captain to wait but he wouldn't, just said that another ship would be in soon and any leftover cargo – that's *us* – could sail on that.'

William, presumably, had not missed the last ship. I thought, if no slave-bearing ship has sailed since midsummer, where is Christopher?

Meanwhile, Brockley, having introduced himself and Dale, had walked over to the cave mouth, carefully avoiding the lumps of fallen rock, and there he had stood for a moment looking out to sea. He then came back by way of the door, which he studied for a few moments before returning to us.

'I can suggest a plan,' he said. 'We can't do much for ourselves at the moment. The lock on that door has no keyhole on this side, and in any case it's bolted on the other side. We can't get out of it until it's unlocked and unbolted for us. The tide is falling and what it leaves behind is a sheer drop to jagged rocks. They're just beginning to poke above the surface.'

'At high tide, the water's deep,' said Dunstan. 'When they want to load us onto a ship bound for the Mediterranean, they'll take us from here at high tide, in a small vessel and ferry us out to where the transport is waiting. They told me as much.'

'Yes. They did,' Eleanor agreed. 'That big fat woman said the same to me only I can't believe it, I can't, this is all a nightmare, I can't believe it's happening . . .' Her voice faded and stopped.

There was a silence. It was the silence of despair. Until Brockley said, 'When they come for us, they'll be expecting to find us still chained. Suppose we sit on our pallets looking innocent until they come to undo us and then pounce on them and chain *them* up, or else throw them out of the cave. Into the sea if necessary. If we have to defend ourselves against the crew of whatever boat comes to collect us, we can swing our chains like weapons. Later on, in the morning perhaps, we can stand in the cave mouth and wave and signal and sooner or later someone will see us and rescue us. We may have a hungry wait but we won't end up in Constantinople.'

I wondered if we could manage it. Eleanor said, 'I don't understand what you mean by pounce. I wouldn't be able to . . .'

'Not on your own, maybe,' said Pearce. 'But we can all help each other.'

'Make sure that you know how to work those wrist gyves,' said Brockley. 'They're hinged in the middle and the two ends just snap to. The last link on the chain, the big link, has to be safely slipped into the fetter before you snap it shut.'

There was nothing to do but wait. Eleanor fidgeted with her fetter, making sure that she understood it. We all stretched our legs round the cave and Brockley once more walked over to the mouth to look at the sea. As he turned to come back, he tripped over something and fell. Dale and I both started forward but he sat up, rubbed his left foot hard, and then looked sharply at something beside it.

'There's an iron ring embedded in the rock here,' he said. He got to his feet. 'Cemented in by the look of it, like that bar we were all chained to. Mooring for a ship, I fancy. This cave has been used a lot. I am all right, except for a bruise or two. The tide's still falling and the rocks at the foot of the cliff look horrible.'

He came towards us, limping slightly, so that Dale, exclaiming 'Let me see that ankle!' ran to meet him and made him stop so that she could crouch and examine the injury.

As she did so, Anna said, 'I heard something. Someone's at the door! I heard a knock.'

We all tensed, listening. Then we all heard it, a decisive knock, the thud of knuckles that meant to be heard. Joseph Dunstan, who was nearest to the door, strode over to it. 'Who's there?'

'Christopher Spelton, otherwise known as Christopher Wood. Is Mistress Stannard or Master Brockley there?'

Brockley shook Dale off. 'It's nothing, just a bruise.' He limped over to the door. I joined him, edging the musician aside. 'We're both here!' I said. 'Is that really you, Christopher? Where have you been? Were you seized and have you escaped? Can you let us out?'

'I have been masquerading as the queen of England, in a red wig, travelling in a gilded carriage and waving to the crowd.'

Christopher's voice was slightly distorted by being projected through a solid oak door, but it was recognizable all the same. 'Did any of you really think that Her Majesty would risk herself – or be allowed to risk herself – in Cornwall just now?' he said. 'She suggested the Progress but she never intended to take part in it herself. See here. I can't let you out. I can draw bolts but I don't carry picklocks and I can't open this big brass lock. Can you open the lock from your side now that the bolts are out of the way?'

I groaned and he heard me. 'Ursula? What's the matter?'

'I can't open it from here,' I said. 'There's no keyhole on my side.'

'Damnation!'

'Damnation indeed,' I said. 'What do we do now?'

'Who is there with you?' Christopher asked.

It would have been churlish to tell him that secret agents ought all to carry picklocks. I gave him the names of our fellow prisoners, and also the names of our captors.

'Penberthy and Nicholas Rowe. We've been partly on the right track,' said Christopher. Brockley, his mouth almost touching the door, demanded, 'How did you find us? Why did you disappear?'

'I was out giving Jet some exercise and I was virtually seized by some of Sir Francis' men. They had had orders to get hold of me if they could, and not let you know where I'd gone. Sir Francis wanted you to think that I had disappeared like the others. He thought that if I vanished as well, then you might be frightened into doing what he had asked you to do and go home. He never did want you involved, not right for women; he said the sooner you were chased home and out of the way, the better. He said I was wasting my time at Cliff House; that I would be of more use if I joined in with the Progress scheme. I told him that I wouldn't consent to anything of the sort and he was exasperated – said you're just like that man Petroc. We wanted him to join us but he said no, he was a free man again and off he went, singing his way the length of Cornwall. As for me, I was virtually kept a prisoner. Well, I did break the monotony once or twice by masquerading as the queen but I was always under the eyes of his guards. I was at the Arwenack House tournament. I saw you in the stands, Ursula. How do you women put up with those bloody awful farthingales and how does the queen put up with the red wigs I've been planting on my bald head? The damn things itch. Finally, I made Sir Francis understand that I must tell you what was happening and that it would be best . . .'

'Do you mean that Sir Francis resented me that much?' I asked.

'Not resented, just believes that you ought to be protected from danger. Doesn't think women are capable of the kind of work you do. You'd think he'd know better, having Killigrews for in-laws but I think he regards the Killigrew women as freaks like two-headed calves only nastier – and that he rescued Lady Alice from their clutches like St George rescuing a maiden from a dragon. Never mind that now. Listen. I said, and kept on saying, that if I told you face to face that I was giving up our enterprise as useless, and urged you to go home, that would work just as well as believing that the enemy had got me and it would be

more honest. In the end, he agreed to that. I came to Cliff House
to tell you the bad news – except that I wasn't going to urge you
to go home; I know you better than that, Ursula. When I got to
Cliff House, your horses were all out in a field and that groom
of yours, Tremaine, was shifty, didn't want to let me go into the
house, said you'd been called away – I didn't believe him. It all
smelt as bad as a guttering lamp. I marched into the house, looked
round . . .'

'Juniper and Nicholas might have been in the house!' I gasped.

'They weren't,' said Christopher briefly. 'I think they intend
to come back, though. The door from the kitchen to the butchery
was open and I could see that the trapdoor was open as well. I
went down into the cold room, got through the crevice into the
cave and I knew at once that it had been used – lit candles have
a smell and it was strong. I lit a lantern for myself and went off
along the passage. I came to the place where that other narrow
passage leads off and because I was being careful to shine the
lantern light in all directions as I went along, bless you, Ursula,
I saw your symbol chalked in the entrance to it. How did you
manage that?'

'Madam was overtaken by the gripes,' said Brockley in a prim
voice.

'I ate too much at dinner,' I added. I heard a snort of laughter
from Christopher.

'I saw,' he said. 'And then I tried that narrow passageway and
I found this door. I wanted to know what or who was on the
other side of it. Since I can't get through it, tell me, who is there
and are you all free to move about?'

Brockley told him, briefly, of my picklocks and our plans to
capture our captors by outnumbering them. He also described
our fellow prisoners and spoke of the position of the tide and
our belief that when it was full again, a boat would come for us.
A rescue could also reach us but . . .

'God knows what might happen if our captors and a rescue
party both got there at once!'

'I'll have to try to race them,' said Christopher. 'There won't
be time to get help from Sir Francis. I expect he'd give it but
he's too far away, at Helston. To reach him, get him to send a
rescue force, on either water or land – it would take hours. I'll

send him word, in hope, but I think I'd do best to raise a force from the Polgillan villagers. I'll go back by way of the trapdoor. I'll ignore Tremaine for the moment but if he tries to interfere, I shall deal with him. I'm armed, don't fear for me. I'll go now. I'll do my best.'

He was gone. We were left to wait, beset by terrors. If the trapdoor was shut after all then Christopher would have to take the long route by way of the passageway out towards the middle of the Lizard. I tried to work it out. He might get a horse from one of the farmsteads but it would slow him down. From one of the farmsteads near that more distant entrance, he might be able to despatch a message to Helston, one that would reach Sir Francis more quickly than if it was sent from Polgillan.

But whether Sir Francis would respond . . . surely he would! He must. As Sheriff of Cornwall, he had a duty to rescue Cornish folk if they were in danger. What was he there for, for God's sake? But it would still be hours before he could hope to reach us and even if he did, he would still need the high tide to get to us and that was just when the enemy would come to take us off. Was there any chance that we would actually succeed in overpowering our captors when they came into the cave to fetch us? Might Christopher think of bringing men down through the tunnels to break the door down? If they could. That door looked as if it had been made to withstand attack.

Too many ifs, too many buts. We could do nothing but wait, and hope.

Time went past, slow and heavy. Brockley kept going to the cave mouth to look at the tide, and eventually he said that he thought it had turned.

'But it will be late before it rises high enough for us,' he said. 'And what will happen then, if rival ships meet in front of this cave?'

NINETEEN
Fighting Over A Bone

'How long,' I asked, of the company in general, 'will it take the tide to reach the full?'

'A little less than six hours,' Dunstan said. 'I was a seaman for a while, when I was young. Went to sea for the adventure and now I sometimes put the sound of breakers into my music.'

The prospect stretched ahead of us like eternity.

Tamzin had the idea of using her red chalk to make a draught board on the floor and said we could use bits of rock, or pebbles, as counters.

'Pebbles?' said Dale.

Tamzin pointed. 'There's a few there, mixed up with that seaweed.'

There were, no doubt tossed there by stormy waves, like the seaweed. Seeing them brought us all to stand and gaze out of the cave mouth. The sea was calm but the air felt close and warm and there was very little wind, just a few fussy breezes that here and then whisked a wave top into foam. The sky had been clear but was now growing hazy. I remembered the earlier rainstorm and eyed the weather doubtfully. Dunstan did the same and remarked that he thought it was changing. 'Let's hope it doesn't change too fast.'

We adopted Tamzin's idea and marked out two draughts boards on the floor of the cave. A few games were played but in a lacklustre fashion. No one could concentrate. The hours dragged and the closeness in the atmosphere grew stronger. The sky was noticeably darkening.

Some relief came when, after a very long time, Brockley saw Griffin Brown's *Sunrise* out in the bay. He recognized the red sails. 'And Christopher's on her – yes, I'm sure he is, someone is waving to us, anyhow.'

Sometime after that, Brockley and I, once more gazing out from the cave mouth, saw that *The Sunrise* had acquired a companion vessel, bigger than herself. We heard shouts flying to and fro between her and *Sunrise*. 'Friend or foe?' asked Brockley tensely.

The tide was well up by this time and *The Sunrise* drew closer. Presently, Griffin, at the tiller, was able to call up to us. 'She be *Cormorant*, Cap'n Jerome's ship. She'm changing course to take you off. Jerome's friendly! When we hailed her, she weren't on course to come this way. Master Spelton's going aboard her!'

Between the spume from the breaking waves, and the increasingly bad light, I couldn't see *Cormorant* clearly although I could make out that she was changing course. As yet, there was no sign of the enemy.

I have taken many sea journeys in my life but I never learnt very much about ships. Two years later, when I was once more living peacefully at Faldene, Christopher came to visit me with his family, and one afternoon, Brockley took the youngsters out riding while Dale and Mildred fell into a happy discussion about embroidery patterns, and I played draughts with Christopher. As we played, we talked and I reminisced about our escape from the Lizard.

I mentioned my first impressions of *Cormorant* whereupon Christopher pushed the board aside and made believe to bang his head on the table. Looking up again, he said, 'If any sailor could hear you! Really, Ursula! According to you, *Cormorant* consisted of three masts on a boat – a *ship*, you landlubber female – with a squat building at each end and a flat part in the middle!'

'That,' I said, with all the dignity of a middle-aged lady who also happened to be a sister to the queen, 'is what I saw. I am not a seaman. Why should a woman know the correct names for such things?'

'Sir Francis Godolphin would say that women had no need to know such things, but the Killigrew women do, I'm sure.'

'The Killigrew women are the wives and daughters of pirates. Some of them *are* pirates. Your move.'

'Forecastle and aftcastle.'

'What?'

'The names of the two squat buildings.'

'Christopher, dear Christopher, I just don't care. I only care that she came to our rescue, and I would rather not think what might have happened to us instead. It came so near . . . so near. If it hadn't been for Dale! *Your move.*'

As I stood in the cave mouth on that terrifying evening, Christopher suddenly appeared on the deck of *Cormorant*, having got himself aboard without me seeing him. From somewhere, probably Jerome's onboard stores, he had acquired a waterproof cape of thick leather. He shouted up to us. 'Jerome's all right except he's got three bottles of Canary aboard. He started out with four but you can guess where one of them has gone. But he'll help us, don't fear.'

The rising sea by now was just below the cave, casting up white clouds of spray, aided by a strengthening wind. *The Sunrise* was manoeuvring out of the way and *Cormorant* was edging into position below us. Then, much to my alarm, Jerome Killigrew appeared on the deck with a long bow and a shaft and shot at us. The shaft fell between Brockley and me, and I shied back in fright but Brockley, quicker than I to understand, merely picked it up. A thin line was attached to it. He hauled it in. Its further end was knotted firmly into a thin cord, the thin cord was knotted into a thicker one and then came a rope ladder with a stout iron hook on it, which Brockley hitched to the ring in the floor. The ring he had tripped over wasn't for mooring a vessel but for securing a ladder.

Cormorant's sails were down and she was edging closer. A couple of sailors were throwing fenders over to protect her sides from contact with the cliff, and tossing looped painters over what I now saw were hooks, cemented into the cliff. This cave had been in use for a long time.

'Just get down the ladder!' Jerome, a grinning face between a leather hat and a kind of leather jerkin, both gleaming with water, shouted instructions up to us. 'Tide won't get much higher. No time to lose! Come down back'ards, one man behind each woman to keep her steady!'

'Let me go first,' said Dunstan. 'I did plenty of this sort of thing when I was a sailor. I . . .'

'Wait,' said Brockley. 'I think that Captain Jerome is about to have company.'

We stood still, peering into what was now a fading light though mainly because of clouds; it was too soon for nightfall. To our right, the cliff swelled out into a bluff, which masked the view from that direction. I thought it was the bulge in the cliff that sheltered Polgillan. A vessel was now rounding the bluff, a fair-sized ship though not a galleon, sails set and full of the west wind.

Further out, Griffin, who was shortening sail on *The Sunrise*, did not seem aware of the new arrival until there was a loud report and a puff of smoke from her, and Griffin shied in alarm as something evidently just missed him. When he realized, he brought the sail down in a rush, and started frantically rowing to get out of range. There was another shot, apparently just to encourage his departure. Then the new vessel was up against *Cormorant*, fenders out so that the two ships could bump against each other. *Cormorant* was being boarded.

'That's *The Shark*!' said Pearce suddenly. 'Nicholas Rowe's ship – everyone knows her – look at that figurehead, like a shark on its tail, with its mouth open!'

'She's attacking *Cormorant*!' gasped Dunstan angrily. 'She's come for us!' Then he swore, with reason.

He was right. *The Shark*'s sailors were swarming aboard Captain Jerome's vessel. We stood in a horrified row, seeing our fortunes, our hopes, cast into reverse. Christopher was seized and flung down on the deck. We heard Captain Jerome shout something in an angry voice and saw him try to brain an intruder with a bottle, only to have the bottle snatched away and applied to the side of his own head. He too went down. Others of *Cormorant*'s crew were up on deck, armed, fighting back, but it wasn't long before we could see that they were getting the worst of it. To me, it seemed that they were outnumbered. The rope ladder was still dangling from the cave edge. And there on the deck of *Cormorant* was Nicholas Rowe, looking up at us and grinning, damn him.

'I seize the day!' he shouted up to us. 'It's quite safe to come down. The ladder's there. Your position is hopeless, better give in gracefully. There's wine and a good meal awaiting you in the galleon we'll take you to. Her crew don't all drink wine but some do and they'll indulge you – it'll be your last chance to taste it. Come along down, my friends!'

'But he lost a valued groom, didn't he?' gasped Dale. 'Ma'am, didn't you tell me so?'

'I suppose the groom was expendable,' said Brockley grimly, unhooking the ladder. 'I wonder how many people that horse has bitten by now?' He hurled the ladder over the edge of the cave. Nicholas jumped out of the way before the ladder could tumble down on top of him but then kicked it aside and came back to where he could most easily shout to us.

'Very well! We'll have to come and fetch you, that's all. It'll take a little while but someone will soon be unlocking your prison door and you'll be marched out and we'll take you off from Polgillan. The villagers won't help you. They won't dare. If they try anything, we'll pop a few of their lusty young men, or a handsome lass or two, into our bag for sale in a slave market. Don't be fools! We'll send the ladder up again and you can come to us by the short route! We'll look after you!'

'Anyone who comes through our prison door will regret it!' shouted Eleanor, unexpectedly joining in with gusto. 'There's cooking gear just outside it. We could all fancy a little roast pirate for our next meal!'

We all looked at her with astonishment. From below came laughter and a few hearty cheers. Nicholas's upturned face was grinning more widely than ever. Even in the bad light, we could see his teeth. He shouted up to us.

'Did you know, Mistress Eleanor, that you were taken because we had been told we were to find a certain type of lady and you matched the requirements so well? Now you seem to match them even better! We were told, there's a buyer for a dignified English lady of standing; there will be such piquancy in having such a one to serve in the kitchen or wash my lady's back. And if she is difficult about it, well, there is much enjoyment in taming intransigent slaves. You match to perfection! You have just raised your price!'

'I'll cut my own throat first!' Eleanor bawled down to him, and then clenched her fists at the sound of Nicholas' laughter.

'Our friend Nicholas has a young army with him!' Brockley

said. 'They're all over *Cormorant* like ants over a caterpillar. This is hopeless!'

From somewhere, however, I could hear some noisy banging, as though a door were being hammered by angry fists. Then, all of a sudden, the odds were changing. With a crash and a roar, a whole lot of *Cormorant*'s crew, who must have been confined below and had now broken out, charged up onto the deck, waving makeshift weapons. One man had a hammer, several others were brandishing splintery shafts of wood, probably from a smashed door, another had what, peering down, I thought was surely the leg of a table. They set about the invaders from *The Shark* with zest and fury. Once again, her decks became a battlefield.

'This is a disgrace!' Eleanor was seething. 'We are being fought over like a bone between two dogs and we can do nothing, *nothing* to intervene and save ourselves!'

Anna, beside her, was cursing like a man, or possibly like one of the travelling mummers she had once lived with and Gervase Pearce was cursing even louder and promising heaven that he would fight until he died. Dale and Tamzin were holding on to each other and crying.

The sky was lightening a little; a shaft of the setting sun was casting a red glow from the west. Down on the deck of *Cormorant*, Captain Jerome, groggy, shaking and still, incredibly, clutching his wine bottle, had been brought to face Nicholas. Two men were holding him up. It looked as though Nicholas was demanding that Jerome should do something because Jerome was shaking his head vehemently. As we stared, Nicholas struck him and then his escort dragged him away.

'I fancy,' said Brockley, 'that Jerome is refusing to call his men off.'

'And I thought we were safe!' mourned Dale.

TWENTY
The Lady And The Shark

J erome was hustled out of sight. Anna let out a cry of anger and pity. Nicholas heard it, turned to look up and favoured us once again with that odious grin of his. He spoke to one of Jerome's men, who was just being dragged past him, and laughed, in a sneering kind of way.

The battle was still continuing and, once again, it seemed that Jerome's men were getting the worst of it, for all their fervour. Nicholas pulled a trumpet from his belt and sounded a call, and about a dozen men who had apparently been kept in reserve, now came scrambling out of *The Shark* to add to the mayhem on deck of *Cormorant*. Jerome's gallant followers were being seized and flung over the side like bundles of rubbish. Anna was sobbing aloud.

All this time, we had been powerless spectators, watching, swearing, sobbing, while others fought over us and our futures were batted to and fro like the balls in a tennis tournament. It was Dale who changed that.

I realized then – not for the first time but this time more sharply than ever before – that I had underestimated her. She had been crying, with Tamzin in her arms, but now she put Tamzin gently back from her and spoke to her. Tamzin at once wiped her eyes and the two of them went to stoop over one of the pieces of fallen rock. It was a heavy piece, a small boulder, in fact, but they started trying to push it.

I called out, 'What are you two doing? You can't move that!' and then I saw that they could, just. They heaved and it rolled, and then they shoved with all their might and it grated on the cave floor but it moved, and then moved again. They were using all their strength. Brockley shouted, 'Fran, Tamzin, what on earth are you doing? You can't possibly . . .' But neither of them had breath enough to answer him and probably wouldn't have tried, anyway. Pushing, heaving, rolling, making the rock scrape and topple and gradually shift nearer to the edge of the cave, they made progress.

Brockley was still expostulating and wanting to pull Dale back but I seized his arm. 'Leave them! Can't you see what they're doing? They've nearly done it! Oh, well done, what a brilliant idea . . .!' I let go of Brockley and ran to help. The three of us worked together. Then Brockley understood and was with us and so was Pearce. The rock moved more easily now. We got it to the edge. Dale peered over and gasped, 'A bit left. A bit to the left!'

We all moved round a little to change the direction of our thrust. Dale peered over the edge once again. Then she stepped behind it and as one man, we stood back and let her have the honour of the final shove. She gave it such a hearty one that she came near to going over the edge herself. Brockley seized her and jerked her back. She sat down with a grunt and he crouched beside her, holding her, saying something to her and from below there was a horrible scrunch and a scream and then a roar of many voices, babbling, cheering, screeching.

The effect on the men of *Cormorant* was astounding. Suddenly, her men with their weird assortment of weapons began to behave as though molten lava had been poured into their veins. A moment ago they had been in defeat but not now. Now, they were fighting like demons and it was Nicholas's men who were being hurled over the side into the unfriendly sea. Those that were still fighting with any vigour had probably not realized what had happened. Others were clustered round Dale's rock. The rock was on top of something, a something that had a head at one side and some legs at the other, all twitching and jerking, while from under the rock, like the juice from apples in a cider press, a crimson juice was oozing. 'Quick!' gasped Dale. 'More rocks! Hurry!'

A few minutes later, almost all the loose rocks in our cave had been thrown or toppled over the edge, *Cormorant* had two holes in her deck and someone down there was waving wildly, trying to say *stop throwing rocks at us!* Nicholas's crew seemed to be surrendering and Jerome's victorious men were making prisoners of them, not in *Cormorant*'s hold which had presumably been wrecked during the breakout of the defenders earlier, but in the hold of their own ship, *The Shark*. Jerome's men were taking her over. Captain Jerome, somehow back on his feet again, appeared on his damaged deck. 'Hold on up there! We'll get the ladder up to you again very soon! Well done! Just be patient a little longer!'

Christopher too had survived. Also limping, but very much alive, he was waving to us. '*Shark* is ours! She's where we're going to drink a toast to the gallant lady who thought of throwing rocks. I saw her do it!'

'I think you've saved us,' I said to Dale, and hugged her.

Brockley was staring out to sea. 'What is it?' I asked him.

'It's hard to see; the light is so poor,' he said, 'but I think there's another vessel out there in the distance. Hove to, I fancy. Not a galleon but bigger than *The Shark* or *Cormorant*. Is she part of all this? Is she going to join in and if so, which side is she on?' He added wryly, 'We've run out of rocks.'

I stared into the distance but I couldn't see what Brockley had seen.

'This is the strangest battle I could ever imagine, or not imagine!' Brockley said. 'Cornishmen are fighting Cornishmen! All these crews probably come from the same set of families. Down there, there were brothers fighting brothers, fathers fighting sons, uncles fighting nephews. This is the weirdest place I've ever known. Cornwall is a world to itself. I've been watching that ship in the distance. I think she's moving off. Whatever she is, she doesn't seem to be reinforcements for Nicholas.'

'God be thanked for that,' I said.

TWENTY-ONE
Cllimbing Down

'That suggestion, that the women should each go down the ladder with a man behind her to steady her, was good sense,' said Dunstan. 'My seaman days may be behind me but I can still climb rigging; I go fishing now and again with a friend in Penzance who has a good-sized boat and I've climbed up his rigging a time or two. Let little Tamzin come with me and we'll show you all how easy it is.'

Before the ladder was once again sent up to us, there had been some rearrangements down below. *Cormorant*, with her broken deck and her angry captives in the hold, had been manoeuvred out of the way and now *The Shark* was below us. The *Serpent* was moving off, and Christopher shouted up to us that as her services were no longer required, she was going home.

As for us, we were thankful to learn that we wouldn't after all have to land on the deck where Nicholas lay crushed under the rock that Dale had dropped on him, and the deck was crimsoned with his oozing blood. I called down to Christopher, to ask what was to be done with him, but Christopher replied shortly, 'He's dead. That was an inspired shot if ever I saw one. We'll treat him with decency, take him ashore and give him a funeral; the Killigrews will expect it. Now, the first pair if you please.'

Tamzin, so timid in everyday life, turned out to have no fears when it came to rope ladders. Young, active and now, it seemed, with excellent nerves, she joined Dunstan on the ladder without hesitation. The two of them receded down it at a remarkable and seemingly effortless speed. They passed through a cloud of spray as they did so and when they landed on the deck where Christopher received them, I heard him say something about *soaking wet skirts; dry clothes in the cabin down below* and saw him point at a door in what I eventually learned was the aftcastle. Tamzin vanished through it.

Jerome came forward, happily brandishing another bottle and shouted for the next pair. Brockley and Dale responded. Dale looked petrified and Brockley's ankle was clearly paining him but she didn't protest and if Brockley's face was grim when he got himself onto the ladder, he still did so with assurance and when he told Dale to turn her back, reach down with one foot and let him position it, she did so obediently. She said afterwards that her success with the rock had given her courage. They went down, slowly, but safely.

We were running out of male escorts but Christopher came to our aid. Though he was clearly injured, he still managed to climb the ladder. He said he would take Anna down and then come back for me. Perhaps Mistress Eleanor could go down with Pearce.

'You'll be safe as can be with me behind you,' said Pearce, grinning at Eleanor.

And then, so to speak, we ran aground. Eleanor could not face the rope ladder. At the sight of it, she backed away, sobbing, saying that she wasn't a monkey, she couldn't climb down that thing; she would fall off for certain and that man Pearce would paw her, too. There could well have been some truth in that, I thought, eyeing Pearce and distrusting his grin. I said I would change places with Eleanor and if Pearce pawed me, then as soon as we reached the deck of *Cormorant* I would hit him so hard that he would think I'd brought a rock along with me.

Pearce promised ardently that he wouldn't paw anyone or misbehave in any way but it did no good. Eleanor would not trust herself with him and she wouldn't trust herself on that ladder either. No one could expect her to, she said, she was a lady, ladies weren't made for such things. She sat on the cave floor and cried. Christopher took Anna down; she was tight-lipped and silent, obviously frightened, but she obeyed instructions with admirable courage and they reached the ground safely. He shooed her through the door to the cabin below and then we saw him in close talk with Jerome.

There were movements aboard that we couldn't make out and then Jerome came up, drawing a rope behind him. As soon as he was in the cave, panting slightly and exuding a wine laden breath, he said to Pearce, 'Help me pull this in. It's heavy.'

The two of them laid hands to the rope and hauled. 'What in God's name is on the end of this?' Pearce enquired, astonished, as a mass of fishing net slid over the cliff edge and into the cave. 'Spread it out,' said Jerome, busily detaching the rope from the net.

Once he and Pearce had spread the net over the cave floor, Jerome said to the tearful Eleanor, 'Sit down in the middle of that.'

Eleanor gasped and protested and Jerome, swearing, pulled a smallish bottle out from some hidden pocket, held her nose and forced a good swig down her, saying that it would give her heart. He then picked the spluttering Eleanor up bodily, dumped her on her back on the net and nodded to Pearce and between them they pulled all the sides of the net together and secured them with the rope. Eleanor squealed in panic, but they ignored her, heaved the palpitating bundle of netting over the edge and lowered it. It passed through a cloud of spray and Eleanor shrieked. But a moment later, it made a gentle landing on the deck and we saw Eleanor being unwrapped by Brockley and Dale.

'She'd have made a terrible slave,' I remarked.

'You think so?' said Jerome. 'One good beating and she'd be using all those tears to wash someone's kitchen floor, meek as a dear little lamb. Would you like to come down with me? Pearce, you can come on your own.'

A few minutes later we were all down, and all drenched from the spray. Christopher said to me, 'After I'd talked to you through the door in the cave, I went back by way of the trapdoor and the crevice into the cold room and while I was in the house that time, I made a dash upstairs and grabbed an armful of clothing from your bedchamber, Ursula, and from the Brockleys' as well. I piled everything into a sack I found in the storeroom. That's where I got all the dry things from. I knew you'd get wet if you had to use that ladder. Down you go. I brought cloaks, as well. Watch your footing on the companionway.'

I went, climbing down the wooden steps, with my soaked skirts clinging clammily round my legs. I reached a lower level and saw a half open door in front of me. Inside I found a cabin, dimly lit through two portholes filled with thick glass. The other women were there, getting themselves into dry gowns, and I thankfully seized a gown for myself. It was one of my own and I didn't forget to transfer the contents of my pouch. I hoped that their bath in seawater spray wouldn't make my picklocks rusty and I made a point of taking them out and rubbing them on my dry skirt. When we were all dry and dressed, we came out of the cabin and called to our equally wet menfolk to come and change their clothes.

When most of us had all reassembled on deck, we found a dark sky and humid air, thin in the lungs. Stormy weather was coming.

The Shark was putting about. 'We're making for Polgillan and Cliff House,' Captain Jerome said. 'My second mate's taking *Cormorant* to Porthleven, the port for Helston and he'll ask Sir Francis for an escort to collect our prisoners from Porthleven. While you've been getting dry we've shifted them into what's left of *Cormorant*'s hold. In chains.'

He emitted a deep, chesty laugh. 'She has two great big holes in her deck. Two of your rocks did that, Mistress Brockley: crashed through into the cabin below them and one crashed through the cabin floor as well, and if I hadn't had some bales of wool in the hold, it would probably have gone through the bottom of the ship and sunk her. But half of the hold is still undamaged and that's where we've stowed them. Mistress Stannard, when we get to Polgillan, will you take us in at Cliff House for a while. I don't like the look of the weather. Most of my sailors have friends in Polgillan; they're all local fellows and I expect they'll get beds and food there. But maybe I and my first mate and Mr Spelton could sup with you while the storm passes. Mr Spelton's below having a cut on his thigh dressed. I have a sailor who is skilled at such things.'

'Of course you can. You'll be more than welcome,' I told him. I spoke gravely and politely, trying to maintain my dignity. Inside myself, I wanted to sit down and sob with relief, the relief of being again among friends, the relief of being saved from . . . whatever would have awaited me in Constantinople . . . the relief of knowing that the Brockleys and nice little Tamzin and indeed all of us who had been rescued from that damned cave were safe along with me.

Captain Jerome looked at me, grinned and shouted something

to a sailor, who grinned back, disappeared below and came back, somewhat predictably, I thought, with a wine flask. Jerome handed it to me with a bow.

'Take a good heartening drink of that, missus. Cures the shakes like magic, that does. Didn't you see it doing wonders with Missus Eleanor there?'

Eleanor flushed, and then raised her chin and turned away. I was tempted to do the same. *Good, heartening swig. Missus! Dries shakes like magic!* I knew quite well that by *shakes* he meant *tears*. I was Mistress Ursula Stannard, half-sister to Her Majesty and I hadn't shed any yet! But they were just below the surface and Captain Jerome knew it. But I owed him a great deal. So, I smiled and thanked him and took the recommended swig. It scorched down my gullet, hit my astounded stomach like a red-hot coal and then, suddenly, spread throughout every vein in my body, imparting warmth and goodwill and quelling any desire to sit down and sob. Jerome said, 'Your man Brockley has an injured ankle, I see. He had better go below and let my medically gifted sailor deal with it.'

'Tell me,' I said, 'how is it that Griffin Brown was so certain that yours would be a friendly vessel and that you weren't as ready as Nicholas Rowe to ship us all off to Constantinople?'

'Griffin's a familiar figure hereabouts. He always ferried Mr Wells to and fro. I know him and he knows me. He is no fool. My fellow Killigrews aren't fools, either. Who wants to conspire with a sot like me? In my cups I might say anything to anyone.'

'He still took a risk,' I said. 'But thank God he did. Master Killigrew, I think that your medically gifted sailor had better sup with us as well. If he wishes to, of course. All the others who were with me in the cave will come to supper as well. Cliff House is well found, believe me.'

TWENTY-TWO
A Tempting Morsel

Night was falling when *The Shark*, under oars, nosed into the little harbour at Polgillan.

Our arrival had been witnessed and a crowd of villagers were waiting to greet us, doubtfully at first, but when they saw Christopher waving to them from *The Shark* and the landing craft being lowered, they ran forward to help us ashore. Griffin, it seemed, had warned them of *The Shark*'s evil intentions. He hadn't seen our victory and none of them knew of it until they saw us arriving in triumph. The first mate of *Cormorant*, Richard Hunt, was with us. He was a businesslike fellow with a square and sturdy build, sandy hair and the far-seeing, blue-grey eyes that so many seamen seem to have. He said that he would see to everything and get the men dispersed among the villagers, some of whom were their friends. One or two, in fact, were their kin. He would then follow us up the cliff; the storm would break any moment and the ladies had had enough.

Jerome said very well, and because I now felt very tired, I suggested that we hire the two mules. Brockley, whose foot was obviously paining him, could ride double with Dale while I could ride with Eleanor. Anna and Tamzin were younger and agreed that they could manage on foot. When at last we were all at the top of the cliff, I led the women indoors while Brockley and Christopher stabled the mules, saying grimly that if Tremaine was there, they would make a prisoner of him.

On the ship, and as we climbed the cliff, the hot stickiness of the air hadn't been so noticeable but indoors, the air was stifling. Dale threw a kitchen window open. Tamzin reached for the wood basket and began to get the fire going and I took everyone else into the parlour. Dale and I set about serving wine all round. Captain Jerome was very appreciative of our Canary. I went back to the kitchen to see how Tamzin was getting on and to decide what kind of supper we could produce, when Brockley and Christopher came back to say that there was no sign of Tremaine, which hadn't surprised them.

'We've got the horses into shelter,' Brockley said. 'And just as well.' He looked towards the kitchen window. 'By the look of that sky and the way it's so sticky . . .'

Without warning, the sky split into a blazing zigzag as though heaven were a furnace and its floor had just ruptured. A split second later there came a huge rumbling crash of thunder, like a cosmic landslide. We crowded to the windows to look. Then, as if the lightning and thunder had released it, a downpour descended.

Simultaneously, as if the storm that released the rain had also released something inside me, the tears of relief, of blessed thankfulness, that I had held back for so long, finally burst forth, streaming down my face. But a sudden gust of wind flung the downpour against the windows and rain blew in through the one that Dale had opened. Tamzin, exclaiming, pulled it shut again and I wiped my tears away with a drying up cloth. They mingled with the rain and no one ever saw them. There was just the one outburst and then I was once more dignified Mistress Stannard, just the same as ever.

Somehow or other, Tamzin, Dale and I conjured up a supper for nearly a dozen hungry people.

The businesslike Mr Hunt had climbed or possibly staggered up the cliff with a codfish wedged into a basket and there were two cooked capons in the cold room. Brockley found an unopened keg of wine in the storeroom and broached it. I don't know what sort of wine it was. It was richly crimson, not very sweet but decidedly strong. It soared into my head as though it had taken wing.

So, while the thunder rolled and the lightning intermittently augmented the candlelight and the rain beat upon the windows, we gathered round the table in the dining room and we ate and we drank and when we had finished our much-needed meal, we drank some more and Joseph Dunstan started to sing, a well-known song that had been sung in every tavern and at every happy gathering for about the last six months. Anna joined in.

Then they stopped and Dunstan said, 'Mrs Stannard, do you have any musical instruments?'

'I brought a lute with me from home,' I said, 'and there's a spinet in the parlour but it's out of tune.'

'I'll see to that,' said Dunstan. 'Madam, please bring us your lute.'

Between the lute and the spinet, rapidly brought to tuneful life under Joseph Dunstan's expert fingers, we created a musical evening. Eleanor turned out to have a very good voice, deeper than Anna's and she not only sang a duet with Anna, but also, with a completely straight face, favoured us with a solo perfor- mance of a song about a bewildered gentleman who had only coaxed a young lady into his bed to keep her warm on a winter evening and was now living with his son, who looked so like her.

She followed that with another song about a sailor who had seven wives in seven countries and each was special because one was beautiful and one could cook and one could dance; another played music but couldn't sing and one sang like an angel but could play no instrument, another could embroider and make wonderful shirts for him and one knew all the games of love- making and another produced the bonniest children but if only he could find a wife who combined all these virtues, what a happy man he would be. She sang that with a straight face, as well. There were some interesting facets to Eleanor's personality.

Our gathering, therefore, turned into a party, a merry, noisy and frankly wine-soaked party. By the end of the evening, Jerome and Hunt were too far into their cups to go down the cliff to their ship. Indeed, Captain Jerome had somehow obtained possession of one entire settle, put a cushion under his head and fallen asleep. I found a rug to put over him, and we organized the rest of our sleeping arrangements, which wasn't too difficult, since we did have six bedchambers and that was quite enough to go round.

In the morning, the storm was gone and the sun was out. Several people (but not Jerome) said they had headaches and didn't want much breakfast. It was a scanty one anyway: yester- day's rolls, butter, cream and honey and a few leftover capon slices. On the previous night, Tamzin hadn't set any bread to rise.

However, the mules must be taken back to Polgillan. Captain

Jerome and Richard Hunt said they would do that. In any case, they wanted to get back to their ship, collect the crew and then sail across the bay to Penzance, at the united request of Eleanor, Anna and Joseph Dunstan. Eleanor and Anna had shared a room and had made friends. Anna was to accompany Eleanor home.

'I think of taking her into my service,' Eleanor said. 'A useful maidservant with a beautiful singing voice can be a good addition to a household. She's a plain little thing but I will soon turn that untidy brown hair of hers into a glossy coil and I have a lotion that will do wonders for her skin.'

Eleanor was reverting to her ordinary dictatorial nature and clearly had no qualms about saying all this in Anna's hearing.

Pearce did not want to go to Penzance. 'My dear late employer Juniper Penberthy has put it about that I drowned Beryon Lander. I didn't but if I walk openly through the town, someone will pounce. If you are likely to see Sir Francis Godolphin, Mrs Stannard, perhaps you would clear my name. He is the Sheriff of Cornwall, after all. Meanwhile, if you'll agree, Mr Killigrew, I'd like to ship with you and learn to be a seaman.'

'I'll give you a trial,' Jerome said. 'Mr Spelton, are you for Penzance as well?'

'No, not yet. I have business to discuss with Mrs Stannard first,' Christopher said.

As we stood outside, watching *The Shark* sail away, I said to Christopher, 'How is it that you were so sure that Jerome could be trusted that you actually hailed his ship and brought him to our rescue?'

'Oh, that. Well, firstly, he's a drunk and therefore a bad conspirator. Secondly, Sir Francis trusts him. I know you don't like Sir Francis, Ursula, but he really is not a wantwit. If he says that Jerome is safe, then Jerome is safe.'

'I see. Well, it turned out to be true. Now, what business is it that you have with me? Aren't you going back to the Progress to go on with your work in disguise?'

'Come inside and call the Brockleys,' Christopher said. 'I want to talk to all of you. You're right, of course. The Progress is a trap but so far it hasn't caught anyone and we're beginning to fear that it never will. But it has occurred to me that you may be able to help.'

When the four of us were gathered in the parlour, Christopher said, 'Sir Francis wouldn't want me to talk about this to you. He was angry with me when I insisted on travelling to Cornwall with you and staying with you in Cliff House to help in your investigation. As I told Mistress Stannard and she has no doubt told you, he has hauled me back to take part in the Progress.'

'She hardly needed to tell us. I've been suspicious of the Progress ever since those harbingers arrived,' Brockley remarked. 'In a real Progress, they would have come months earlier.'

Christopher grinned. 'The whole idea came from the queen, of course. Impersonating Her Majesty is a serious matter. Few people would ever have had such a notion – would never have dared to have it, let alone put it into action. We tried to put a reasonably convincing entourage together even if it is only a tenth the size that a real one would be. Sir Francis hired some travelling players to help out. Some actors are so used to playing female parts that they're more convincing females than real ones. They can play the ladies-in-waiting as well as put on helmets and look like soldiers. Also, Her Majesty helpfully packed her own band of players into wagons and sent them to Cornwall at a fast trot and the use of the royal remount system. They were here in three days.'

'But surely . . .' Dale was puzzled. 'The people you stayed with while the Progress travelled – did they know about the pretence or not?'

'One or two. Most of the time, we've tried to make our hosts truly believe that they're entertaining Elizabeth. We do it by keeping whoever is playing the queen so closely surrounded by ladies and guards that her hosts never get near enough to look at her properly.

'We have had to let town councils into what is happening,' Christopher added regretfully. 'We do that as we go along. No one has objected – no honest man wants Cornwall to be a hornets' nest of slavers. It's bad enough at ordinary times, with the corsair attacks that we've never managed to prevent. Our so-called Progress assembled on the Devon side of the Tamar, crossed the Tamar in style, and made the first stop in Cornwall when it reached Launceston. Our unfortunate hosts, whether in the know or not, have had to lay on entertainments and find housing for people and animals at high speed. And all the while, we've been trying to give any interested slavers every chance to snatch her ersatz majesty but have they?' said Christopher bitterly. 'No, they have not, and the Progress is nearing its end.'

'The slavers have probably realized that it isn't genuine,' I said.

'I hope not. We've put on a good show. Very likely, the perpetrators aren't familiar with the way Progresses are organized – we've gambled on that. But alas, no one has tried to kidnap any of our Elizabeths though it's been made easy for them. Her Majesty three times took it into her head to ride on Bodmin Moor with only a small escort, and she kept outdistancing them. No one interfered, alas.'

'Bodmin's inland, in the middle of bleak and empty moors,' I said. 'There's nowhere to hide, no way of going to ground, as it were.'

'No doubt. Well, Penzance is our last chance. Our best chance in a way, since it's deep in the heart of the district where most of the disappearances have happened. Ursula, whoever is running this nasty trade has still evaded not only capture but kept his name, or their names, hidden. Juniper Penberthy is part of it but she's not its head. She hasn't the . . . stature, the intelligence. And that isn't just Sir Francis' opinion; I agree with him and so do others of his household, people who know her. All that is clear is that there is – there *must* be – big money behind this, and an organization too big to be disbanded just because we have our eyes on Juniper. We also have our eyes on Alexander Killigrew, by the way.'

'Why him?' I asked, surprised.

'We've been suspicious of him for a long time. He doesn't make a living from rents, in a proper, gentlemanly fashion. He trades. His *Serpent* is bigger than either *Cormorant* or *The Shark* and regularly makes trading trips to Constantinople with woollen cloth and tin and a number of her crew are Turkish. We have been watching him.'

'Why hasn't he – and Juniper – been taken and made to talk . . .?' Brockley asked.

'We . . . that is, the queen, Lord Burghley, his son Sir Robert Cecil, and a few agents like myself, have come across large-scale

plots before. One thing is a feature of most of them. The individuals involved don't know too much about each other. That
way, even if one of them is caught and handed over to Richard
Topcliffe, he can't get much out of them. Often enough, they
just die on his hands and little is learned. Besides, we aren't sure
they're guilty. So, for the moment, we've left them alone, hoping
that one of them will lead us to their principals.'

Brockley said, 'I thought I saw another vessel hovering out at
sea but the light was too bad to be sure. But if Alexander
Killigrew's ship is one of those that transports captives to the
Mediterranean, what I saw could have been the *Serpent*.'

'Indeed?' Christopher was interested. 'You may well be right.'

'You said I could help,' I said. 'You haven't yet told me
how.'

At that point, Tamzin appeared with a tray containing a jug
of wine and four glasses. 'Fetch a glass for yourself and join us,
please, Tamzin,' I said. To Christopher I said, 'Tamzin was
kidnapped with us. She was in danger of being sold into slavery
along with us. She has lost the man she was going to marry. We
shan't get William back. He must have sailed before us. She is
entitled to know all this.'

I looked at Christopher very straightly, and after a moment he
nodded. 'Very well,' he said. 'This is a most unusual household,
although Mildred would very likely feel as you do. Pour wine
for yourself, Tamzin. I have something to tell you.'

In brief, he repeated what he had told me, and at the end of
it, received a surprise.

'Well, who'd have thought it? A pretend Progress, processions
and so on and they harbingers. Only, sir, I more or less did think
it. You see, I thought I recognized one of they harbinger men.
Couldn't think where I'd seen him afore, kept wondering, thinking
about him and only a few nights ago it come to me. He's an
actor. Seen him at a play I saw last year in Penzance; out in the
marketplace on three evenings, lucky with the weather, it was.
Three warm summer evenings one after the other. That St Leger
fellow was the hero. He's no courtier, I thought. And then it all
started coming together. If one of the harbingers isn't a real one,
then maybe none of it's real. All a pretence business to catch the
kidnappers, that's what I thought.'

'You must keep silent,' I began, but Tamzin was nodding. 'That I understand, Mrs Archer.'

I turned to Christopher. 'I suppose you sent me those imitation harbingers because I would probably expect them.'

'You think we were trying to fool you into believing in the Progress? We were, against my will. I would have told you all about our plans but Sir Francis forbade it. He said it would just complicate matters. Let her get on with her ladylike investigations, he said, and we'll get on with the real ones.'

I snorted indignantly, but Christopher just laughed. Then he said, 'What I want from you is simple enough and I haven't consulted Sir Francis about it. You can help by coming to Penzance, abandoning your pretence of being Mistress Archer, presenting yourself as Mistress Ursula Stannard, half sister to the queen and saying that the queen has asked you to join her retinue while she is in Penzance. Your real name is quite well known, even in Cornwall.'

'Then why was I pretending to be Catherine Archer?'

'Because you are *also* a distant cousin of Edmund Wells and came to Cornwall to look after his property in the hope that he will return; if not, to see to his estate. It was a private family matter and you wished to attend to it in private. But now that the queen is in Penzance and therefore close to you, she has called you to join her. I want you to act as evidence that the Progress is real. You are to be its guarantee, as it were. You are to talk about it, whenever you can, in an indiscreet fashion. Not too obviously but indiscreet all the same. It is such a privilege to be with her on this occasion, you were so touched to be asked, the queen likes Cornwall so much, has eaten shark for the first time, has admired the Cornish hedgerows that are made of patterned brick . . . you will know what to say.'

'To whom?'

'I will arrange for that.'

Tamzin had poured the wine. We had all sat down by now and begun to sip. Christopher said, 'There is one part of our trap that I want you to know about. We've played it many times in vain but we still have hopes of it. When you came to the joust at Arwenack, did you notice a blue tent?'

'Not especially, no.'

'Wherever we stay, some of our entourage has had to sleep in tents. There always are some. The blue tent has a special purpose, however. No one sleeps there. It is put up near to the so-called queen when she's watching a play or a joust or hearing a debate. Whenever she's watching an entertainment outside.'

Christopher was smiling broadly. 'It's a bright blue tent, longish. It's a retiring room for the queen, where she can go between events or the different scenes of a play. She can take one or two of her ladies with her or not, as she pleases. She can change her clothes. Wine and snacks are always ready there. Inside, the tent is divided into two. The refreshment room is the larger one and the smaller one is a necessary room. Each compartment has an outer door of its own and inside, there is a door between them. When Her Majesty – or whoever is playing her part; several of us take turns at that – wishes to use the blue tent, we so arrange matters that she goes alone across an open space. It's an unspoken invitation, as it were, but so far, no one has accepted it.

'Another thing we do now and then is to drive a high-sided cart up to the other side of the tent, seemingly to make deliveries – of food and drink and so forth. That too is an open invitation to them to send a cart of their own, pretending to bring deliveries but really to seize the so-called queen and rush her away. We have also had a couple of Sir Francis' men going out into taverns, appearing to get themselves sodden on ale or cider and gossiping about that blue tent. Not too much, that would be suspicious in itself, but a little.

'But as yet,' said Christopher regretfully, 'no result. The blue tent is something else for you to gossip about when you come as yourself, Ursula. I am also to be part of an ambush in the blue tent when the queen's in the marketplace in Penzance.'

'What programme has been arranged for the royal visit to town?' I asked him.

'A throne has been set up in the marketplace, where the queen can sit to listen to an address from the mayor. It's in the open air, though if the weather turns bad it will all have to go inside the town hall. Anna is to sing a song specially written for the occasion. Women don't perform in public, so she will be behind a screen, and the songwriter – he did both the music and the words – will take the bow for them both. Then the queen will retire for a short rest and after that she will return to her throne to watch a short playlet and the children of the town will perform a dance. Then Her Majesty will withdraw again. She is scheduled to begin her journey home the next day. Only that is to be by sea, as far as Portsmouth and then by land – privately, not as Progress – to Whitehall. Now, will you and you Brockleys, come to Penzance tomorrow and set about making our imitation queen look like a really tempting morsel?'

I said, 'Exactly when does this tempting morsel arrive in Penzance?'

'Next Tuesday, the twelfth day of July,' said Christopher. 'And perhaps then, if you play your part convincingly, the enemy will think that after all, the queen really is here in Penzance and they will try to seize her, which will bring them into the open. We will lay hands on them. I don't deny that there will be danger though we will protect you as well as we can. You will always have armed men near you. For your part, you have only to talk, to say the right things to the people I indicate. Will you do it?'

The Brockleys were looking harassed already but only one answer was possible.

'I will,' I said.

TWENTY-THREE

Apparition

We set off for Penzance the next day, which was Saturday. Tamzin was frightened of being left alone in Cliff House and I sent her home to her parents for a week. I paid her for that week and added something extra so that she could give some money to her family.

Griffin took us across to Penzance as usual. I began my new task by explaining to him that I was not Mistress Archer but Mistress Stannard and we were all taken aback to learn that Griffin had had his suspicions. Apparently Wells had several times stated quite firmly that he had no relatives at all. But here was a lady saying she was his cousin, and after all, even if it were a few years back, Mistress Stannard had been to Penzance before – he'd seen her then and I looked like her. I told him that my royal sister had asked me to join her other ladies during her stay in Penzance and I added in a firm voice that whatever Mr Wells might have said, I really was his distant cousin. Wells had probably just forgotten that I existed. Griffin said he could well believe that, and he'd be in the crowd when the mayor gave his speech.

At Penzance, Christopher met us and took us to The Good Catch, where he said we were to stay until the Progress was finished. Here, I once more embarked on my task and told the landlord's wife that I was really Ursula Stannard, half-sister to the queen, only I was also Mr Wells' distant cousin and had come to look after Cliff House in his absence or deal with it if he proved lost for good. I had wished to keep my business private, but the queen, knowing that I was in the district, had called me to join her and what a privilege it was! To my own ears I sounded fulsome and absurd but the landlord and his wife seemed to find it all quite reasonable.

I praised the comfort of the room they had given to me and the landlord's wife brought out a comestible I had never seen before, saying that it was a dish called a Cornish pasty. I enjoyed it and wondered if the queen would be offered one when she arrived.

After that, throughout Saturday, Christopher whisked us all from place to place. He took us to see the men of the Penzance fishing fleet. Several of them already knew me as Catherine Archer. I duly trotted out the story of my pretence and burbled about the impending visit by Her Majesty, how she had heard that I was in the district and had called me to join her and what a privilege it was.

After the fishermen, Christopher led me round the market, where I talked to suppliers of flour, kegs of ale and wine, firewood and candles and I admitted that I wasn't Mistress Archer but Ursula Stannard and oh, what a privilege it was to have been summoned by the queen . . .

By the end of the morning, I was growing hoarse and Christopher said we had better stop. To overdo it would look suspicious. Tomorrow I would go to church, elegantly dressed, where I would meet some of Her Majesty's escort, who had come on ahead of the main Progress. They would greet me as a friend; to any watching eyes, it would all look genuine. On Monday I would let myself be seen in the town and I might do a little more prattling but not too much. On Tuesday, when the Progress arrived, I would join it.

I carried out these orders. At church on Sunday, I was recognized by Sir Francis Godolphin, who was also present and gave me a sharp look, not at all friendly. I hoped that no watching eyes would notice *that*. After the service, I got myself and the Brockleys away quickly and hurried us back to the inn.

On Monday we went out again and watched Penzance adorning itself to meet the Royal Progress. If the town council were in the know, and presumably they were, they had entered into the spirit of the thing with enthusiasm. I saw bunting being strung across streets or along them, house to house, tree to tree. Colourful pavilions were going up on the outskirts of the town and there was a constant sound of music in rehearsal. On one side of the marketplace, a platform was being constructed, with a throne on it, where the queen would sit to hear the mayor's address, and yes, there behind it was a long blue tent.

I studied this with interest. There was no fencing between the back of the royal dais and the tent, only a cobbled space. There was fencing behind the tent, but this had a wide gate in it, wide enough to let a horse and cart through. A small white tent beside the gate was presumably a guardhouse. It all looked a little ramshackle, somehow.

'It *looks* like a trap,' I said to Brockley. 'Could anyone possibly be fooled?'

'The whole thing seems to me quite absurd,' Brockley said. 'I don't think it can possibly succeed.'

On Tuesday morning, the market was closed but crowds of people were out in the town, all dressed in their best. We too had dressed for the occasion. The storm had refreshed the air for a while but hot weather had resumed since then. Dale and I chose open-necked styles that didn't clutch at our throats. My ruff stood out splendidly behind my head and we both had impressive farthingales.

I said, 'You two had better find somewhere to stand while we listen to the address. I shall have to be with the queen, sitting at her feet on the dais, I expect.'

'It's bound to be longwinded; these addresses always are,' Dale said dolefully. 'My back will start to ache. I wish Tamzin were here. I have been teaching her how to massage me when my back hurts me.'

Tamzin was a dear girl, I thought, and my heart ached for her. William was gone and with him all their hopes and plans for a life together, were gone as well. They might have talked of their possible children, perhaps even planned names for them. Gerald and I had planned Meg's name before she was born.

'If we have a daughter, I would like to call her Margaret,' he had said to me. If Tamzin and William had talked in that way, then Tamzin must now be like someone whose home had fallen apart all round her. She was living amid the ruins. I could only hope that one day – soon – there would be somebody else. And that whoever paid money for William would treat him well.

I found good positions for the Brockleys, just as the sound of hooves and the first part of the queen's mounted escort came clattering through Penzance. This was followed by the so-called queen, on horseback. She was much more convincing than the blue tent arrangements were. A small crown glittered atop the beautifully dressed red wig, and behind the wig rose a mighty ruff, patterned with pearls. Her gown was of white satin embroidered with deep pink roses and she had long ropes of pearls about her neck and from her ears hung earrings of pearls and diamonds. Her side saddle was of scarlet leather with gold edging for cantle and pommel and her red leather reins were scalloped.

This was as good an impersonation of Elizabeth as one could well imagine. In fact, for one staggered moment I wondered if this was indeed the queen. But Elizabeth would never have taken such a risk, or been allowed to, either. And surely, even the craziest kidnapper would realize that. This ridiculous impersonation had no more chance of success than a flea in a furnace.

The imitation ladies followed on, in simpler but still costly array, riding together in a group. A crowd of gentlemen, all dressed in the queen's favourite black and white, came next. Last came a whole lot of wagons, pulled by workhorses (probably local, borrowed, hired or simply grabbed from Cornish farms), presumably containing beds, cooking gear for large numbers and luggage in boxes and hampers. There was one whole wagon full of servants.

It was impressive. It was also all wrong. In a real Progress, those wagons would have come on ahead. Such practical and unlovely items would never be part of the queen's own procession and the servants would have arrived on the previous day or perhaps earlier, to make sure that all the preparations were as they should be. I supposed that there were practical difficulties in creating a complete facsimile.

I left the Brockleys and went to the town hall where I joined the mayor and other dignitaries and waited for the queen to arrive, when they would be presented to her and I would quietly join the ladies who would be with her. This took place as planned, except that the queen, though she did not embrace me, recognized me and welcomed me, her dear sister, who had come to share this auspicious day with her. There was a hum of voices all around me and I couldn't hear the queen very well. I certainly couldn't recognize her voice.

After that, came some refreshments – wine, slices of cake and, I noticed, some pasties – and then the queen was escorted outside to the throne on the platform and the mayor went to a lectern on a humbler dais, facing it. One of the attendant ladies told me that I was to come with her; we were to sit on the steps up to the platform. A fanfare of trumpets sounded, and accompanied by me and three other ladies-in-waiting who looked to me so real that it was very hard to believe that they were male actors, the queen stepped up to her throne.

Four chosen ladies including myself sat on the steps below her. Other attendants, undisguised male ones, stood guard on either side. Opposite to us, behind his lectern, the mayor nervously fingered his chain of office, cleared his throat and began his address.

Longwinded it certainly was though when at last it was over, Anna's singing was worth waiting for. There was an intermission after that, and one of the male attendants announced, in a stentorian voice, that Her Majesty the queen would retire for a short time. On her return, there would be a playlet telling the tale of a young maiden who was afraid to marry a man her father had chosen for her but was obedient to her father and said goodbye to the young man she loved, but then was freed when, at the very altar, proof was brought that groom was married already, and only sought this bigamous wedding because of the maiden's dowry. Her Majesty would then dine with the town council and rest for an hour, and after that, the children of the town would perform a dance.

The queen left the dais and went towards the blue tent. Her four ladies including myself provided an escort as far as the door. She went to the left-hand door, which led straight into the necessary room. And then, with a jolt in the pit of my stomach, I noticed that a small, high-sided cart drawn by a single horse was just approaching the tent, apparently making for the gate on the far side.

If this was one of our own pretended deliveries then it was badly timed. No cart that we had arranged ought to arrive while a royal visit was actually in progress. I supposed that a cart *might* be badly timed by accident. But how careless, how badly arranged . . . and where were the guards who should have turned it back? There was no sign of them!

And that was when, despite the nuisance of my heavy swinging

skirts and the farthingale which banged into people and brought
forth exclamations of annoyance, and the fact that I was supposed
to be part of a decorous group of ladies walking behind their
queen on her way to her retiring tent, I broke away and ran.

Leaving the other ladies behind, I raced ahead of them, holding
my skirts up, afraid I might trip on the cobbles. I stopped outside
the canvas door through which the queen had gone and shouted,
'Are you all right?' There was no answer, yet I heard something,
a kind of scuffle; what sounded like an oath and then something
that was surely a masculine shriek. I plunged through the door.

I am not likely to ever forget what then confronted me. To
this day, or perhaps I should say *night*, I see it in nightmares.
Not often now that I am old, but still, sometimes. Sometimes, in
those dreams, I even smell it.

For the first thing to hit me as I rushed through that door was
the hot, metallic, revolting smell of blood. Choking, I saw before
me a rent in the canvas wall of the tent and through that, I caught
a brief glimpse of a cart. Even as I saw it, it vanished, the horse
started from a stand to a gallop, urged by the crack of a whip.
Horse and cart were gone in an instant.

Here within the necessary room, the floor was covered with
sheeting, originally white but now mostly scarlet. Sprawled on the
floor there were two bodies. Both were male. One looked as though
it had died of a stab wound to his heart; the man had died clutching
his chest and much of the blood had pumped from his wound.

The other was merely a body. It didn't have a head.

Standing over it, sword in hand, was Queen Elizabeth.

For a long, ghastly moment, I almost believed it. The figure
in the white silk gown, with its pretty roses and its ropes of
pearls and its crowned head, looked so utterly and perfectly like
my royal sister that my muscles were twitching in readiness for
a curtsey before I took in that the costly gown was liberally
splashed with blood. The sword the figure held was reddened
and that in its left hand, held away as though for inspection at
a distance, grasped by its thick black hair and dripping sluggish
blood onto the sheeting, was a severed head.

I didn't faint and I wasn't sick. This wasn't because I was hard-
ened, but because I couldn't believe that what I was seeing was

real. Then I saw that though the figure had brown eyes like Elizabeth, they were not her golden brown. This being had eyes of a deeper, warmer shade. A shade I knew. After a moment, waveringly, I said, 'Christopher?'

He laid the head down, carefully, against the neck of the dead man on the floor. All three of the imitation ladies I had abandoned now burst through the door behind me and I realized that in the interior door to the retiring room, two armed men were standing, as paralysed as I was, though with drawn swords. Christopher now wiped his own sword blade on his ruined silken skirts. I said, 'Who is it? Do you know him?'

'It's Jago,' said Christopher. 'The fellow on the floor looks like one of his sons. He is careless with his sons. He cut the throat of the one that hated what his father was doing and threatened to betray him. Oh, Jago said as much, boasted of it, in the few moments while he still thought I was his captive before I sliced his head off. He was trying to convince me that I was helpless in the grasp of a ruthless man. I fancy the madman who rushed out of here just now, through the hole they'd slashed in the canvas, was another of his offspring. This whole thing is very big, Ursula, much bigger than just Juniper on her own. Jago used deep-sea fishing as an alibi while his sons gathered their victims together. They had a cave prison of their own. I daresay there are others like them. Ursula, this horror isn't fit for you to see. Go and collect the Brockleys and go home. We are not at the end of all this yet, not by any means. For now, just get yourself out of it.'

I said, 'But . . .' and then stopped, not knowing what to say.

Christopher said, 'I must maintain the queen's reputation. Our Elizabeth would wish to appear courageously indifferent to a little thing like an attempt to murder her. But you get yourself and the others away. Go on!'

I was passing the lectern on my way back from the town hall, where I had made suitably tearful farewells, when the announcement began. The mayor had a powerful voice and I was passing close to his lectern. I heard him clearly.

An attempt has been made on the queen's life. She is safe because her bodyguard were at hand. The playlet will be performed later, after the queen has had time to rest and has then dined with the town council, as planned. After the playlet, the children of the town will perform their dance. Her Majesty has herself insisted that this should be so. The day's programme will be followed, a little later than intended, that is all.

TWENTY-FOUR
Chess With The Butler

I found the others where I had left them, wondering why I had rushed away as I had. 'Come with me,' I said. 'There was an attempt to abduct the queen, only she's Christopher in disguise and he's swiped the head off one of the would-be abductors. I saw him behead someone once before but it's still a horrible business. We're to go home and I for one can't get there fast enough.'

The Brockleys were as thankful to be going home as I was. I took us to the harbour where we found that nearly all the fishermen had gone into the town to see the queen. However, we did find one gnarled old man who wasn't interested in queens and was taking the chance to laze in the sunshine with an ale flask beside him and a pasty in his hand. He wasn't interested in ferrying us across the bay, either, but money talks and the bribe I offered him had a persuasive voice.

While I was negotiating with him, we heard a voice calling *Mistress Archer* and looked round to see Tamzin running towards us. 'Saw you, I did, just going away from the market!' She was out of breath when she reached us and her words came in gasps. 'If you're going home, can I come? No room at home . . . sleeping on the floor . . . looking after . . . dribbling baby twins. Left them with my sister . . . she's right welcome. Can I fetch my bundle . . . and come? Ma . . . only five minutes from here!'

I said yes, of course. Our ancient ferryman's boat was pulled up on a stretch of shelving beach and it would take a good few minutes anyway to get it launched. In fact, he had just got her afloat when Tamzin came back. As we set off across the bay, she wanted to know what had happened, but Brockley shook his head at her, glanced at our boatman, who just then was busy with his sail, and mouthed *later.*

Most of the Polgillan people, of course, had gone to Penzance for the day, but we found an elderly couple who gave us permission to take the mules. They also offered us some prawns, which Brockley bought. He and Dale took one mule, Tamzin and I the other. Dale was feeling the heat while I was feeling badly shaken, no matter how I tried to hide it, and although Brockley's ankle was now much recovered, the cliff path would still have made it ache. We were all glad of the ride.

Once at home, and by now we really were thinking of Cliff House as home, I filled two flagons with the strong red wine that Brockley had found in the storeroom. Then we sat round the kitchen table and I told them what I had seen.

It was as well that we had the wine at hand. I poured us all a glass before I began, and Dale went so white when I described the apparition in the necessary tent that I seriously feared she would faint. I picked her glass up and thrust it at her. Even Brockley turned a little pale while Tamzin sat there with mouth open and eyes distended. My voice shook as I told them what I had seen. Describing it brought it back to me, much too vividly.

It was true that I had once seen Christopher take a man's head off with a single sweep of his sword. But he hadn't been dressed as Queen Elizabeth at the time. The spectacle in the blue tent had had a new and ghastly quality that had shocked me deeply.

We sat in silence for a few moments, absorbing the horror. Brockley was the first to speak. 'You say that Christopher sent you away, madam. Are we still on duty, or not? If Jago and his sons were behind all this, then surely it's all over? Those sons would be his means of roaming around this end of Cornwall, looking for people who matched the descriptions he'd been given. They could go anywhere and who would ever notice?'

I said, 'I don't think even Jago can have been the top man. Christopher said *we are not at the end of all this yet, not by a long way.* Those were his words. I think we are still on duty, as you have put it, Brockley.'

'But who else could be the one?' Dale wanted to know. 'Not Sir Francis Godolphin himself, surely?'

'I've wondered about that too,' I told her. 'But how we're supposed to find out, is a mystery to me. Alexander Killigrew is another suspect and a likelier one. Perhaps Christopher will contact us soon and then we can talk to him. Meanwhile, we can forget our pretend names. We always were forgetting them, anyway. Brockley, Tamzin will want things from the cold room and would like your escort when she fetches it. We had better have some dinner now.'

'I'd prefer a dozen or so of the real queen's personal guard to escort *me* when I go down there,' said Brockley. 'I must find a way of blocking that crevice up. But I'll fetch what you want, Tamzin. Just tell me. I brought some prawns up from the village. We can have prawn omelettes. You'll want eggs, I suppose.'

'And cheese,' said Tamzin, pulling herself together. 'And there's some honey cakes as well.'

We had a late dinner of prawn omelettes and yesterday's bread and some honey cakes, and then Dale and I went upstairs to rest. A rest was something we both needed, badly. When we came downstairs again, a little over two hours later, we found that Tamzin had taken the mules home and returned and was now planning a supper of salad with veal pies and a gallantyne sauce which could use up some of the old bread. She had set next day's bread to rise. We were fortunate in having an oven. Ovens were expensive because they used up so much fuel. Mr Wells had not been short of money.

We gathered in the kitchen and sat talking. I remarked that since Tremaine had now vanished, it was presumably he who had attacked William and taken him away by means of the cold room trapdoor. Tamzin began to cry and I was trying to comfort her when there was a knock at the door and we heard a familiar voice calling to us. Dale let Christopher in.

'The door wasn't locked but I didn't want just to walk in on you,' said Christopher. 'It should have been locked, by the way. We dare not be careless. Your back and front doors should be kept locked even if it's a nuisance. Am I in time for supper? Can you feed me? I have spent hours and hours answering questions, considering what should be done next, finding out things and cleaning myself up. I made the landlord's wife at The Good Catch bring me three kettles full of hot water and a tub to put it in and I fear I may still smell of blood, even so.'

He sat down at the kitchen table. 'Alexander Killigrew,' he said, 'is now known to be part of this selected slave trade. He has disappeared. So has his ship, the *Serpent*. There's no doubt about it. Before you killed him, Dale, Nicholas sent a boatman from *The Shark* to tell him what was happening – they had expected just to collect you from the cave and Jerome was an unwelcome interruption. You were all to be taken out to the *Serpent* and Alexander would transport you to Constantinople. He had more room on his ship for passengers than *The Shark* has. We took a good many of *The Shark*'s crew prisoner and handed them over to Sir Francis. He had them questioned. We now know who the boatman was and he's been pulled in. The ship you thought you saw in the distance, Brockley, was the *Serpent*. I understand that Nicholas hoped Alexander would send him some help but Alexander evidently decided to get himself out of it. The *Serpent*'s men weren't all that eager to talk, but Sir Francis was insistent. They have been persuaded.'

No one commented, let alone asked how.

'We know quite a lot now,' said Christopher. 'But not as much as we would like. So many of the men we questioned knew very little themselves. Which is what we expected. However, one thing was now clear: Alexander certainly wasn't and isn't the only captain involved in transporting captives abroad. He was just one cog in a complicated machine. He is not its head. You all had a very narrow escape, though.' Christopher spoke with great seriousness. 'If Dale hadn't turned the scales of fortune with a rock, you would have been on the high seas now.

'Well, Nicholas is dead and Alexander has got himself away. I expect he has a pleasant little house in Italy or maybe Spain, ready to go to in an emergency.'

'Alexander didn't apparently think to send a boat ashore to collect Mrs Penberthy,' Brockley remarked. 'He'd have had time. He could have got her aboard by midnight.'

'No, very unchivalrous,' Christopher said. 'At first, of course, she didn't know that she needed to escape. A local lad who regularly delivers milk and cheese to her – and is also now in our pay – went there yesterday. A maidservant took the delivery indoors but the lad did a little snooping. He was noticed and turned away by a couple of indignant grooms but not before he had managed a peep through a window and caught sight of Mistress Penberthy. She was playing chess with her butler.'

'Just calmly playing chess?' Dale gasped.

'Yes, just that,' said Christopher. 'Sir Francis says that he has
let her be, as he did with Alexander, in the hope that she would
lead us to her controller but she has shown no signs of doing
any such thing and so he said he would bring her in. He set about
it personally and took a squad of men to her house. I wasn't one
of the squad but I have heard all about it. When Sir Francis and
his men arrived, she was amazed to find that she was to be
accused of kidnapping you and the others. She exclaimed that it
wasn't her. It must have been someone disguised as her, perhaps.
She has been at home all the time, looking at some chess puzzles.
They help to pass those dark winter evenings that lie ahead. Or
perhaps, well, was Mrs Archer – or Stannard – she said that with
an arch smile . . .'

Brockley made a noise that could only be described as a growl.

'. . . was she ever really kidnapped at all? She is a wealthy
woman and can pay well to persuade others to uphold her fantasies . . .'

'Her *what*?' I shouted.

'She said it was sad but true,' said Christopher, who now
looked as though he was stifling laughter, 'that women of a
certain age did, well, have fantasies sometimes, and such a one
as Mrs Archer – or Stannard – could afford to pay others to
uphold them. If she only had, say three people willing to lie for
her, that would be enough. There would be people who believed
the lies and would pity poor Mistress Stannard and bring her
comforts and make her important.'

'I can't believe any of this,' I said. 'To create an illusion like
that, anyone would need to be as puffed up as a great big pillow
and as conceited as Lucifer!'

The full nature of the insult that Juniper had thrown at me
was gradually revealing itself. I recoiled from it as though it were
the edge of a precipice. 'No one but a madwoman would dream
of such a thing!' I gasped. And was then seized by outrage.

'*Women of a certain age!*' I shouted. I then added, 'I am in
any case past that certain age and when I was in it, I didn't have
any foolish imaginings. I had migraine headaches, that's all. I
have them very rarely now.'

There had been a time when anything like the day's events
would have brought one on but I didn't fear one now. I hadn't

had a headache now for so long that I hoped they were now a thing of the past.

'She can't get away with a tale like that!' Dale said angrily. 'We can *prove* . . . we have witnesses! All the others! Who would even try to bribe Dunstan, or Eleanor? This Penberthy woman is running mad. Is the moon full just now?'

'No. Waning,' said Christopher.

I demanded, 'Is she still at large? Wasn't she arrested?'

'No. Sir Francis pretended to believe her and took his squad away. He thought that as his visit might have upset her enough to stir her, at last, into leading the way to whoever is her master. She may turn to him for help. We don't think it was Jago, by the way. Oh yes, Sir Francis thinks he was well up in their hierarchy but even he didn't have the . . . the stature. As things are, the organization is probably still in existence and we must take great care. Of you, Ursula. You are a prize. You are the sister of Queen Elizabeth. You are as precious as a bag of rubies.'

I was still concerned with Juniper's offensive accusation. 'Does Juniper Penberthy seriously accuse me of bribing sea captains and complete strangers like Pearce and Anna Clay and Eleanor and Dunstan, to act out a silly fantasy?' I said. 'I would like to talk to the woman who made that monstrous accusation. Yes, I would very much like to visit Mrs Penberthy. Tomorrow, perhaps. Escorted, naturally. I can't guess what may come of it, but I shall get a good deal of pleasure out of it. And maybe some information. Who knows? She is a secret Catholic, is she not? That could be a weak chink in her insufferable armour. I may find a way to thrust a chisel into it and see what happens. I am happy to try. But above all, I wish to look this woman in the face, this impertinent lady who calls me a woman of a certain age, subject to insane fantasies and throwing my money into making them seem real. If you give me protection so that if she has a door in her cellar, leading into a system of caves, I won't be seized and dragged into them, I will face her and face her down. Will you allow it?'

'Why not simply take her in and make her talk?' asked Dale reasonably. 'And why not just call the other witnesses? Anna, Eleanor, Dunstan, Pearce. Hasn't Anna spoken of her experience? She was part of the entertainment for the queen, in Penzance.

They can all testify that the kidnap was no fantasy, and that Juniper was there.'

'I wish to see her,' I said quietly. And also ominously. 'Fantasies, indeed! Woman of a certain age! The only danger is that if it's her washing day and she shows me round the house again and we go into the laundry room, I may push *her* head into the washtub and drown the bitch.'

TWENTY-FIVE
The Messenger From Hell

'Madam,' said Tamzin, as I prepared to set off the next morning, 'you are dressed to kill, as the saying is.'

I was, and for more than one reason. I very much desired to face the woman who had put such an insult on me, but even though I would be accompanied by Christopher and Brockley and two soldiers borrowed from Elizabeth's genuine royal guard, I was afraid of Juniper Penberthy.

She had made a prisoner of me; had put gyves on my left wrist and I still had abraded skin to prove it. I might talk about wanting to drown her in a washtub but at heart I quailed.

So, I wore fine clothes not just to impress but because they gave me confidence, like putting on armour. I had brought one court dress from Faldene, a rose and green damask open-fronted gown, worn over a kirtle of ruched green silk, with matching slashings in the sleeves. My headdress was covered with green velvet and my jewellery consisted of a pearl rope and pearl earrings. My ruff was a starched lace shield for my head, my farthingale so huge that when Brockley fetched a mule so that I could ride behind him down to Polgillan, I could only perch awkwardly sideways and when I was aboard Griffin's fishing boat, I couldn't get into the little amidships cabin and Griffin said gloomily that he hoped it wouldn't rain. It was an overcast day. We all had hooded cloaks with us, to protect our finery, just in case.

Brockley, Dale and Christopher were also carefully clad. Dale was in her very best blue velvet, which was brighter than the one she had worn at Arwenack House. Brockley and Christopher were in their soldierly buff with stout leather jackets over it, and they were armed. So, secretly, was I. Expensive brocade notwithstanding, this dress had my usual pouch inside it and the pouch carried my picklocks and my purse. And my dagger.

There was a little drizzle in the air when we arrived at Penzance, but our cloaks kept us dry while we went to The Good Catch where we were fortunately able to hire two sturdy nags, capable of bearing weights. Brockley took one and mounted Dale behind him, Christopher took the other and I sat sideways behind him, holding on to his belt. The soldiers marched beside us. We crossed the town, turned into the gate of Juniper House, rode past the curiously shaped, grey-green juniper trees and dismounted at the door.

As before, two grooms came hurrying to take our horses. This time Brockley did not try to go with them but remained grimly by my side. Simmons received us without any apparent surprise. We followed him inside. I thought he would want to send the soldiers to the kitchen but he did not. We were taken, all together, to Mistress Penberthy's parlour.

Our hostess was doing embroidery. As one generally does, for the sake of the light, she was seated on a window seat. She had a frame in her hands, and the fall of fabric below it suggested that she was working on a sleeve. She looked up as we came in, smiled, pushed her needle into her work and laid it down on the seat beside her.

'I thought you might come, dear Mistress Archer – or Stannard,' she said graciously. 'And you have brought an escort, as I also expected. But there is nothing to fear from me.' She turned to the butler. 'Simmons, bring wine for my guests, and some pastries. And now, Mistress Stannard, or may I call you Ursula, do please seat yourself – all of you seat yourselves – and Ursula, please introduce everyone to me.'

I was beginning to have a sense of unreality. I was glad to have the Brockleys with me, glad of Christopher's solidly reliable presence, very glad indeed of the two stolid soldiers. I cast a sideways look at Christopher. The open-air life of West Leys farm had browned his skin and the top of his bald head and it gave him a look of health and vigour. His martial dress too was reassuring. My companions were all real. I held on to that. However, the urge to drown Mistress Penberthy had left me. I no longer felt angry, but much more inclined to turn round and run away from this house and away from this woman who wasn't what she seemed.

With an effort, I pulled myself together, sat down as invited, arranged my skirts with care, and said, 'I am here to ask you to correct some strange notions that you seem to have told to those who called on you yesterday. They could not believe their ears.'

'No doubt. I could hardly believe mine, when they told me why they were here. You must have sounded very convincing when you talked to them about me. Dear Ursula, how *could* you?'

'How could I what?'

'Tell such shocking lies about me. I visit you at Cliff House just to see you and perhaps arrange for you to come to my house one day to play chess and if you were not too busy, to have a game straightaway. But you were in such a strange mood . . . I felt unwanted. I went away. The next I hear is that you have accused me of trying to kidnap you and sell you to the corsairs! What did I ever do to you, that you should treat me so? I know that you are perhaps suffering from the troubles that so often afflict women in middle life . . .'

'I am not a woman in middle life and you kidnapped me as well,' said Brockley coldly. 'You put chains on us. My left wrist is still sore.'

'Now, come, Mr Brockley. I know your mistress is wealthy and that you are very loyal to her. No doubt it was easy for her to buy your testimony—'

Brockley gasped with outrage but was checked by a sign from Christopher, who said, 'I found your prisoners, all of them, and I summoned rescue. Your pretences are nothing to me.'

'You too, Mr Wood – or Spelton. Or can it be that you were actually fooled, that this poor lady, full of delusions, did indeed cause you to find her in a cave and so appear – even to believe – that you were rescuing her.'

'Never did I hear such a dung pile of rubbish!' Dale was crimson with wrath. 'We were kidnapped by you and Alexander Killigrew and only saved because Mistress Stannard left a mark on the wall of an underground passage and Master Spelton traced us by it!'

Juniper gazed at me, smiling again, and her voice was gentle as she said, 'Do you often play these games with your friends, Mistress Stannard? They must love you very much to indulge you so – or do you merely buy their help? What did you pay for that blue velvet gown your tirewoman has on?'

She picked up her embroidery frame, lifted the needle and with perfect calm, began her stitchery again.

Around me, the very air seemed to be wobbling. Juniper was so calm, so assured, that I felt as though my own mind was faltering, as though, perhaps, she was the one in touch with reality and I was . . . had . . . had I really been acting out a fantasy, persuading or buying others to join in, and then let it all spin out of control like a wheel coming off a wagon? Confound it, we *were* rescued from that cave! There had been a battle between the crews of two ships. Captain Jerome Killigrew could speak for us!

Brockley and Christopher were almost choking and Dale was still scarlet. Even the two soldiers seemed uneasy, shuffling their feet and glancing at each other. They didn't know me. And Juniper, however ugly she might be, was still the perfect lady, with her embroidery frame and her meticulous stitches and her gentle, untroubled voice. She was trying to put an enchantment on them and she was very near to succeeding.

A maidservant came in then, with the refreshments on a tray, and broke the spell. 'Simmons is dealing with a man at the door, madam. I heard the man asking to speak with you and Simmons telling him that this is the wrong moment and please will he go back to Penzance, find himself an inn and come back tomorrow but . . .'

'Of course she will see me!' The new arrival's voice rang through the house. 'Don't be such a fool, Simmons. You know me, she knows me, and I have other errands, that won't wait. Don't waste my time. My orders are to place what I have brought into her hands and no others. What if she has people with her? The only people she would ever entertain are our friends. I've left my horse standing. Get out of my way!'

The door behind the maidservant had closed itself after her, swinging on noiseless hinges. It was now thrust roughly open again and a man in the plain riding dress worn by messengers everywhere, strode in. He checked for a moment when he saw us all but then stepped boldly on, went down on one knee before Juniper, held out a little leather bag, tied at the neck and bulging, and with a little scroll attached to it and said, 'My master's compliments, madam, and here is your payment. You are serving him well.'

His English was perfect but he had an accent. I tried to place it and could not.

'Unfortunately,' said Juniper, 'although I tried, I have so far failed in the service he requires most of all. Our numbers are depleted, too. Jago is dead and so is Sir Nicholas. But our work can continue. Perhaps, before long—'

'You . . . Jago is . . .?' The messenger seemed to become fully aware of us for the first time. He rose quickly to his feet, looking round at us, questioningly. Christopher and Brockley rose too, moving as one man. Brockley seized the bag from the messenger, shook it and detached the scroll. He handed it to Christopher.

'There's money here. You'd better read this.'

Christopher was already breaking the seal. He unrolled the scroll, which was very small. 'It's in Spanish,' he said. 'Fortunately I know the language well enough to read it. It's very short. *To Mistress Penberthy, my trusted servant, from her royal Master King Philip of Spain, greetings. Payment for your loyal service is sent to you herewith.* It has King Philip's signature. I can recognize that. There are some figures. In English currency it would amount to five hundred pounds.'

Christopher said to the soldiers, 'Get him!' and they obeyed at once, seizing the messenger, who stood rigid in their grasp, staring.

One of the soldiers said, 'What now?'

'I take it that King Philip is your master too. What is the service for which this is the payment? I'm sure you know. Come, speak!'

The messenger stared back at him and then turned his head to address Juniper. 'Mistress Penberthy, who are these people? Why are they here if they are not our friends? On whose authority do they lay hands on me?'

Christopher said to the soldiers, 'We'll never have a better chance. Get it out of him! If he won't talk, we'll have to get it out of Mistress Juniper but I would find that distasteful. Do it!'

It took them several unpleasant minutes. His legs had given way and he had fallen to the floor, bleeding from his nose and from a

cut lip and groaning from the pain in his belly where brutal fists
had hit him before he told us what we all wanted to hear.

King Philip of Spain. He's building a new armada. *He is
financing these enslavements, paying for the use of ships' holds,
paying captains and crews and Cornish agents to find and abduct
the new slaves and transport them to Constantinople and Algiers.
In return, the Ottomans will help him to create his* armada. *They
will provide trained men, warships, weaponry. He greatly desires
that one of the captives will be Queen Elizabeth of England. He
doesn't wish to have her brought before him. He burns heretics
but to burn a queen . . . no, no, let her live out her life and die
as a humble slave in some rich Ottoman family. And her sister
too, if hands can be laid on her.*

Brockley said, 'Dear God!' and Christopher whistled softly. I
felt as if I had always known it. It was as though something had
suddenly fallen into place, as though a key had turned in a lock.

Philip! Yes, who else? There had been money behind all this,
much money, hatred and a passionate desire to conquer England
and force the Catholic religion on us. Philip, the invisible hand
moving pawns on a chessboard between him and Queen Elizabeth,
seeking to take our queen. And oh, how happy he would be to
think of her, an unbeliever, enslaved in the hands of great unbelievers still. And me, her sister, enslaved with her.

Philip was paying for the abductions and yes, they were expensive to organize, of course they were but it was cheaper than
building an *armada* himself. It would buy the assistance of the
Ottoman countries. They would help him to put a truly deadly
armada together. The news that the queen meant to make a
Progress into Cornwall must have made his heart pound with the
same hope and joy that a stalking cat must feel when the prey
it is after comes within reach of one pounce.

'Philip,' Brockley said wonderingly. 'Here's the messenger
from hell, with the devil as his lord.'

'Take him away,' said Christopher to the soldiers. 'And take
her away as well.' He pointed to Juniper. 'We are tired of her
pretence that Mistress Stannard is out of her mind. Ignore her
silly stories. Take her to London and let rackmaster Richard
Topcliffe question her. She is mad for money, a slaver, a traitor,
a catspaw of Spain. She may have much to tell us.'

More than once, in the past, I had had the unhappy experience of seeing a personality dissolve in terror and despair. Now I witnessed it again, although this time there was a difference. The others had cried for pity, for mercy. Juniper Penberthy dissolved into rage, a noisy fury that took us all aback and brought Simmons running, to be knocked to the ground by Brockley and quickly fettered by one of the soldiers. I hadn't even realized that they were carrying fetters with them. What was happening to Juniper took all my attention. I was still afraid of her and wished that they would fetter her as well. The hatred in her eyes as she looked at me was terrifying.

'*You can sneer! You can call me traitor and slaver and catspaw of Spain! You can say I was mad for money, well, yes, I was, and I am and why shouldn't I be when money is all that can buy me a life worth living? What do you know about being born ugly and never noticed by any man even when you're young! My father bought me a husband but when he found out that I couldn't have children, that was the end of any pretence of love! Yes, he left me property and money and he left me his faith. He was a secret Catholic. So now am I! If I can help King Philip conquer England and return her to the true faith, then I'm glad of it. If it makes money for me then I am glad of it even more. Yes, I desire money. It buys me the power, the attention, that my looks could never win. I hate you, Ursula, because you were beautiful once and you still are, as befits your age. You are one of the loathsome ones, who so despise me. Aha! You didn't despise me so much when I watched while you were put in chains! As for Elizabeth, I hate her and her heretic rule! I hate all pretty women and all the men who play chess with me but never, never love me, I am full of so much hate that I am ready to burst into flames!*'

She sprang. I was half expecting it and shied away from her, away from the angry fingers, curved into claws, that were reaching for my eyes. It was Dale who snatched me away and parried Juniper's attack with a cushion before Brockley got hold of her and the other soldier brought out his fetters and secured her wrists behind her back. I was shaking. I was out of her reach and yet the hatred in her eyes still frightened me.

'You will get flames in plenty,' said Christopher. 'You have sought to abduct and sell into slavery the queen of England herself. That is treason and the penalty for treason, for a woman, is burning. But not until you have told everything there is to tell.'

She talked, of course. Most people who were questioned by Topcliffe did. It had begun with Alexander and her. A casual conversation over a chess game. He had heard of a man in Turkey who wanted a skilled gardener to create a special garden for him. Juniper knew of one; she had used his services herself. Suppose they were to get together, abduct him and ship him out. The scheme worked. Word came that three or four other wealthy men – corsairs probably – desired to have special people as their slaves and were willing to pay. Jago was drawn into it. He and his sons between them could range over Cornwall and finger the right prey. He had always had a bad reputation, they thought he would agree. He did.

After a little while, emissaries whom Philip had sent to Constantinople to negotiate with the Ottomans because he wanted assistance with another *armada*, heard of the scheme. They sent word to Philip and he replied encouragingly. It was agreed that if Philip would take over the financing of this expensive slave snatching service, then the aid that he wanted would be forthcoming.

He need not build ships and train men. The Ottomans already had a fleet of warships they could lend him – or hire out to him would be a better word. There were trained men to go with them and the latest artillery.

The scheme grew and swelled, until it was big enough to become dangerous, to become noticeable and I was sent to investigate in secrecy, while an imitation queen would travel through Cornwall as a decoy, a honey-trap.

Much of this, of course, I learned later, once I was back home in Faldene. I did not have to attend Juniper's trial; Christopher was able to provide all the necessary witness statements. He told me how, when the sentence was passed, Juniper had screamed and actually vomited there in the courtroom.

Under the persuasions of the notorious Master Richard Topcliffe, Mistress Penberthy had confessed to the murder of Beryon Lander. Gervase Pearce, now at sea with Captain Jerome, had been right. She had overheard something that told her what Juniper and Alexander were about and had tried to bargain with Mistress Penberthy and be paid for her silence. During the trial, Christopher told me, she had tried to justify herself because Beryon was a greedy little chatterbox and deserved what she got.

Juniper, however, was also forced to admit that she had schemed to have Queen Elizabeth abducted into slavery and that was high treason, and for that, only one penalty was possible. Juniper was burned.

I was invited to attend but hers was a fate I wouldn't wish on anyone. Dale and I spent the morning of her execution in the little church of St Mary's in Faldene village, on our knees, praying for her soul and for her body too, asking God that death would find her quickly. I never found out – or asked – whether my prayer was answered or not. I doubt it. Christopher, returning from London, told me that the execution had taken place but added that I wouldn't like to hear the details.

He spoke quite calmly and at once dismissed the subject and began to talk of something else.

Once, at court, I had overheard a courtier saying – I think concerning something the queen had said or done – that all the Tudors had a chip of ice in their hearts. Thinking of Queen Mary's persecution of heretics, and knowing that my father sent two women, women he had loved, to the block, I thought he might be right. Indeed, I was well aware that Elizabeth had a little piece of coldness in her heart. So had I. Without it, she would not have been the successful queen that she was and I could not have done the work I did. But now, looking at Christopher's calm face and hearing his calm voice when he spoke of something that must have been utterly appalling, something that he and I had been partly responsible for, I felt that his heart contained a bigger chip of ice than mine did.

Christopher had a friendly manner, and he was a good husband and father to his stepdaughter as well as to his own children. But if I had married him, as he once wanted, I would never have been truly happy with him. I would have sensed that piece of ice and recoiled from it.

But the trial and its aftermath came much later, of course. What happened immediately was that the prisoners were taken away to be held for a while in cells beneath Sir Francis' house at Helston, before being taken in carts to London, to the Tower and the attentions of Topcliffe. Criers in Penzance declared a reward for information leading to the capture of Thomas Tremaine but he was never found. The guess was that he had gone to sea with Alexander Killigrew and would not return to England. Nor would Alexander, who had utterly vanished, perhaps, as Christopher had suggested, to a home in Spain.

Sir Francis asked us to stay on at Cliff House for a while, so that it could be made ready to be let. Sir Francis didn't want to leave it empty. He wasn't averse to turning an honest penny, he told me. But it would be a difficult house to let, unless it was in really good order. Please would we tell him if it needed building repairs. As the landlord, he would have to pay for those himself.

We did not realize then what had become known as the Selected Slavery Scandal wasn't quite over.

TWENTY-SIX
The Homecoming

'Thank you, my good friend, for everything,' said the tall man, pressing a small but heavy bag into Captain Tredgold's hand. 'I mean it. You have taken a grave risk for me. Take my advice and don't go back to Constantinople – ever. Go on a voyage to the New World, or better still, go round the Horn and sail for Cathay.'

Captain Tredgold weighed the little bag in his palm in a pensive manner. 'I only did what a decent brother-in-law would do. If I had left you there, I would never have forgiven myself. My wife – your dear sister – would rise from her grave and haunt me!'

'There isn't as much in that bag as I would wish,' said the tall man. 'It comes from gratuities I was given now and then, from a few coins saved when I went to buy books and maps for my pupils or ran errands for my owners. I shall miss Mustafa's children. I was growing fond of them and they were bright little things, learning fast. I hope he finds another good tutor for them. He treated me well, you know. He sent for me personally! He didn't just ask for a learned man to teach languages to his youngsters. He knew of me because I correspond with learned men in many places. I never thought it would be such a dangerous occupation. But I have savings here in England – at least, I hope I have. I will bring you more as soon as I can; you've earned it, God knows. Only I had to use a little when we called at Athens. I needed a shirt and breeches that were really my own and I saved some money by buying a second-hand doublet.'

Captain Tredgold laughed. 'You were welcome. I didn't do much, after all, beyond seeing that your beard was shaved off and staining your face and your arms with walnut juice and darkening your hair. And putting you in sailor's clothes and sending you into the rigging while we went through the Bosphorus

Strait. I hardly breathed until we were safely through and bound
for open water.'

'I never breathed until I was down from the rigging,' his
brother-in-law said with feeling. 'I had to cling on with my eyes
shut for most of the time. If I looked down I felt as if the world
was turning beneath me.'

'You'll have to take care you're not snatched again,' said
Tredgold. 'I wouldn't stay in Cornwall if I were you. You know
you'd be welcome in my home in Bristol. Kate would take you
in with pleasure. Before I left England on this voyage, I heard
of mysterious disappearances, just like yours, in this part of
Cornwall. Cornwall's the home of dragons, my friend, and you
don't resemble St George.'

'I must see my house first, even if it's risky. It's home! I've
longed for it . . . you can't know how much. I suppose the vicar
will want to welcome me back into his flock with a ceremony.
He may want to baptize me again, since I've been so earnestly
pretending to be a Moslem. That's how I won the freedom to
come on my own to the quayside. I pretended that I was a secret
Believer and that I hated the Christian world. I said I was thankful
to have been rescued from it. I made my master trust me and I
was sorry that I had to deceive him. But all the time I ached for
home, *this* home. I love my tower of a house and watching the
stars from its topmost rooms!'

There was a bundle lying at the tall man's feet. He now picked
it up and positioned it on his shoulder. It was fastened with a
cord that had a long loop, which its owner took into his hand.
'I'll be on my way. Give my love to Kate. I won't thrust myself
on her if I can help it. Home is where I want to be. Thank you
again, for everything.'

'The boat's ready for you,' said Tredgold. 'It's not a long pull
from here. Then I'll berth at Penzance.'

'Come and see me when you can. Goodbye.'

'Godspeed,' said Captain Tredgold.

The tall man, balancing his bundle, which was not very heavy,
for it held only the few belongings he had purchased when the
Mary Pengelly called at Athens on her way home, gave the captain
a final pat on the shoulder and made his way to the rope ladder
that led down to the boat rocking gently on the water below. The

red-headed seaman who had removed the tall man's beard before the *Mary Pengelly* had even sailed from Constantinople, was waiting and caught the bundle as its owner threw it down. The tall man climbed down the ladder after it. He had learned a lot about climbing during the voyage and descended with agility.

He was silent as they sailed across the short stretch of water between the *Mary Pengelly* and the rock-strewn southern edge of the Lizard. He was looking about him, marvelling at the clear Cornish light and the remembered, beloved outlines of the Cornish coast and the tang of these Cornish seas. He had dreamed of home for so long, and for a long time had feared that he would never see it again.

The little harbour was empty. The fishing fleet were all out at sea. The tide was low, but there were steps up to the quay. He shouldered his bundle, stepped lightly onto the quay, pressed money into the boatman's palm, waved farewell to him and made for the cliff path.

At the top of the cliff, he found that the gate to the house was open. He walked in. He saw smoke coming from the chimney and felt a qualm. He had felt the same qualm several times during the voyage. He had been gone a long time. Would there be strangers in his house now? Would he be turned away from his own door? Well, if so, he would go to Sir Francis Godolphin and seek his help. Meanwhile . . . he squared his shoulders, hitched his bundle up again, walked to the front door and pushed it. It was open but he paused on the threshold and called, 'Is anyone home?'

A girl appeared, hurrying from the kitchen. She stopped short at the sight of him and then her eyes widened with recognition. He knew her too, and said, 'Tamzin! You're still here!'

'I don't believe it. I can't believe it! Dare I believe it? Mr Wells! Oh, Mr Wells! You've come home!'